Jack Boys Vs Dope Boys 2

Romell Tukes

Lock Down Publications and Ca$h
Presents
JACK BOYS VS. DOPE BOYS 2
A Novel by *Romell Tukes*

Lock Down Publications
P.O. Box 944
Stockbridge, Ga 30281
www.lockdownpublications.com

Copyright 2022 by Romell Tukes
Jack Boys Vs. Dope Boys 2

First Edition September 2022
Printed in the United States of America

Lock Down Publications
Like our page on Facebook: Lock Down Publications @
www.facebook.com/lockdownpublications.ldp

Book interior design by: **Shawn Walker**
Edited by: **Jill Alicea**

Stay Connected with Us!

Text **LOCKDOWN** to 22828 to stay up-to-date with new releases, sneak peaks, contests and more…

Thank you!

Submission Guideline.

Submit the first three chapters of your completed manuscript to ldpsubmissions@gmail.com, subject line: Your book's title. The manuscript must be in a .doc file and sent as an attachment. Document should be in Times New Roman, double spaced and in size 12 font. Also, provide your synopsis and full contact information. If sending multiple submissions, they must each be in a separate email.

Have a story but no way to send it electronically? You can still submit to LDP/Ca$h Presents. Send in the first three chapters, written or typed, of your completed manuscript to:

LDP: Submissions Dept
P.O. Box 944
Stockbridge, Ga 30281

DO NOT send original manuscript. Must be a duplicate.

Provide your synopsis and a cover letter containing your full contact information.

Thanks for considering LDP and Ca$h Presents.

Acknowledgments

First and foremost, I would like to give praises to Allah. Thank you to all readers who continue to rock with me. Free everybody stuck in the system. Thank you to all my friends and family. Shout my city 914, shout my Yonkers team CB, Spayhoe, Lingo, YB, SG, Baby James, King Hound, and Elm St. Shout Melly from the BX, shout OG Chuck from BK. Much love to Chi'raq. Shout to da guys, shout to my boy Youngsta from Texas-Lubbock. Shout out to Spazz from Brooklyn Bed-Stuy. Big shout to LDP and Ca$h for all the support and guidance on this path Allah created for me. If it's up then stuck shoot for stars. Pop Smoke shit. . . .

Romell Tukes

Prologue
Bronx, NY
Six months ago

Knight and his crew went to war for their turfs in the BX against Fats and his army of killers.

Nobody had a clue Fats' nephew from Virginia was Knight's cellmate when he did jail time in VA for drugs. When Knight found out Don was Fats' nephew and he was warring with his crew, the friendship they once shared went out the window.

While Money and his friend Troy were trying to slide into the Bronx and Brooklyn to gain turfs, they gained enemies instead.

Bree and Official had Brooklyn on lock, so when Fats sent his goons to take over, it started a heatwave of killing and a big war.

Eventually Knight's crew and Bree's crew linked up to go against Money's people as shit got litty in the streets.

Don started fucking Mita, a DA chick from Manhattan, until he fucked up. Mita's father was a judge who got killed by Money and Troy. The hit was put on the judge by Fats.

Money and Troy became two of the FBI's most wanted until Troy got killed by the police.

Money went on the run to Albany, where he was raised.

Mita and Knight had a long good solid friendship for years. They knew a lot about each other. She knew he lived a different type of lifestyle but she still had love for him - enough to not send him to prison.

Knight killed Uncle Pimp's family and Uncle Pimp sent two killers back at Knight and his crew. He sent Cassey and India.

Paco ended up killing India while Cassey crossed sides with Kazzy and fell in love with him.

Cassey told Kazzy everything, from Uncle Pimp's operations to how he was holding her little sister for ransom so she would do as he pleased.

Eventually, they were able to save Cassey's little sister in a house raid, but Uncle Pimp got away.

Cassey was more than happy to have her sister back, but that didn't last for long. Cassey came home from shopping one day to see her little sister overdosed on heroin - the same drug Uncle Pimp gave to his women.

Not too long after Cassey got pregnant, she was killed by Uncle Pimp, who was coming for blood.

***

Bree's soldiers got knocked off by Money, Don, and 50.

Fats got shot up and both of his daughters went to visit him, but when Paco's girlfriends D'Arcy and Jadaya found out they were sisters, they felt disgusted.

Fats found out D'Arcy was dealing with Paco and killed her for the disrespect.

Lil K and Red tried to focus on the Muslim ways of life, but it was hard since Red's memory was still blurry from getting shot in the head.

***

Less was running around turning up with the guys, fresh home, until he got killed.

Less' brother D Fatal Brim was still in prison and the loss of his brother crushed him.

D Fatal Brim married a beautiful Mexican woman from Cali named Marie and she was a different type of woman.

Julie cut ties with Bree because of the rumors and she couldn't trust her.

Bree ended up dealing with Khalid, who supplied her with mountains of dope and coke.

The main problem was the rumors of the new crew trying to take over the city.

The Cubans were paying hustlers to flood the city. Everybody knew the BX was off limits.

Chapter One
East Hampton, Long Island

Knight stood on his upstairs balcony early in the morning, drinking a strong cup of coffee his maid had made.

The new 23,496 square foot mansion he recently bought from a former NFL football player was one of a kind. The gated home had six bedrooms and four master walk-in bathrooms with marble floors and sinks. There were two levels, walls of glass, expensive chandeliers, a family movie room, a large high-end chef kitchen, a private lounge, marble slab floors, a private elevator, and a large backyard with a heated pool. Knight still had a few condos around the city, but he loved his new home.

This was the type of life Knight felt he deserved after years in the game robbing, killing, and hustling. It was time to reap the benefits.

Six months ago, his life was in a twist while he was dealing with Khalid, who blackmailed him into selling work for him. Knight came up with his own plan to rob Khalid and find a new plug in Miami. His scheme worked perfectly because his new plug Julie was the truth.

Since dealing with her, money been flowing in at an all-time high. Julie kept it strictly business even though he saw the chemistry between her and Kazzy every time they went to Miami.

Knight was living the single life. He still dealt with Mita, the DA chick, but it was more so on some lover and friends shit.

The crew was good. Everybody was focused on getting money. His rivals, Fats and Money, had been M.I.A. for the past six months, but word was Don never left Brooklyn after Red killed his little brother 50.

When they lost Less, it hit home hard, especially to him because Less was like a brother. Lil K told him after Less' death that Less wanted to get out of the game and wanted to live a regular life. Knight felt bad because he had brought this lifestyle back into Less' life when he came home from prison.

Everything seemed as if it was falling into place except for one big problem Knight heard a while back. A new crew was trying to set up shop in the Bronx, Washington Heights, and Harlem. Knight heard it was a heavy crew of Cubans paying blacks to sell dope for them, making them rich. That was all Knight had been hearing about for the past six months and he wasn't feeling it. Someone coming in the Bronx trying to take over his blocks and city wasn't happen.

He spent months doing research on the crew, but he always came up empty-handed. Knight knew it would only be so long until they expose their hand and slipped, and then he would make his move.

"Come back to bed, baby," a female said, lying across in his bed. She was a sexy thick Colombian woman with a pretty face whom he had met in Atlanta last week.

Knight went back inside and fucked the soul out of the woman before putting her back on the flight to Atlanta.

Today he had made plans to speak with investors about some big business plans into some legit shit. Nowadays, he knew it would be best to have legit people clean his money up for him, because he knew the drug game only lasted for so long.

***

East Hampton, Long Island

Up the block from Knight, a forty-year-old Cuban man was cutting his grass in his backyard. The man's name was Batista, and he had lived in a beautiful mansion for nearly seven years now. He and his wife shared the home. Their two children were both grown and living in the city enjoying their lives, working for big time investment companies.

Being Cuban in New York, you had to work extra hard to be successful. When Batista came to the United States when he was a young boy, he came off the boat with nothing expect dreams. It took years to learn to speak English and how to write in English, but when he did, he learned to speak better than most Americans.

Batista grew up in a city called Guantanamo, Cuba. His father's name was heavy in Cuba and still was. His father wanted him to come to America for many reasons, but one was so he could learn how it feel to come out of the mud, from the nothing, and become something, the same way he did.

Batista's life looked like a fairytale, but there were always two sides to a story.

Batista grew up in Cuba, later moving to Manhattan, but he had been selling heroin in Boston and the Delaware area for over twenty years now. He locked down Red Hook in Brooklyn recently. He was a Cuban drug lord and now he felt like it was time to take over every section in the city of New York.

In the last couple of months, he had been having his nephew flood the streets with heroin for a low price. Competition was the last thing on his mind because he was paying killers and crews for protection and to sell his product.

The only name he been hearing about was a kid named Knight in the Bronx who had shit on lock, but Batista planned to take the crown.

Romell Tukes

Chapter 2
Downtown, Brooklyn

Fats rode in the back of a Maybach on his way to a doctor because he had been having health problems. Being overweight caused him to have a heart attack last week, so now he was on his way for a checkup.

Fats smoked a cigar, feeling like the boss he was moving keys throughout the city.

He had spots in Staten Island, and now his little cousin EJ was moving keys for him.

Don was still in Brooklyn doing numbers in the East New York section, holding shit down since erasing Official from the picture.

The only person who still had a piece of Brooklyn was Bree. Don also had a crew in the Soundview section of the Bronx. The Soundview hood hated Knight and his crew, so linking up with Don was the best thing that happened to them since Big Blazer and Glock.

Every day, Fats thought about how he had to kill his daughter D'Arcy. He haven't seen his other daughter Jadaya since he was in the hospital. Killing D'Arcy hurt him, but when he saw her with Paco one day, he couldn't believe it.

Fats was still dealing with Gotti, who had been supplying him with an endless supply of coke.

He had still been on the hunt for Knight, but his focus had been on a new crew he had been hearing about taking over Redhook. Word in the street was that a crew of Cubans were moving a lot of dope in the city, and that was slowing down his money.   He was investigating this new crew but had found nothing yet.

**

Uptown, Bronx

Lil K drove down White Plains Road, passing blocks filled with Jamaicans selling drugs who were posted up on the curbs and in front of the corner stores. He had left Red home asleep while he creeped out of the crib because he knew if he told her where he was going, she would have wanted to come along.

Over the past few months, Lil K had been taking back over his old hoods. He was moving weight in a few projects in the Bronx. Shit had been a little crazy because there was news of a new crew trying to take over.

That wasn't the only issue at hand. Don had a crew in Soundview selling his work. Lil K and his crew stayed outta the Soundview area because everybody wanted them dead for the murder of Big Blazer.

Tonight, Lil K and Paco planned to go on a mission like the old days. Lil K liked selling drugs but taking drugs from drug dealers and dopeboys was his love.

Since the death of Less, every day he thought about him. Even though they never saw eye to eye, Less was still the bro.

He pulled into a fast-food restaurant parking lot to see Paco waiting for him in an older model Honda Civic sedan.

***

Paco had mostly been spending his time in Washington Height getting money, but this new Cuban crew was snatching up a lot of killers and workers.

"What up, son?" Paco hugged his boy, then tightened his black hoodie.

"What da lick read?" Lil K asked.

"My boy Mike G live a few doors down from them niggas he hate them but he just texted me letting me know two inside," Paco said, re-reading the text.

"A'ight." Lil K got in the Honda.

***

Soundview, Bronx

X and Ro rolled up their fourth blunt for the night, waiting on their homies to come back with some hoes they had gone to pick up.

"Pass me da Dutch Master, boy-boy," X told Ro from the kitchen as he warmed up some pizza from earlier.

"Nigga, get it yourself. I'm counting this money and bricks. How we only got twenty left, yo?" Ro yelled from the living room.

"I thought it was twenty-five?" X shouted, hoping Don didn't trip.

"Me too, bro. I'm starting to think that nigga Messy on grimy time," Ro said, coming back into the living room.

"I'll kill that."

X saw the man climb through the kitchen window with a Glock 45 in hand with an extended clip attached to it. Before he had a chance to fire his own weapon, shit got crazy.

Blocka! Blocka! Blocka! Blocka!

Ro and X each caught two bullets to the chest. Ro's body spun around and his body collapsed into the living room table.

Lil K stepped over X's dead body and took all the money and drugs.

"That's all?" Paco laughed, thinking they were moving 500 keys or something.

"They small level hustlers," Lil K said, thinking this was a waste of time, but he knew Don supplied Soundview, so this would send a message to Rilla and Don.

Romell Tukes

Chapter 3
Park Slope, BK

Don took the elevator to the penthouse in the expensive luxury condo for which he paid top dollar. He just wanted to take a shower and go to sleep.

Moving to New York was somewhat of a curse and blessing. Don had been a go getter since he was a kid out in VA trapping with his crew, but things changed. When he came to New York, his life changed for the better besides going to prison for two bodies someone planted in his trunk. Don got sentenced to 75 to life, but he ended up giving his time back and coming home.   Unfortunately, his grandfather Rick was killed by Bree, so he came home to a new plug: his Uncle Fats.

A couple of months ago, he lost his little brother 50 to the war they had going on with Knight's crew. Losing his little brother fucked him up. He felt like it was his fault because he was supposed to protect him.

Don had leveled up and took over a few hoods in Brooklyn and the Soundview part of the Bronx with the help of Rilla. Controlling Soundview was big to him because it was in the Bronx, and Soundview niggas hated Knight and his crew, so it was a perfect fit.

Don thought about Mita from time to time. When Fats told him who she was, he couldn't believe it. He knew he had to kill her before she found out who he was. Little did Don know she already knew Don's whole background. Money told him he had a shootout with Knight and she was with him.

Tomorrow, Don had to meet up with Rilla to see what the fuck was so important were he couldn't wait until their next meeting.

***

Brewster, NY

Uncle Pimp's ranch style home was located in a quiet area surrounded by his own land, ten acres of field and dirt roads. He sat on his front porch as he watched the eight women train by running up and down the long driveway, which was as long as a football field.

Since losing his best shooters, Cassey and India, he had been focused on his new recruits. Uncle Pimp had his women moving keys up and down the highway to Delaware and Philly, where he was coking it. The past few months he had been laying low, trying to mastermind a solid plan to get back at Knight and his crew. Pimpin' and killing didn't mix in da game he played, but Knight killed his family and hoes.

He never hated a nigga so much as he hated Knight. He wished death on him and everything he loved every day.

Uncle Pimp was sipping on Dom P out of his pimp glass, watching his beautiful women sprint up and down the driveway in bikinis. After running, the women had to swim laps in the pool, so they were dressed and ready.

***

Washington Heights, NY

Dyckman was the spot to be at on summer nights because everything was going on: hustling, dice games, whore houses, gambling spots, and after hour spots.

Drop and his crew were all in the building cutting dope and bagging up the heroin they just got from Drop's plug Paco.

Growing up in Washington Heights, Drop learned how to hustle and get to a bag. He was one hundred percent Puerto Rican and he loved his people.

Three of his workers wore masks and gloves, cutting the dope with all types of chemicals the fiends loved.

"I'm out," Drop said, leaving the apartment, tucking his 9mm handgun in his Louis Vuitton belt.

Minutes after Drop left the apartment, the workers took a break because their hands were starting to lock up.

Boom!

The door flew open and four Cubans ambushed the crib with assault rifles only the military had.

Tat! Tat! Tat! Tat! Tat!

The Cubans killed all of the Puerto Ricans and then left the crib, leaving the drugs and money.

Romell Tukes

Chapter 4
Washington Heights, NY
Two Days Later

"Are you sure, bro?" Paco asked.

"Paco, I saw two Cuban niggas enter the building, then I saw a few more coming up the block. but I thought nothing of it." Drop said, pissed off about losing his people. He heard from a neighbor that they saw a few Cubans leaving the apartment Drop trapped out of with weapons.

"This shit don't make sense, bro, because there ain't a lot of Cubans out here. They could have been Dominican," Paco stated.

"Paco, I know the difference between a Dominican and Cuban. I'm Puerto Rican, my nigga."

"Let me figure this shit out, bro, because this may have something to do with them new niggas trying take over turfs. I don't know if they Cubans, blacks, or what, but I'ma find out," Paco said, walking off to his car across the street.

Before he even made it off the curb, he saw a pickup truck pull up a little too close to him. When he saw a Cuban man climb out the window with a weapon, he ducked.

Bloc! Bloc! Bloc! Bloc!

Drop saw the moving truck and fired shots while Paco was on the ground shooting at the tires. The pickup truck got away, and Paco now knew everything Drop just said was facts. He saw the Cubans, and now he planned to kill any Cuban he ran across for the attempt made on his life.

***

Miami, FL

Julie lay on the beach, getting a tan and listening to music. Today was her chill day and she was enjoying it to the fullest. A little later, she had made plans to attend a yacht party with a group of clients and rich people.

Things in Julie's life had been bittersweet, but she learned how to take the good with the bad.

Knight turned out to be her favorite client because he was buying so many keys she couldn't keep up with him and his orders. Cutting Bree off was good because she was dead weight. Knight was copping two times the amount of her orders every round. As long as her supplier sent the drugs, she would be forever rich and wealthy.

Julie had been exercising extra hard and her body was looking amazing thanks to her personal trainer.

***

Bronx, NY

Red came out to the local park near her home to get her fresh air. Every other day she came out here to clear her mind and try to remember her childhood. Losing her memory took a lot out of her because lately she had been having flashbacks of her younger days.

Hers and Lil K's relationship was good. He took good care of her, and she saw all he was doing. She had been building feelings for Lil K through sex and their chemistry. She really was starting to love him all over again.

Red had been having an itch to kill again. Her last kill was 50 and it felt so good. Last night she asked Lil K when the next time she could play is and he knew she meant kill. Lil K told her soon and she could not wait, because her patience was starting to wear thin.

Chapter 5
South Bronx, NY

Kazzy hopped out of the Maserati coupe with three chains hanging down from his neck.

"Yoooooo!" Kazzy came out to Mill Brook projects to check on his investment. He flooded the projects with dope and coke and he was seeing at least a million dollars in a week's timing.

"Shit smooth out here, boss. We out'chea getting to a big bag," Nippy said with his childish voice, but he was twenty-seven years old.

"I hope so, family, but check it. I'ma give you a promotion since Zack on the Island."

"Good looks, big bro. You know I got you, cuz," Nippy said, happy that Zack was on Riker's Island fighting a body since last week.

Kazzy saw Paco calling him telling him to come Hunt's Point as fast as possible.

"Yo, I'ma swing by here tomorrow. I'ma have something for you," Kazzy said before jumping back in the car.

Kazzy pulled off, wondering what Paco wanted. He knew his trap was recently robbed, so he had a feeling that what he was calling about.

For the past couple of months, Kazzy had been holding down the hoods in the south Bronx area while Lil K focused on Uptown and the Westside part of the town.

Kazzy and Julie had been texting and calling each other every day for a while now, starting to build a real friendship outside of business.

***

Hunts Point, BX

In an abandoned factory outside was a line of dumpsters the city used every morning to store garbage.

Paco had a Dominican nigga tied up and pistol whipped so badly his nose was hanging from his face. Paco got word a Dominican nigga from outta town was trying to open up shop in his hood yesterday. After losing his soldiers in the home invasion, he had been on all bullshit, ready to flip the city up, but the Dominican kid fell right in his lap.

"You thought my people would not find you?" Paco asked as he saw Kazzy's car creeping through the area as if he was lost.

Paco flagged him down and he pulled over.

"What's up, cuz?" Kazzy got out of the car, staring at the Dominican cat who looked like Paco, but a little darker.

"Damn, boy fake look like you," Kazzy joked, but Paco's face didn't crack.

"This fool tried to take over my spot."

"Who sent you?" Kazzy asked the man, who had blood clots in his eyes.

"The Cubans paid me to find workers in the Heights and the Bronx, man. Please, I only did what any nigga would," the man said.

"Who are the Cubans?" Paco wanted to know.

"Batista and his son Diaz. They crazy people, I'm telling you. They offering people a lot of money to take over blocks. If not, they will kill their family." The man's words sounded so believable.

Kazzy and Paco looked at each other, shocked, because they had heard of a young nigga named Diaz.

"A'ight, son, we appreciate you, boy." Paco's voice was cold. Boc! Boc! Boc! Boc!

"Let me go holler at Knight and tell him the street gossip," Kazzy stated.

"You believe him?" Paco asked as they walked off.

"Yeah. Nine times outta ten a nigga gonna tell the truth on his last words," Kazzy added before he got back in his car.

Paco climbed in his Jeep on his way home to make love to his baby Jadaya. Things between them were good, but Paco wanted to bring another woman into bed with them to spice shit up. Jadaya's pussy was natural good and he refused to give that up. He really wanted to marry her, but she wanted him out of the streets first. Paco told her he was married to the streets for life, and she didn't like that shit.

Now with this new problem at hand, Paco had too much on his plate, and he hadn't forgotten about Fats and them niggas.

Romell Tukes

Chapter 6
New York City, NY

Paco had an expensive condo downtown he shared with Jadaya, but he was barely there nowadays. Lately, spending time with Jadaya wasn't at the top of his list, but tonight he devoted himself to her.

"Ohhhh fuck, Paco," Jadaya moaned as Paco pushed her legs all the way back towards the wall.

He buried his cock in her wet tight grip, grinding his hips into her lower ass cheeks.

"Im about to cum, babyyyy!" she shouted, letting go of an orgasm.

The loud slaps of his balls clapping on her ass turned him on, but he felt himself about to bust so he pulled out. His pole was covered in her creamy juices.

"Can I suck it?" Jadaya saw how hard she came on his cock and wanted a taste.

"Go ahead," he said watching her crawl to the dick.

She placed her lips around the head and made love to his manhood, twisting her neck and doing tongue tricks.

Jadaya's head game almost made his knees lock up on him, so he had to stop her.

"Bend over," he said.

She did as she was told like his personal sex slave. He saw her bare plum peach poking out and her tiny asshole. Paco started to eat her ass out, making her go crazy.

"Paco, oh my fucking God!" she screamed, putting her head down, choking on air. Jadaya had never felt so good, especially when he placed two fingers in her wetness while still eating her booty.

After that, he fucked her doggy style, and that was the nightcap for them both. She was ready to have Paco's baby after the way he just ate her ass.

***
Queens, NY

Diaz waited in a strip club alone, drinking and minding his business. The club scene wasn't really his thing but he had come out for two reasons. One reason was because his girl Summer worked here as a bottle girl. She was a bad Dominican bitch from Washington Heights. The second reason was to meet a client to discuss prices on keys of dope.

Diaz was twenty-one years old, handsome and very intelligent, of course. He ran mostly all of his dad Batista's drug operation in New York State. When his dad finally came up with the idea to start taking over cities like Brooklyn, the Bronx, and Washington Heights, he couldn't wait. Diaz knew it was smarter to pay and feed local drug dealers into moving their product instead of trying to muscle their way into niggas' hoods.

Summer walked into the VIP section with a bucket full of Dom P, wearing sexy lingerie. At 5'2", her ass was too much for her to carry, but Summer could have been a video vixen. Her beauty stood out from most women with her golden complexion, colorful eyes, and tattoos covering her body. Her sex game was above average. She wasn't nothing to be reckoned with at all.

"Can I get some dick, papi?" Summer asked, leaning in to kiss him.

"When I'm done, ma. My people just walked in the building," Diaz said, seeing a crew of blacks walk into the strip club entrance.

"Okay, I'll see you when I get off," she said, walking past a handsome black man who was looking at her sexually.

"Diaz, what's good? Who dat? Her ass phat," Yala said, leaving his crew outside the ropes.

"A friend. Good to see you, Yala. I hate coming out here to these clubs." Diaz's English was perfect. If he didn't look Spanish, one would never knew he was full-blooded Cuban.

Diaz had a hood swag to him and he knew how to dress. He had real drip. That's why the women loved him.

"I know, but I believe public places with loud music are the best place to handle legal business," Yala said, pouring himself a drink, looking at Summer at the bar. She was watching their every move, ice grilling him.

"True. But how many you wanted to get and how is the takeover coming along?"

"A hundred is good, and I will always have Harlem on lock, son," Yala said, meaning every word.

The meeting went well on both ends, as always.

Chapter 7
Atlanta, GA

Buckhead is where Khalid resided in his $19.7 million home sitting on eighteen acres of land. Khalid and his newest wife Chai lived here alone. Chai was a thirty-two-year-old trained killer from South Korea. Chai was a beautiful woman with a nice body, but due to her Islamic religion, the only person who saw her body was her husband when she wasn't covered up in her Islamic garment.

Chai spoke good English because she attended college in Atlanta. When she met Khalid she had nothing except the clothes on her back. Even after graduating college, she was working in a sweat shop in downtown Atlanta for eight years to make a living to pay bills. When her apartment caught on fire and burned down two days after she lost her job, she had nothing left. She became homeless, and that's when she met Khalid and he took her in as a wife. Following his lead, Chai had recently turned Muslim. Khalid explained the teachings of Islam to her, in regards to Muslim men being permitted to have four wives as long as he treated them equally. At first, Chai resisted it, but she eventually accepted the culture in totality.

The first time Khalid made love to her, he got addicted because her pussy was extra tight and good. Khalid asked her if that was her first time because he saw he had popped her cherry and she said yes. Now Chai loved taking cock up her anus, down her throat, and in her pussy. She loved the pain and pleasure feeling.

Khalid walked into his backyard to see her catching a tan on her pale skin in a Gucci two-piece bikini.

"I'ma step out. I'll be back later, okay?" Khalid said as she nodded.

Khalid looked at her bikini stuck between the slit of her phat coochie and couldn't help himself. "Take them off," he said, walking in between her long legs, helping her slide her bikini bottom off to see a phat bold pretty pussy so big it looked like a pouch. Khalid sucked on her swollen clit, using his finger to play in her gushy wetness.

"Ohhhhhhhh, daddy!" she cried, leaning her head back, letting him please her.

It didn't take long for her to climax everywhere.

When Khalid got up to leave, she stopped him and lifted up his garment, taking his erect pole out of his shorts. Chai started at the base of his shaft, using her tongue and lips, making her way up to the tip. She sucked and slurped on the head, then took him down her throat, picking up the speed.

"Ummmmm," Khalid moaned as she did her thing.

When he finally nutted, she caught most of it and rubbed it all over her face like make up.

Khalid left feeling drained. Chai always took good care of his sexual needs, unlike his other wives in Africa, whose pussies were whack.

Khalid had a few clients in Atlanta. They copped a good amount of weight, but nothing close to what Knight used to get.

Coming to the States, he was ready to kill Knight and everything he loved. He had trust in his daughters except one of them, for some reason.

Bree was a good customer, but Khalid knew her track record, so he didn't trust her one bit.

***

Atlanta, GA

In Zone 4, the drug flow had been in high traffic since Money came down. Money flooded Zone 4 with the best coke he got from Fats in New York. Being back and forth from Albany to Atlanta on the run was rough, but luckily he had fake ID's and shit to get him outta a jam if he ever got into a legal situation.

Atlanta was beautiful. Money had a condo in the downtown area near all the big name clubs. The women were different in Atlanta, unlike stuck up New York bitches who acted like their pussies don't stank.

He still thought about how Knight and his crew took everything he loved in a matter of a few years. Money knew sooner or later he would be captured for killing a DA agent and a judge in New York, but until then, he was running up a bag, trying to get richer.

In Atlanta, Money knew a few Bloods in Zone 4 and they were fucking with him heavy because he was a big homie from New York, so they looked up to him.

Money had his boy Twist selling weight for him and they had Zone 4 on lock now. Twist was moving fifty keys a week in his hood because the grade of the product was killing any competition. Twist was twenty years old and ugly, but the dancers loved him and his momma.

"Damn, shorty, I got four of dem thangs left." Twist walked into the trap house, seeing assault rifles and women all over the place.

This was Twist's older sister's crib. She was a stripper and scammer. She had been fucking Money on da low since he been in the city.

"I got you tonight, son," Money said, about to leave after he just got done fucking his sister in the back.

"How come you ain't tell me you was coming? I would have had da paper ready, shawty," Twist said, sitting on the couch, seeing his sister come from the back with her hair wild in just a bra and panties, showing her curves and flat tummy. She was a bad dark-skinned chick with ass and titties.

"I just swung by," Money said, looking at Twist's sister smiling, then at her large camel toe.

"Bitch, put on some clothes! Nobody trying to see all dat," Twist told his sister.

"If you only knew." She laughed and told two of her girls to come to the back so they could hit a line of coke before going to work at Magic City, the strip club.

Romell Tukes

Chapter 8
Soundview, BX

Since being shot in the home invasion a few days back, Ro would never be the same. Ro survived the shooting because the bullets missed his heart and luckily medical help arrived on the scene while he was still breathing.

Yesterday he got released from the hospital, and he planned to lay in his baby mother's crib to heal up. Losing his boy X hit him hard. He had looked into his friend's eyes as he took his last breath.

Ro had never been robbed before, but he knew that home invasion was more than a regular jacking from the way the two shooters were talking.

"Ro, you got company!" Pam yelled from the front room.

When the door opened, he saw his homie Rilla step in the room with two soldiers dressed in all red.

"Y'all niggas wait for me out there, son." Rilla looked back at his two goons with his serious face because he never smiled.

"Rilla, what's goody? I was gonna hit you today, son. I just got out the hospital. I'm just glad I got out the hospital," Ro said as Rilla sat down.

Rilla was the quiet killer type. He lived a militant lifestyle: no drugs, no gambling, and on demon time. He was from down south, but he grew up in Soundview and he also spent all of his teens and twenties in the prison system. Rilla's family played a big part in the Black Panther Party before he was even thought of.

Selling drugs wasn't Rilla ideal dream, but he was left no choice when his mother got killed in a shootout from a stray bullet years ago by a cop. His mom was walking home from work when a cop and a teenager wanted for a robbery got into a serious shootout and she got caught in the middle.

"Ro," Rilla said, taking a deep breath, taking off his Cartier frame glasses.

"What's up, big homie? I can get you that money back." Ro saw Rilla laugh

"Have you ever read a book called *The Art of War?*" Rilla asked.

"What?"

"I don't like to repeat myself, brother." Rilla's voice was strong, letting Ro know he meant business.

"I think I read it when I was up top."

"Nice."

"What does that have to do with anything going on? Niggas killed X," Ro stated.

"You killed X," Rilla shot back.

"What? I ain't kill the bro."

"You did, because you ain't protect him." Rilla pulled out a gun and Ro's body tensed up.

"Rilla, you bugging, son. I got hit up too!" Ro shouted loud enough so Pam could hear him and help.

But Rilla's goons had Pam in the living room and were running a train on her.

"You will see my point of view one day."

Bloc! Bloc! Bloc! Bloc!

Rilla shot Ro in his dome before walking out of the room to see his men finishing up with Pam before killing her.

Rilla didn't trust Ro. He felt like he had something to do with the robbery and killing of X, so he had to clear any doubts he had in his thoughts.

Don asked Rilla to come out to BK sometime today, so he decided to go after he checked on his sister Nika at Bronx Community College.

***

Harlem, NY

Jen walked the dark streets, looking for her late night hit with $15 dollars to her name. In her early thirties, Jen was still beautiful besides her rotten teeth and dirty skin. She was Puerto Rican and white with a nice frame, but the drugs had turned her out.

Coming from a rich family, Jen chose the wrong path to life, unlike her dad, Judge Santana, who got killed last year. Her sister

Mita was one of the top DA's in New York City. There were many times when Jen tried to get help by going to rehab, but it never worked. Drugs had her soul.

A black luxury car with tints pulled up to her. The car was so nice that Jen knew it had to be fresh off the show lot.

"Miss, you're Mita's sister, right? I have a thousand dollars for her," the handsome man said, catching her body language.

"I'll give it to her," Jen said quickly, smiling while adding up how much crack and dope she could get for all that easy money.

"Lean in," the man said, reaching for something as Jen's face was inside the car.

Boom! Boom!

Don pulled off, leaving Jen's body painted to the curb with her blood.

Romell Tukes

Chapter 9
Washington Heights, NY

Drop sat on the block playing cards for money, surrounded by his soldiers. Today was a nice warm day so beautiful women walked the streets and hustlers played every building, selling pills, nutcrackers, weed, bricks of coke, dope, or molly. Drop had placed more security on every block. In case the Cubans ever chose to come back, he would be waiting with a hundred round drum on his Draco.

"Drop, we have a problem," one of Drop's friends said, rushing up to the table, outta breath as if he just ran fifty miles up a deep hill.

"I'm busy. Can this wait?" Drop asked.

"No. It's your little brother Freddie."

Upon hearing Freddie's name, Drop stopped the card game and got up, following his friend Joa with his crew. They rushed up two blocks until they made it to a baseball field, where all the kids played baseball at. Drop saw his thirteen-year-old brother hanging from the fence with a slit throat and a Cuban flag tied to his feet and wrists holding him to the gate. Freddie's feet were crossed and his arms were stretched out like Jesus on the cross.

Drop's goons couldn't believe what they were looking at, but the crazy part was how Freddie's eyes were cut out.

***

Clinton Hill, BK

Bree had just got done feeding her newborn. A few months back, she had a baby girl she named Bridgett. Her daughter became her world. Motherhood kicked in as soon as Bridgett came out of her womb.

She had moved out of her Park Slope condo into a nice brownstone home in Clinton Hill, a few houses away from where Biggie Smalls the rapper grew up. Bree also had a condo in Atlanta because she had been spending a lot of time out there.

Since losing her crew to the war with Fats, she had to start from the ground up. She had a few workers in Redhook and Fort Coreen projects, Official's cousins who were loyal to her, but Bree also had drugs moving in Delaware and Boston.

After parting with Julie in Miami, she was happy to have met Khalid, who now supplied her with an endless amount of heroin and coke. In a few days, she had to make a trip to Atlanta to meet with Khalid about her next order.

Bree hadn't heard or seen from Knight in a while, but she did hear stories about a new crew in town, and she knew that was never good.

She went to take a warm bubble bath and listen to slow jams since her daughter was asleep, because relaxation time was not a question with a newborn baby.

***

Millbrook PJs, BX

"Nigga, take off all that shit and give me that ice," Nippy said, snatching the Cuban link chain off the man's neck with a gun pointed at him.

"I'm just coming to see my grandmom, bro," the man said, stripping ass naked.

"You look Cuban," Nippy stated.

"I'm Dominican, bro, please. I don't want no drama, man."

"Nigga, shut up! Where your gun at?" Nippy saw that he was clean.

"I'm not in the street. I work a 9 to 5. My grandmom live here."

"Get dressed. Next time check in, nigga," Nippy said before leaving the stairwell with his crew.

Ever since Kazzy told him to be on the lookout for Cubans, he had been G-checking any nigga who looked Cuban or close. The Bronx was filled with Dominicans and Puerto Ricans, but Nippy didn't know the difference nor did he care. Any nigga that wasn't from the projects had to check in with Nippy and his young crew.

***

Staten Island, NY

EJ stopped at a red light on his sports bike with a bookbag on full of keys of heroin for his homie Juggy. This was EJ's hood - S.I. He was born and raised here since he could remember.

Whenever someone mentioned Staten Island, EJ's name came up. He was the man in S.I.

Fats was EJ's cousin and plug since three months ago because EJ's old plug caught a fed case. Fats was EJ's last choice because he had heard a lot of snake shit about Fats.

EJ's crew was moving keys all through the city. He was now the man in charge, but he tried to keep a low profile because he wasn't trying to go back to federal prison.

Two years ago, EJ came home from a five year bid in the feds for scamming.

Chapter 10
Brooklyn, NY

Fats and two of his goons chilled in a local bar, watching a basketball game, yelling and shouting. Basketball was Fats' love. He placed big money on bets. Even though he had been too out of shape to play ball since he was a kid, he still loved the sport.

"Come on, Lakers, I need to hit this ticket," Swab said, sitting next to Fats, his boss and childhood friend.

"You dumb enough to put money on dem bum-ass Lakers, you deserve to lose." Fats laughed.

"Whatever. But I thought you said Don was coming?" Swab asked because he liked Don.

"He on his way to the Bronx, I believe." Fats was shocked that Don had managed to squeeze his way into the Bronx, but he was proud of him.

"That kid brings you a lot of paper, Fats, just like Glock," Swab stated, taking a sip of liquor.

"Facts." Fats smiled. His phone rang and he saw that it was an important client from Philly calling.

"Time to go?" Swab saw the look on Fats' face and knew it meant business.

***

Outside, Kazzy and Lil K waited patiently in a two door muscle car. Kazzy got wind that Fats always came out to this sport bar for big games.

"Bro, why you ain't bring Red?" Kazzy asked, looking across the dark street at the nice bar.

"She only talk about killing shit, bro. It's to the point where she talk in her sleep about killing people. Bro, she even told herself to kill me in her dream," Lil K stated.

"Damn. But you can't hold her hostage, bro. Let her out, let her kill, let her open up or she gonna go crazy," Kazzy stated.

"I feel you, son, but I'm not trying make shit harder on her. She still don't remember her name." Lil K shook his head.

"There he go," Kazzy said, picking up his Glock 40 with a long clip dangling from the end.

Lil K and Kazzy jumped out, not giving Fats a chance to get away again.

Bloc! Bloc! Bloc! Bloc!

Fats ducked, seeing one of his guards get hit. Swap fired back at the two gunmen Fats knew to be his ops.

Lil K ran behind a car when Fats started to fire rounds at Lil K as Swap and Kazzy focused on each other.

Boom! Boom!

Fats looked to his left to see Swap catch two head taps and his body dropped on the sidewalk near his other guard.

"Oh hell nah!" Fats said, running off down the street.

"Son can run for a big boy, cuz." Kazzy laughed, not trying chase Fats all through Brooklyn.

***

Soundview, BX

Don drove through the famous Soundview projects to see so many tall buildings it looked like the Times Square area.

Out in VA, it was rare to see projects like Soundview because every project had flat land and small apartment complex buildings.

Rilla was his connection to the Soundview area and Rilla was making him a lot of bread. Don still had people out in VA hustling for him, but he was loving New York so much he didn't want to leave. Another reason for his stay was to find Knight and his crew for the death of his little brother. If Don would have known years ago that his cell buddy in prison, Knight, would turn out to be one of his number one enemies, he wouldn't had believed it.

Rilla waited for Don on the side of a big blue dumpster. Don liked Rilla's style. He was militant and solid.

"Don, what's going on, big bro?" Rilla embraced the man who had been making him hood rich.

"Everything is in order for tonight, bruh. Have your people on point. You heard anything about what happen to your spot?"

"Yeah, some Bronx niggas. Nothing I can't handle." Rilla's words were confident.

"Any names I can help with?" Don asked.

"Nah, Knight and his crew is different. They been beefing with Soundview since D Fatal Brim was home." Rilla saw the look on Don's face.

"They back to get at me. It's a long story, but this is only the beginning."

Don left knowing what Knight was trying to do.

Romell Tukes

Chapter 11
Miami, FL
Two days later

Knight and Kazzy had just pulled up in Miami on their way to meet Julie again. What Knight didn't like was how Julie told him not to come to her city without Kazzy. Knight liked to keep shit focused on straight business, but when Julie and Kazzy got around each other, they were like two teenagers.

"Kazzy."

"What's up, cuz?" Kazzy said as he looked out the Maybach's tints as the luxury car drove down the street.

"I'm not feeling how you letting your feelings come between our business arrangements with Julie." Knight had been wanting to open up to Kazzy about this for so long, but he knew how his brother was emotional.

"Nigga, I'm a grown-ass man, cuz. When the fuck did I have to check in with you about a connection I find with a woman?" Kazzy got so upset he drooled on himself.

"You missing the point, my nigga. Julie is our plug. Stop thinking with your dick and use your head," Knight said as Kazzy stared at him.

"Fuck your point. Me and Julie just close friends, I ain't have a bond like this in a while since Cassey." Kazzy's voice lowered when mentioning Cassey's name because even though she was dead, she still had a piece of his heart.

"Don't mess up my business. You know firsthand how hard it is too find a plug, son." Knight's words made Kazzy shut up because he did know how hard it was to find a plug and he understood business.

The rest of the ride to Julie's was silence. You could hear a pin drop.

Julie's driver peeped in the mirror, hoping the two men didn't kill each other in Julie's backseat.

***

Dade County, FL

When they pulled up to Julie's 27,827 square foot mansion, it was breathtaking. The elegant stone home had a royalty entrance with a red carpet leading to the Brazilian oak double front doors. Julie had paid $19.7 million for the home which had nine bedrooms including the guest house, seven bathrooms, dual staircases leading up three levels, private bar and lounge, rooftop pool and backyard pool, high 30 foot ceilings, two family rooms, and expensive floor tiling.

The double doors flew open as Knight and Kazzy walked up the stairs. Julie was about to jump into Kazzy's arms, but he walked past her and her guards, going to the back.

"It's like that?" Julie said, looking at Kazzy's backside, wondering why he just played her. Julie and Kazzy talked on the phone almost every night, something Knight didn't know.

"What's up, Julie?" Knight said as she gave him a flat look as if she didn't want to talk.

"Come into the private office," Julie said, walking through her home as her guards watched Knight's every move.

"Your delivery will be shipped a few days late now," she said with an attitude, sitting down and crossing her legs.

"What? I thought we was on for Saturday?" Knight asked, confused, because this never happened.

"Things change. You have yourself to thank for that." She put on a fake smile.

"What do you mean by that? Julie, I been straightforward with you." Knight wasn't in the mood for games. Kazzy already had him uptight.

"You play with my happiness; I play with you." She was straightforward with him.

"This is because of Kazzy?"

"What, you think you're smart, Knight?"

"Y'all mixing business with pleasure. It's bad for business."

"Knight, me and Kazzy's business has nothing to do with you, playboy."

"It does, because what if shit goes bad between you two? That shit will fall back on me!" Knight shouted, seeing she didn't blink an eye.

"Let me say this loud and clear. I don't give a fuck how you feel about me and Kazzy. We have a bond. I don't know if you jealous or miserable but stay out our business or we will have a problem. He's special to me - period." Julie stared him down.

"Fine. I washed my hands. I'm out." He got up to leave.

"Bree is dealing with Khalid, so if I was you, I'd keep my eyes open. Kazzy will be staying here. I don't like to see him upset, so bye." She waved him off.

Knight couldn't believe the way Julie just carried him. He was pissed as he left the mansion.

Romell Tukes

Chapter 12
Atlanta, GA

Jadaya was so happy to be out of New York. She couldn't stop smiling since being in Atlanta. She and Paco drove to Atlanta for a week's vacation because they both needed peace of mind in another city for a while. Jadaya wanted to take a flight to the A, but Paco refused to travel without his guns.

"What we doing first?" Paco asked, carrying her bags as they just checked into a nice expensive hotel downtown.

"I got the whole week already planned out, so have no worries." Jadaya smiled, glad to be able to spend time with her man without having to worry about him being shot at or him shooting at someone.

"Can we have sex and take a nap? We been driving nearly sixteen hours," Paco complained as they opened the door the hotel room.

"That's why I sucked your dick at every rest stop. You know I'm on my period, Paco." She looked out the tall glass windows, looking over the city.

"Your asshole ain't," Paco said, seeing her frown because she disliked anal sex.

"Don't play with me." She made him laugh.

"So what you want to do?"

"I wanna go to the Underground Mall over there where that big-ass Coca-Cola thing is at," Jadaya said, pointing at the big Coca-Cola stand they could see from their window.

"A'ight."

***

Hours later

Jadaya loved everything they had in the Dior store. She was going crazy. She already ordered some shit online two weeks ago and she came to pick it up. Paco liked to see her smile and live life because she deserved it.

"You like this?" Jadaya said, lifting up a blouse, showing him.

"If you like it," Paco said, peeking at it then putting his head back in his phone, texting Kazzy back and then Drop.

"Babe, don't do that. You told me this week's for us." She sat in his lap making sure he had her full attention.

"Yeah, a'ight." Paco put his phone down and did some shopping for himself because he saw some nice outfits in the store.

Once Jadaya was finally tired of shopping, she was ready to go and prepare for dinner out on the town. Outside, walking back to the car, Paco thought he was tripping when he saw a nigga with a red Yankee hat that looked like Money, his op. The closer Paco got, the more his blood pressure rose. Paco handed Jadaya the bags since their car was a few feet away.

"Get in the car now," Paco said, pulling out his gun before Money and his friend could realize what was going on.

Blocka! Blocka! Blocka! Blocka! Blocka!

Money ducked and ran between two cars as his friend got hit in the neck and face, dropping him.

When Money saw Paco, he thought he was dreaming. Since he wasn't strapped, he got the fuck out of there.

Paco saw Money run off like he was at a track meet so he got in the car with Jadaya as she drove off upset.

"Same shit, and people never change. If you wanted to kill people, you could have stayed in New York," she scolded him.

***

USP Canaan Prison, PA

Marie looked beautiful in her Gucci sundress with her long hair in a bun.

She was in the visiting room waiting on her husband D Fatal Brim to come out so they could talk face to face, because talking on the phone only did but so much.

Marie had a home in York, PA and one in New York for when she wasn't in her city Los Angeles, CA. Being one of the biggest queenpins on the West Coast, she had a lot on her plate, but it was the life she chose.

Marrying D Fatal Brim was big for her because she had never cared or loved a person as much as she did him.

Every day she prayed he would give his life sentences back and come home, but she knew the chances of that were slim.

Romell Tukes

Chapter 13
Manhattan, NY

Gotti arrived in New York with three of his best shooters from VA. He had a nice condo in the city he recently brought for $4.7 million just to stay in when he came to New York.

He was currently on his way to Brooklyn in a limo with his goons to meet with Fats and Don at a sports bar. Gotti had come to meet up with Fats to talk business and to see why Knight was still alive. When Fats promised him he would take care of Knight, Gotti believed him, but now he had second thoughts.

Gotti also realized Fats' net worth in the amount of drugs he used to cop had been decreasing a lot.

Coming to New York took a lot out of his time because he had a lot of shit going on in VA.

***

Downtown Brooklyn, NY

Fats and Don saw Gotti and three young niggas walk into the sport bar Fats went into a partnership with.

"There he go," Don said, taking a sip of liquor, looking at Gotti approaching the table.

"Gotti, what's going on, big dog?" Fats said with a fake smile Gotti saw through.

"Why the fuck is Knight still alive, and why I feel like we had this damn conversation before?" Gotti said.

"You have to understand, Gotti, this kid disappears every month. I have to wait and let him come to me," Fats said.

Gotti's facial expression said it all. "Fats, I've known you for a long time and I know when a nigga scared, and it seems to me this Knight kid got you shaken over here." Gotti made Don laugh because Gotti was right.

"I will never fear no man who bleeds the same blood I bleed" Fats said, upset his connect was trying play him in his city.

"That's what they all say," Gotti shot back.

"How's business, Gotti? I know you didn't come out here for nothing?" Don asked, hoping to clear the bad air in the room.

"I came up here to find out what the fuck is going on because you not copping like you used to, Fats. What's going on? You getting high or some shit?" Gotti said, making his goons and Don laugh because he was on a roll today, crossing every line.

Don was starting to lose respect for Fats.

"I don't do drugs. There been rumors of a new group of drug pushers hitting my city and I'ma look into it," Fats said.

"What does that have to do with you?" Gotti needed to know because when Fats slowed down, so did his money, and Gotti had a plug to pay off as well.

"I'll take care of it," Fats repeated

"I heard that before, but I hope so. I'll be around. I'ma chill in the Big Apple for a while." Gotti got up to leave, shaking his head at Fats.

When Gotti stepped outside after talking shit about Fats, he saw two bare-faced gunmen about to strike. One had a grill in his mouth and looked familiar.

Tat! Tat! Tat! Tat! Tat!

One of Gotti's goons got hit in the shoulder while the other two shooters let off shoots at Kazzy and Knight.

Boom! Boom!

Kazzy side-stepped the bullets falling off the curb as Knight fired the AR-15 assault rifle.

Gotti and his crew managed to climb in the limo and pull off onto the thin one-way street.

"Man, you in the way, nigga," Knight said to Kazzy as they got in the car pulling off.

Knight was still in his feelings about what had taken place in Miami with Kazzy and Julie. He felt like they were both starting to fuck up his shit.

They heard Fats had a new hangout spot at a sports bar, so they slid out there. When Knight saw Gotti, he knew it was now or never, but seeing him in New York made him wonder what the fuck he had going on.

"I feel shit happens. I ain't see the curb. And what you on my dick for, nigga?" Kazzy said as Knight got on the expressway back to the Bronx.

"I'ma let that slide, my nigga." Knight stopped talking.

The ride home to the BX was quiet.

Romell Tukes

Chapter 14
Harlem, NY

Lil K and Red had been parked on 117th Street for a few hours, watching the brownstone home in the middle of the block. Two Cuban men had gone into the home an hour ago with bags, letting them know they had the right spot.

"How the fuck is these niggas spreading out all over the city so fast?" Lil K said out loud as Red sat in the driver's seat cleaning her Glock 40 with her shirt.

"They trying lock down different cities at once. It'd be brilliant if this was the 1960s," said Red.

Lil K ain't hear a word outta her all day until now, but he was used to that at times so he just gave her space. "Whatever happened to that doctor in the city I used to take you to? The one who used to call to check up on you once a week?"

"Oh, that one? I killed him," she said nonchalantly.

"Okay." Lil K knew he needed to get her some real help.

Lil K had been thinking about sending her to a mental hospital, but he had a strong feeling she wasn't going to like that. Red thought she was completely fine and normal because she only saw what her mind let her see.

"I have a question, baby," he said in a calm voice.

"Shoot?"

"Would you go to a special type of hospital for me for a while?" he asked. He saw the devil in her colorful eyes.

"Over my dead fucking body, bitch," she said, drooling out of her mouth.

Lil K never had never seen this side of her. The car got silent for few seconds and he felt uncomfortable.

"Lil K?" Red said in a happy voice, fucking Lil K's mind up.

"Yes, Red?"

"Happy birthday, baby."

"Thank you." Lil K played along even though his birthday wasn't for six more months.

"Can we go play now, please?" she begged like a little kid.

"Put your mask on," Lil K told her while putting on gloves and a ski mask before picking up his double barrel shotgun.

***

The two Cuban men spoke no English, but they knew how to count money and weigh keys of dope and pure coke. They transported drugs for Diaz. Normally the two men would bring money and drugs to this stash house and leaving it here for 24 hours then the money and drugs would be moved to another location. Diaz had a good smooth operation going on in Harlem thanks to Yala helping him.

The door got busted open and both men jumped up, wasting no time shooting at the masked shooters.

Boc! Boc! Boc!

The shots missed the shooters as Red and Lil K dipped into the cut, shooting out the living room lights, making the crib pitch black.

Boom! Boom!

Lil K's shotgun bullets tore through a Cuban's chest, knocking him over the living room couch. Red hit the last Cuban man in his stomach then ran down on him to hear him say something in Spanish.

Boc! Boc!

Once the Cubans were dead, Lil K and Red bagged up all the money and drugs they saw on the table before leaving the crib.

***

Long Island, NY

Knight brought out his new Bentley Continental GTC today to check out some foreclosed business establishments so he could open a club in the Long Island area. He pulled over at a gas station because his tank was on empty. There was a Spanish man pumping gas into a new blue McLaren 600LT Spider with the top cut off.

"Nice car," Knight told the man, who was looking at Knight's Bentley.

"Same to you, young man." The man saw the diamond grill and wondered how many diamonds the man had in his teeth.

Romell Tukes

Chapter 15
Long Island, NY

Batista pulled out of the gas station in his McLaren, hitting the gas pedal, feeling something off about the man with the diamond grill in his mouth.

He had to go meet his son in the Times Square area to see how shit was going. Then he had made plans to have lunch with his daughter on Wall Street. Batista was planning to take a trip to Costa Rica with his wife, then hit the United Kingdom. Traveling with his wife was something he loved to do at least twice a month or more if it was possible.

Driving down the highway and letting the wind take his breath made him feel like the true boss he was born to be. But Batista just couldn't get the man with the grill outta his head because East Hampton was a wealthy area and there were a few blocks. To see a young black man in a $200,000 car with expensive jewelry and dressed in designer suits was rare to him. In his eyes, there could only be one Jay-Z in the world. Everybody else was a low life.

***

Hempstead, L.I.

There was something about the man Knight saw back there at the gas station that stood out to him. Knight knew a boss when he saw one.

Knight parked in a shopping center parking lot where the fore-closed building was at with a realtor waiting in the front. Walking to the young white man in a suit, he could tell it would be easy to lower a price if he didn't like what the numbers were.

The outside had dark glass windows and two double doors, but the place looked spacious.

"Hey, I'm Harold." The white man shook Knight's hand with a tight grip and a big smile.

Knight knew the man only wanted his money and Knight only wanted the establishment, so they were both in it for something.

"I want it," Knight said, looking at the outside of the building, which was surrounded by other stores.

"But you didn't even see the inside of it," Harold said.

"It's the outside that matters, and location when it comes to clubs or bars. Now let's talk prices. Talk nice or don't talk twice."

"Okay, let's go inside and figure this shit out." Harold smiled walking inside the place.

They closed the deal in less than twenty minutes. Knight already had a blueprint mapped out in his head, so fixing the place up would be easy. He wanted to make the establishment into a hookah bar.

***

JFK Airport, NY

Kazzy had a flight to catch to Miami real quick. Julie said she had a surprise for him.

Driving into the airport, the traffic was heavy this morning and he started to get annoyed, beeping his horn.

A Jeep Wrangler pulled up to the driver's door. The truck had no doors and was full of beautiful women in bikinis. It was hard to stay focused on entering the airport parking lot when he saw all the beautiful women.

At the drop of dime, Kazzy looked into his rearview mirror to see Uncle Pimp in a Ferrari behind him, smiling. Kazzy looked at the women to see them all reaching for guns.

Bloc! Bloc! Bloc! Bloc! Bloc!

Kazzy swerved out of the lane, crossing into the emergency lane, driving off and ducking the hail of bullets hitting the back of his car. Kazzy couldn't believe he almost got caught slacking in traffic.

Kazzy parked and rushed to catch his flight to Miami, wondering how Uncle Pimp knew he was coming to the airport - unless he had been tailing him.

***

Miami, FL

Kazzy got off the flight still tired because he didn't get any sleep on the flight thinking about what happened at the JFK.

Walking into the Miami heat, he saw Julie there in a sexy short sky blue minidress, standing in front of a two tone white and sky blue Rolls-Royce Wraith.

"Kazzyyy!" she yelled, jumping into his arms.

"You happy to see me today? What you up to?" he asked, holding her slim waist, admiring how good she looked.

"I'm not up to nothing. I just wanted to see my bestie,"

Julie and Kazzy had never had sex, but they were close. When they went places, people would think they were a couple.

"Oh, so you missed me? Because all that shit you be popping, I knew you be fronting," he said, making her laugh.

"Whatever. But do you like your gift?" She pointed at the Wraith.

"This for me?"

"Dunnnn." She smiled, handing him the keys as he thanked her, kissing her lips. They were sharing their first passionate kiss, and she embraced it.

"You're a good kisser, but next time let me make the first move," she said, kissing him now.

Kazzy and Julie went out to eat and then went back to her place to cuddle and watch movies, but no sex. Kazzy woke up with blue balls.

Romell Tukes

Chapter 16
West Hollywood, Cali

"Ohhhh! Mmmm!" Marie screamed with her legs wide open as one of her close female friends ate her pussy.

Marie and her friends would have foursomes and orgies with all women. She told her husband about her sex sessions with women and he was all for it. D Fatal Brim told her she can do as she pleased, but she told him she didn't need no dick. She only wanted his. Most women that told their boyfriends that in prison were lying, but Marie was an honest chick.

Marie came again and the sexy thick Mexican naked woman between her legs continue to suck and lick on her clit.

"Get the fuck off!" Marie said, pushing the women outta her legs as Marie's juices went everywhere.

The other women saw Marie get up to go to her nightstand to get a toy or something to please her with.

Marie faced her friend with a big custom designed Louis Vuitton Glock 45.

"You stole my iPad, bitch," Marie said as she saw the fearful look on her friend's face.

Mare saw yellow piss coming out the slit of her friend's vagina. Boom! Boom! Boom! Boom!

"Stupid bitch." Marie put on her robe over her naked body. She went into the living room and told her maid and bodyguard to clean up the mess she just made.

Marie had to get ready to fly out to PA after a meeting with a cartel family in Mexico City.

***

Manhattan, NY

Mita left her crib so she could be at work a little early to start a few new cases before she started a trial for a big 162 man indictment. When she was a block away from the DA's office, a Honda motorcycle pulled up on her, making a lot of noise. When Mita saw it was Don on the bike, shots were fired.

"Ahhhhhhh!" she yelled.

Don got away after airing her Benz- C-class out, hitting her twice in her chest.

Luckily, Mita had worn a vest since her sister got killed, just in case there was an attempt on her life.

Mita took off the vest, winded after being hit up. She called Knight on her personal phone and busted a U-turn.

There was no way she was going to work today or going to the police. She was ready to take matters in her own hands.

Money killed her father and he was still on the run, so she was taking justice into her own hands. Mita used to fuck with Don, so he knew where she lived, but a few months ago she had relocated for her own safety.

***

Washington Heights, NY

Drop and a bad bitch were parked across the street from Dyckman basketball courts.

"Ummm," Drop moaned, getting his dick sucked about to say a prayer because the woman was going crazy on his rod.

She took him down her windpipe then came back up, using her small hands to twist the base like a salt shaker.

Before he could get his nut off, the woman stopped and pulled out a gun from between her legs.

Boc! Boc! Boc! Boc!

The Cuban woman climbed out of the car and rushed up the block, where a truck full of goons awaited for her.

"He dead?" Diaz asked as the driver pulled off.

"Yes," she said in her Spanish accent, picking up the bottle of mouthwash from her purse to rinse her mouth out.

Once she spit the mouthwash out the window, she dove into Diaz's lap, pulling out his penis slowly, sucking the tip while massaging his balls.   The woman was a professional killer and oral sex expert. That's why Diaz kept her as his wild card.

***

Atlanta, GA

Khalid met up with Bree in a barber/hair salon parking lot where people were coming and going, making it a busy area.

"Bree," Khalid said, approaching Bree.

"The money is being dropped off at the address you sent me. Where is my shit?" Bree had an attitude because she was on her period and she disliked coming to Atlanta to confirm every order if she wasn't in the city already.

"Slow your roll, little lady, and learn some respect before I detach your head from your shoulder," Khalid said seriously.

"Okay, I don't want no smoke. I just want what I have coming," Bree stated.

"You will have everything, Bree, in a matter of hours."

Khalid walked off to go pick up his wife from the salon.

Romell Tukes

Chapter 17
Brewster, NY

Uncle Pimp relaxed in his mansion, eating shrimp and lobster with expensive sauce as his hoes ran around with water guns, having a good time.

Missing the attempt on Kazzy's life had him very pissed because he had been laying on Kazzy for two weeks prior to the shooting at the JFK airport. Now he needed to come up with another plan before they come for him again and he knew he wasn't a cat with nine lives.

Uncle Pimp heard his doorbell ring. He had cameras all over the place just for Knight, but he saw three men he never saw outside.

"Daddy, someone is out front," one of his women said with an AK-47 assault rifle cocked and ready.

"Let them in, and if you see any funny movements, UK, take their heads off," Uncle Pimp told the cute slim white girl he bought from the United Kingdom in a gambling spot for five hundred dollars.

Gotti and his men walked into the dining room with a bunch of women with assault rifles behind them.

"Gentlemen, how can I help you, and how the fuck you know where I live?" Uncle Pimp asked as he stopped eating his shrimp.

"Nice set-up here. I'm Gotti from VA and we can help each other," Gotti said.

"Okay, that answers the first question, now back to the second. How do you know where I live?"

"The day you brought moves on Kazzy at the JFK airport and fumbled, I was there, so I followed you back here," Gotti said.

"How can you help me?"

"We can help each other," Gotti corrected him before taking a seat at the round table.

***
Uptown, Bronx

Sunny waited outside his stash house for his little cousin and his runner to come outside with the money he had to give to his plug Lil K. Sunny ran half of Uptown thanks to Lil K putting him on. Sunny was Blu's cousin and a solid nigga with a heavy name Uptown around the Gunhill section.

"These young dumb niggas need to hurry the fuck up," Sunny told Rain, his best friend and personal bodyguard.

"That BMW truck parked down there moving real funny, son," Rain said with his crazy eyes. Rain smoked a lot of PCP. He was what niggas considered a dusthead in the hood.

"Bro, how can a car move funny if it's parked? Yo, you need to leave that wet alone or I'ma cut you the fuck off again," Sunny said, seeing his workers come out with two gym bags full of money for his re-up. "About time! It's all——"

Tat! Tat! Tat! Tat! Tat!

Sunny couldn't finish his sentence as bullets went through his back. Sunny's workers and Rain fired wildly because they didn't see the shooters.

Boc! Boc! Boc!

Rain saw a shadow, but Diaz fired two rounds into his head and then his goons shoot both of Sunny's young workers.

Diaz took the bag of money just to send a message, but he grabbed a handful of money and tossed it in the air.

One of the young boys was still breathing as Diaz pulled off and someone came out of the building, calling 9-1-1.

***

Staten Island, NY

EJ had been dealing with a baddie he met a few weeks ago in a lounge in his hood. Shawty had a new luxury car and she was a fly bitch. She asked him to come out to a riverfront surrounded by restaurants and fancy clothing stores. His Audi pulled up behind a white Porsche that belonged to his new boo. EJ never had no pussy or head so good where he would check in with a bitch every other hour.

"What's up, boo?" EJ hugged her, grabbing a handful of her big ass as an older couple looked at them a few benches down.

"You so nasty." The women laughed.

"You know dat. But what's the vibe?" EJ sat down.

"First, let me ask you a real question?" she asked.

"Sure."

"What means more to you: pussy or money?"

"I'm sorry, but I'll pick money over any chick," he said.

"Even me?"

"Hell yeah, my nigga! Don't get it wrong, you sexy wit' some good-good but I'm in it for the bands, not the wedding plans." He made her laugh.

"Let me get to da point. I don't care about you. To be honest, you fuck like a crippled nigga. I need you to help me make some big money out here because I see how you do."

"Who the fuck are you, police?"

"No, dummy, I'm Bree"

"I thought you was Tiffany?" EJ asked, knowing she played him.

"Listen, honey, are you trying to make some money or not? If not, lose my number, little dick," Bree said, standing up to leave.

"What's the number?" EJ asked, ignoring her rude remarks.

"I'll give dem to you a few points lower then what you getting dem from Fats for," Bree said.

EJ could tell she did her research on him.

"Okay. I hope it's not trash."

"It's way better than your sex. I'll call you tomorrow," Bree said, walking off, laughing.

EJ felt bad crossing sides, but Fats had been dragging him and he was about his money.

He just hoped Bree was who she said she was.

Chapter 18
Miami, FL

Julie walked into the big mansion with two of her guards to meet with a Cuban man named Alfonso.

"Julie, follow me to the gazebo." Alfonso said outside in the back, opening the door for the beautiful woman he liked so much. Alfonso was an older man who had retired from the drug game years ago, but he was still a major player in the game and well-respected.

"It's nice out here," Julie said, looking at the garden.

"Thank you. I have a lot of free time nowadays, so I try to use it wisely. How can I help you? I been hearing a lot about you."

"Is that right?"

"Yes. You're doing great out here. I'm proud of you, Julie. You may be the biggest thing out here since before my time," he said, making her smile.

"That's sweet, but I'm here on the behalf of a good friend of mine," she stated.

"Okay, I'm listening."

"Do you know any Cubans in New York trying to take over the city?"

When she said New York, she saw the look in his eyes. "Is this friend your people?"

"Does it matter?" she shot back, feeling his shifted energy.

"Yes, it does, because the Cuban you speak of is named Batista. He is a very powerful, dangerous man with a lot of connections to Cuba," Alfonso said strongly.

"Let me guess: you're connected to him too?" she asked.

"Good guess."

"He's trying to take over New York, and I have a lot of money up there. Batista is stepping on my feet, Alfonso," Julie said.

"I had no clue you were moving weight in NY," he said.

"Now you know."

"I can make a call, but Batista is the type that when he has trained to do something, he goes for it, and his son Diaz is the same," Alfonso said.

"How are you connected? Do you supply them?"

"Oh no, I'm retired, Julie, but his wife Cynthia is my daughter," he said.

"Bonded by marriage."

"Yes," he said, seeing Julie reach into her designer bag and pulling out something.

Bloc! Bloc! Bloc! Bloc! Bloc!

"Now you bonded by blood," Julie said after killing him.

When Kazzy told her about the Cubans while pillow talking, she knew it had to be bigger than what he said.

***

Soundview, Bronx

Rilla and his boys were all outside shooting dice, hustling, and turning up, but Rilla was talking to his sister.

"You need to go put on some damn clothes," Rilla told his cute, thick, brown-skinned sister. Niggas had been trying to get at her for the longest, but they didn't want that problem with Rilla.

"Rilla, I'm nineteen. That's not fair You treating me like a thot," she said, upset.

"You dressing like a thot. You have to respect yourself," he said as she walked off, about to cross the street as a Jaguar pulled up speeding a little too fast.

Rilla never saw the Jaguar, so he got off the wall to see two gunmen hop out with MP5 assault rifles.

Tat! Tat! Tat! Tat! Tat!

Nippy and Lil K jumped back in the car while Paco drove up the block, leaving seven people dead. One was Rilla's sister.

Rilla cradled his little sister's dead body with tears as he shut her eyes for her.

People were crying, screaming, and going crazy for the deaths of their family members.

Chapter 19
South Bronx, NY

Knight drove his snowflake-white Range Rover through the city he had a lot of sleepless nights in, but he loved his city. The Bronx was in Knight's flesh. Wherever he went, the city still had a grip on his heart.

As a Lil Durk album blasted in his custom speakers, he noticed a black BMW truck had been tailing him for ten minutes. When he went left or right, so did the truck. Knight saw a female driving, but he couldn't make out a face behind the wheel.

Knight pulled into the small parking lot of an Auto Zone store. He parked and got out with his weapon tucked as if he was going into the store. Out the corner of his eye he saw Mita behind the wheel staring at him.

"What the fuck?" Knight mumbled, walking towards her to see her bang on her wheel as if she was mad that he caught her.

"Mita, why are you following me and what's going on" he asked, seeing a Glock on her passenger seat and bags under her eyes like she hadn't slept in days.

"I- I-I need to talk to you," she said, fumbling over her words.

"Stalking me ain't the way. You have my number." Knight could tell Mita had something big going on.

"He tried to kill me," she cried in tears.

"Who?"

"Don. Who else?"

"When was this, Mita?" he asked, seeing she was scared.

"Does it matter, Knight? He's gonna kill me."

"No, he's not. Where you been staying at since it happened?" Knight asked, hoping Don was following her so he could kill him once and for all.

"At a hotel."

"I can't let you do that. Come stay at my place. It's safe."

"No, Knight. You're a killer and drug dealer, just like him." She wiped her tears, trying to get herself together.

"That's why it's best I take you in, so I can protect you. Mita, put your pride to the side. I'm not asking you to live with me. I just want to make sure your safe until this shit over," he said, seeing her thinking.

"Where?"

"I got a few spots," he flexed on her, but Mita had a bag also, so she saw him trying shine on her.

"The safest?"

"My East Hampton mansion. Here is the addy. Let me see your phone." He placed his addy in her iPhone.

"I hope you got a guest room?" she asked.

"I got a lot of rooms." He smirked.

"You still the same." She smiled before driving off.

When Mita got out of the lot, Knight saw Don trying to lay low in a hoopty. Knight pulled out his blicky with thirty shots and ran down on the car.

Boc! Boc! Boc! Boc!

Don ain't even have time to get out and bust back as bullets tore through his car door and window. Don felt a burn in his arm but he knew it wasn't a gunshot because he would have been in more pain.

Don made it out of the lot and with a graze to his left shoulder.

***

Atlanta, GA

Behadi and Nasma had recently moved to a nice Atlanta area in an apartment with three bedrooms and two master bedrooms and two walk-in closets.

"I'm going to get my nails done. I'll be back in a few," Behadi told her sister Nasma, who was on the living room floor doing military push-ups.

"Ummm," Nasma mumbled because she disliked talking.

Both women were extremely beautiful. Instead of killers, they could have been models. Being born and raised in Africa, their outlook on shit was very different and serious.

"Don't forget, we here to do jobs, not makeovers," Nasma said, going to the back room to take a shower after her daily workout to keep her body nice and toned.

Behadi paid her miserable sister no mind as she left and went to get her nails done at a shop up the street.

The African sisters were the daughters of Khalid and he had them out here on a mission, but Atlanta was only their rest stop. The main mission was in New York City. Behadi didn't know what her father had planned, but she had no choice but to follow his orders.

She only hoped Khalid wasn't about to send them up to New York on a dumb mission or to kill the one man who had been playing in her dreams since she saw him a while back.

Romell Tukes

Chapter 20
Mount Vernon, NY

Diaz had a little crew in Mount Vernon. It was a short walk from Mount Vernon to the Bronx. A young black kid named Shark G ran a block called 3rd Avenue and he had a crew of young shooters and hustlers. Shark G now had keys of dope and coke flooding the streets thanks to a man he met on the humble tip a few months ago.

Diaz met Shark G at a food spot. He liked the way Shark G moved and offered him the chance of a lifetime.

"Yo Shark, it's a nigga around the corner looking for some work?" Lace said, walking up to his boy's car window as Shark G was watching his TV in his car.

"What the fuck you telling me for, son?"

"He want a lot, bro," Lace said. He only had 37grams left from his day of trapping.

"What's a lot?" Shark G asked.

"A few keys."

"He police?"

"Nah, bro, he don't look like dem boys. Son Crip," Lace stated.

Shark G got out of his car to walk around the corner to see a nigga with a diamond chain on and a blue sweatsuit. "What's up? Who you?" Shark G sized the man up.

"Penny Loc from Brooklyn," the man said with a bookbag full of money.

"How can I help? I see you pulled up by yourself." Shark G didn't see too many niggas come to other niggas' hoods and post up.

"I need five keys."

"How come you ain't get it in BK?" Shark G made all his goons look at Penny Loc because he had a point.

"I heard you got some fire."

"You heard right," Shark G boasted.

"Can we do business?"

"Talk a walk with me." Shark G led the man around the corner, where he hide his keys of coke and dope.

Once in the alleyway, a dude and a chick popped out with guns and all his drugs.

"You set me up," Shark G, said shocked.

"Facts. Now tell me about Diaz," Kazzy said with a gun to Shark G's head as Red and Lil K listened.

"I don't know him. I only met him three times. He's a Cuban nigga. He be in Harlem and the Lower Eastside a lot."

"Good enough," Red said before firing twice in Shark G's face, killing him.

Kazzy knew she was tripping now. "Why you kill him so fast?" Kazzy asked as a gang of shooters ran towards them.

Bloc! Bloc! Bloc! Bloc!

Lil K shot first, hitting two shooters in the face as more niggas continued to come with guns.

"Get in the car," Kazzy told Red.

Lil K covered them while shooting at the gunmen down the street.

They all made it in the car safely, getting off the block and heading back home to the gritty Bronx.

"You talk too much," Red told Kazzy out of the blue.

"You doing too much, Red," Kazzy said as Lil K gave him a look to shut up.

"It was clear you wasn't doing enough, fucking bozo," she said, ending the convo.

Kazzy was upset, but deep down he laughed because even though she had lost her memory, she was still Red.

Kazzy's mind went to this Diaz nigga.

***

Lower Eastside, NY

Diaz sat in his quiet condo living room, enjoying the rest of his coffee, preparing to go to church. He was a strong Catholic man and God-fearing.

The news of his worker Shark G's death made him a little upset, but he only hoped he had kept his mouth shut and died with honor. Diaz had a lot of shit going on in Harlem, so Mount Vernon didn't really matter.

It wasn't hard to put two and two together. He knew Knight and his crew was the ones who robbed his spot and killed his people.

After Paco's death, there was no doubt in his mind that it was time to turn up in the streets. He knew the war was just getting started, and he lived for that shit.

There were six men downstairs waiting on their boss to come down for church. Even after a week of killing and drug dealing, he made Sunday God's Day and family day. On Sundays, he would visit his dad and his kids. Today was the best day of the week in his country.

Diaz was planning a trip to Cuba in a few weeks. He had a lot of family out there.

Romell Tukes

Chapter 21
New York City, NY

Knight and Paco went out to a bar/nightclub in the city with Paco's crew from the Heights. Knight wanted to check the place out to steal some ideas for his new club in Long Island.

Mita had been staying in his mansion in L.I. for the time being and her company was great. She cooked and knew how to play chess.

"When you plan to open your new club?" Paco asked, seeing all the good-looking women in the spot tonight.

"I want to do it now, but I had to put it off until we can get this little situation handled," Knight said as a gang of Hispanic niggas blocked off their section ropes.

"These niggas came out of nowhere. I don't get it," Paco said.

"We was sleeping and they were scheming, son, plain and simple, boy," Knight said, drinking a bottle of water because he had to fall back on the liquor. Too much shit was going on at the moment.

"Facts of life. But yo, B, I been meaning to ask you, what's up with Kazzy flying out to Miami every day, yo?" Paco had been meaning to ask Knight this for a while but he had been busy.

"He fucking the plug." Knight saw Paco choke on liquor.

"Kazzy gay?"

"No, nigga, the plug is a bad Hispanic bitch," Knight said, shaking his head to see movement outside the ropes. When Knight saw who was on the other side of the ropes he didn't know what to do. "Let that bitch in," Knight said, seeing Bree and her crew.

"I'm a bitch now?" Bree sat across from both men in a sexy Prada dress with cuts on the thighs.

"What do you want?"

"Hey to you too, and Paco."

"I'm not impressed you know my name," Paco stated, trying not to look at her sexy legs, but he had to be honest, Bree was looking like a snack.

"I don't know why you here, but we about to leave. I'm sure Khalid won't approve of this sit down." Knight laughed, getting her upset.

"I'm grown, and that beef y'all have is between y'all. I ain't come on that time, Knight," she said, looking into his eyes. "I'm a boss, so talking to workers isn't my type of vibe," she shitted on Paco.

"You lucky I'm still letting your dirty feet-ass talk," Paco spoke up.

"Look, Knight, I know we got different plugs but we still in the town together and we should link up again." She got straight to the point.

"This a joke?" Knight asked.

"No, and I'm willing to do anything to prove my loyalty to you," she said sexually.

"That's not going happen. I learned my lesson fucking with you, ma, and we good on this side. You better take that shit to Delaware." Knight saw an evil grin appear on her face.

"Well, when the Cuban chew you up and spit you out, I'll be here to laugh," she said.

"That's cute," Paco said as both men stood to leave.

"By the way, a nigga named Gotti is looking for you," she said.

"I ain't hard to find," Knight told her.

"He outside with Uncle Pimp and three black cars full of shooters, but the back exit is open." She finished Paco's bottle of D'ussé.

"I really don't like you and we don't duck no rec, When you see Khalid, let him know we outside, ma."

Knight and his crew walked towards the front door with their straps out.

***

Gotti and Uncle Pimp both sat in a gray Rolls Royce Wraith a block up from the club, waiting for their ops to come out.

They had three cars full of men and women ready to go crazy on Knight.

"We going to get him tonight. Ain't no way he getting out of this. I only wish I could watch him take his last breath," Gotti said.

"I hope we get him. Knight is like a cat with nine lives," Uncle Pimp said.

The club doors opened and Knight ran out shooting at the gunners parked across the street. Knight and Paco aired out all three black cars full of shooters who were waiting to jump out on them, but their plans backfired.

Boc! Boc! Boc!

Boc! Boc! Boc!

Paco and his crew saw a few shooters crawl out of the car but they ran down on them, killing all of them.

The body count was twelve in all when they were done.

Gotti and Uncle Pimp couldn't believe what they just saw as they made a U-turn and got the fuck outta there.

Romell Tukes

Chapter 22
Atlanta, GA

Nasma and Behadi were talking to their father outside of the restaurant where they sold food and drinks at and where you could purchase uncooked Caribbean food.

"My favorite daughters, you both look so healthy." Khalid smiled.

"Can we get to business please?" Behadi saw Khalid flip.

"Don't ever cut me off." Khalid got serious.

"Sorry."

"Now did y'all get the crib over in New York?" he asked the both of them, looking back in and forth.

"Yeah. I did it a few weeks ago," Nasma said proudly.

"That's why you're my number one," Khalid told her, making her smile as Behadi leaned back.

"What's the mission?" Behadi was starting to get impatient with the whole meeting.

"When the two of you get to New York, I will fax you all the info y'all need. This mission should be easy because we know these men very well - especially you," he said, looking directly at Behadi before he got up to leave with his goons, who were all posted up on the wall.

"What's he talking about?" Nasma asked her sister.

"We will find out, I guess." Behadi's mind flashed to Lil K.

***

Long Island, NY

Mita and Knight made a bet in a card game that if one of them lost, they would have to do the winner's exercise.

Knight was doing Mita's exercise. At first he assumed it would be easy, but they were going in on the second hour.

"Remind me to never exercise with you again." Knight sat on a bicycle next to her, watching her camel toe and thighs in her leggings in front of him, timing his exercise.

"Time is up," she said, ready to take him to the yoga area so she could teach him some shit.

"Can we take a break?" Knight hadn't worked out in a while, so he was winded.

Knight couldn't stop thinking about how good she was looking. He hadn't fucked Mita since the last time they were together.

"Why you be giving me them eyes?" She smiled, hitting his arm. She knew what he was thinking and it wasn't happening - at least, no time soon.

"I don't know what you mean, but I have a question?" he asked, sitting down at a beach.

"What's going on?"

"Do you ever plan to go back to work?" asked Knight.

"Hell yeah, once this Don shit is done. Why you ask?"

"I have a close friend behind bars and I need your help on getting his case returned, please." Knight saw the look on her face.

"Knight, you know how hard this will be?"

"Yes, but you can use your time now to look over his case and make better judgements. I really need you." He gave her the sexy eyes he knew she couldn't resist.

"You get on my nerves, boy. I swear I'ma do it this one time, but I'm not going back to work until Don is in jail or——" Mita didn't finish her sentence because she didn't want to be a part of any murder case.

"I got you. Now let's finish this corny-ass workout." Knight got up and did thirty minutes of yoga with her before leaving.

As they walked out of the gym to their car, Knight saw a familiar face. It was the man he saw a few weeks ago at the gas station in the nice McLaren.

The two men nodded their heads at each other while taking a quick glance at each other's Richard Mueller watches, then the man went into the gym to do his daily exercises.

***

Miami Beach, FL

Julie was on her way to the Miami International Airport to pick up her boo thing Kazzy. They had finally made it official over the phone and she was head over heels for his love and affection. Today she planned to surprise him with his own mansion in the Miami Beach area.

She knew Kazzy had business to attend to in New York, but he also had her to attend to now. Julie wanted to tell him about the news she heard about the Cubans. She knew his life could be in danger up there because she knew how they got down.

The day was beautiful as she stopped in front of a red light next to a beach that was popping today with people. A gray Caravan pulled up next to the luxury car she drove around on a daily basis, but before she even got a good look at the car, shots were fired through the Rolls Royce.

Tat! Tat! Tat! Tat! Tat! Tat!

The shooting killed both of her guards before she had the chance to slide out the side door with her gun.

Boom! Boom! Boom! Boom! Boom!

Julie shot one of the attackers before running off into the crowd like a madwoman.

Julie saw the gunmen's faces. They were Cubans, and she knew who sent the hit.

Romell Tukes

Chapter 23
Washington Heights, NY

"Mel, have my money in two weeks, bro, or you a dubb, homie - on gang! The only reason I'm still dealing with you is because I fucks with your older brother," Paco said while placing the bag of dope on the kitchen table. Melo's older brother Fudge was a close friend of Paco. They basically grew up together until Fudge got killed in prison a few months ago.

"Paco, come on."

"Nah, you be fucking up," Paco said because he had given Melo four chances to get money and Melo always fucked up. But this was the last time.

"I know, son. I was down bad getting high on coke and shit after I lost my daughter," Melo told him, glad he was giving him a chance again to get a bag, but he had child support, bills, and car notes to pay.

"Why you got the window open?" Paco walked towards the fire escape to close the window, but then he heard the front door get kicked in. He got his gun out and saw Cubans with AR-15 assault rifles. Paco had a Glock 40 with a long clip full of 50 shot.

Boc! Boc! Boc! Boc! Boc!

Paco hit two gunmen, making them spin and drop, but the rest of the gunmen were sending round after round at Paco.

Tat! Tat! Tat! Tat! Tat!

Paco's only exit was the window so he rushed out of it, racing down the fire escape. When he hit the pavement, he ran into the front of the building to see two Cuban posted up in front.

Boc! Boc! Boc! Boc! Boc!

Paco fired at both men, knocking their heads off with head taps from a close distance.

A few niggas on the block asked Paco what was going on, but when they saw three Cubans with guns coming out of the building, it was on.

The Cubans hit three hustlers on the block, killing them. Paco sent four bullets back, killing one of the Cubans as the rest took off running down the dark street.

Paco was starting to feel like shit was going all wrong again.

***

USP Canaan, PA

D Fatal Brim's name was called for a visit. He had just spoken to his wife on the phone. Marie was out in Cali doing some business, as always.

Knight told him today he was coming so he didn't plan to do anything like cook food or work out on the yard.

D Fatal Brim walked through the metal detectors they had in the unit and walked out of his E-2 unit. He walked past other buildings to see niggas in the window throwing up gang signs.

Walking through the yard into the building there was the mess hall and visit room. He saw a lot of his homies coming from work or going to a visit. Today the visit room was packed, as it usually was on a Saturday.

"Big homie, what's good?" Knight smiled and his diamond icy grill shined when the light hit it.

"What's really good, son? I like that shit."

"It's Dior, something light for a nigga. But how are you?" Knight could see the stress on his boy's face and he was starting to look old.

"I'm blessed." D Fatal Brim always kept a good spirit.

"You ain't gotta do all the extra tough guy shit with me, bro. I know what it is," Knight repeated.

"If you know what it is, then why ask, nigga? I can't even get a good sleep at night knowing this is where I'ma be for the rest of my life." D Fatal Brim's face got serious because he knew Knight ain't really feel his pain.

"I got good news."

"What's that?"

"I been dealing with this DA chick for a while now, and——"

Before he could finish, D Fatal Brim stopped him. "What you mean by dealing, bro?" D Fatal Brim had to ask because normally when people had any dealings with the law, they were snitching, in his world.

"I been fucking her for years, bro, nothing like that. She my people. When I was in VA she was pulling up on me, you heard?" Knight said.

"A'ight, but how can she help me?" D Fatal Brim wanted to know.

"She can try to get you back in court so you can give some time back because you have a lot of loopholes in your case."

"I know."

"She can help."

"What's her name?" D Fatal Brim asked.

"Mita," Knight stated.

"Santana?"

"Yeah, how you know?"

"Long story, but she vicious. She put a lot of good men in here bro, facts," D Fatal Brim said.

"So I heard." Knight had heard stories about Mita also, but he didn't let that affect the way he felt about her because she was a civilian who believed in justice.

"You think she really gonna help?"

"She looking at your case at my house now."

"Damn, you doing it big, son." D Fatal Brim couldn't believe he was fucking the top DA chick in New York.

"Facts. I got you, bro, trust me. I have to go. I love you." Knight got up to leave.

"Love you more, brotty."

D Fatal Brim couldn't believe the news his friend just told him. He was happy and he had hope now.

Romell Tukes

Chapter 24
City Island, BX

Lil K took Red out to eat at a seafood spot because they had been laying low in the house chilling all day.

"You look beautiful tonight," Lil K said. She rocked a dress with heels, looking like the true diva she was when he started to fall in love with her.

"Thanks," she said dryly, not even eating her food.

"Damn, I get a dry 'thanks', ma? Let me know the vibes then," he said, feeling something was wrong with her.

"I'm on my period, and I don't think you truly understand my situation, Lil K," she expressed herself.

"You can't be serious? Because I care about your feelings more than I do my own!" he shot back.

"I'm not saying that."

"So, what are you saying?" He needed to get to the bottom of this because her energy was off.

"It's hard to look at you every day knowing we shared a deep chemistry. I have no emotion now. I can never love you the way I used to. That don't bother you?" she asked, looking into his eyes.

"No."

"Why?"

"Because I love you and I know deep down there is something still there from the way you make me feel, and I see it in your eyes," he said, making her blush so hard.

She laughed, but when she saw a familiar face, she knew something wasn't right.

When Lil K saw Red's attention turn to the door and her face change, he looked to see Uncle Pimp and two women walk into the food spot.

"Your time to shine," Lil K said as he pulled out his gun and Red followed his lead.

Luckily there were only five or six civilians in the back of the food spot.

Bloc! Bloc! Bloc! Bloc! Bloc!

Uncle Pimp saw his girls embraced with slugs and turned, running full speed out the exit. He was caught off guard by the shooters. He didn't even get a chance to see who was trying to kill him.

Lil K and Red ran outside to catch Uncle Pimp, but he was already pulling off in Bentley. Lil K forgot how fast Uncle Pimp was. He had to laugh.

"I guess the dinner date is ruined for the night but we can still do something," Red said, getting in the car.

"What's that?"

"Sex on a roof somewhere. I want to fuck next to the stars," she said. It was her fantasy.

"Okay, I'm down," Lil K said, rubbing her thighs as she drove, getting up to her wet phat coochie.

***

Harlem, NY

"Who let these niggas in da hood, bro?" Future said, standing in the apartment building in Grant Projects.

"The boss nigga. Who else?" Sticks said, looking at the two Cubans take keys of coke out of a trash bag for them.

Future and Stick were moving keys in Grant Projects. They fucked with Yala. He was their plug. But when he told them Cuban niggas would be dropping off their drugs, he got tight.

"We should rob these niggas, son. Facts," Future said as the Cuban was in the kitchen counting bricks.

"Nah, because they with Yala. We don't need that issue, cuz," Stick told him.

"I agree. I just hate them." Future heard the door open up but when he looked behind him, it was too late.

Boom! Boom! Boom! Boom!

Paco and Kazzy ran up in the spot with shotguns letting off.

One of the Cubans fired a 9mm handgun back, but Kazzy shot him twice while Paco killed the last man standing.

"Bag all that shit up. We jack boys, son," Kazzy said as Paco tossed everything he saw on the table into the trash bag.

Paco had been hearing about Cubans in certain parts of the city hustling and he was coming for them.

Chapter 25
Chicago, IL

Knight flew out to Chi-Town to visit his daughter and his baby mother. He was in an Uber on his way to a park to see them on this nice day. Knight loved leaving New York City for a while this was his peace of mind. The Uber pulled up to the park and saw his daughter and Valentines looking beautiful with her hair in a bun.

"Hey you," Knight said, looking at how beautiful his daughter was and how big she had gotten since the last time he saw her.

"Come say hi to your daddy you been asking for," Valentine said, paying Knight no mind.

Knight felt her cold shoulder. He hugged his daughter, not trying to get emotional, but he knew this is what he needed.

"Daddy," the little girl said in her childish voice, almost making Valentine cry, so she walked off a few feet away to give them privacy.

"Yes, I'm Daddy, my little princess." Knight saw her little smile and finally shed a tear because this was missing in his life.

"Dada," she said.

"Yep." Knight spoke with his daughter for a few minutes and then went to speak to his baby mother. "How's everything?"

"Good."

"Okay. Thanks for letting me see her," Knight said

"Anytime."

"How's life?" Knight asked

"I got something to tell you, Knight."

"What?"

"I'm getting married to a cop," she said. He looked disappointed.

"Oh, okay, that's good," Knight said going back to his daughter.

"I love you, but I have to go. I'll be back," Knight told his daughter before walking off to see Valentine was in tears.

***

Queens, NY

Julie came out of her city, Miami, to spend some time with her man Kazzy. She really needed to speak to him so she was waiting for him at the airport and he was late. Last night she told him her flight was landing and to be there at 7 a.m. and it was 7:15 a.m.

A sky blue Audi pulled up playing loud music. Kazzy hopped out, diamond chain and Rolex on.

"You're fucking late." She placed her hands on her hips, giving him an evil eye.

Kazzy grabbed her waist and kissed her, not even responding to her statement.

"Damn, you think it's that easy?" she said when he pulled back until he kissed her again.

"You still poppin' shit," he said.

"Nope, as long as I get some of that dick," she joked with a serious vibe.

"That's a fact." He opened the door for her as cars started to pull up to let people out to catch their flights.

Kazzy drove off. He hated coming to the JFK airport because of his bad experience last time.

"I missed you," Julie said, holding his hand.

"How you miss me if we talk all day?"

"Don't be smart, asshole," she said.

"Okay, you got it." Kazzy got on the highway, happy for her to be out here in the city.

"We have to talk." Julie got very serious.

"What da vibes?"

"Stop wit' all dis vibe language." She had heard the word vibe so much she had started using it.

"It's the swag. You be living like an old lady. You need to enjoy all that money," Kazzy said.

"I do live life."

"No you don't."

"Yes I do, Kazzy. I just be focused on business. This is my life. I run a real business. You don't understand. I had a rough life and when I leave this world, I want to leave a legacy."

"You will, but it's okay to spread your wings, ma," Kazzy got on the Sprain Brock Expressway.

"I had a sit down with a man who is well-respected with the Cubans."

"And?" He got upset hearing the word Cuban.

"I found out who's been sending people to take over your blocks and city."

"Who?"

"A man named Batista. He is from Cuba. He has a lot of family and they run Cuba. He is a very dangerous man."

Kazzy knew if Julie said someone was dangerous, then it had to be serious.

"What the fuck is a Cuban nigga doing trying to take over the Bronx or Harlem?" he asked himself out loud.

"I don't know, but I do know he lives in New York."

"So he should easy."

"No, Kazzy, you don't understand who you dealing with."

"Tell me."

"This nigga just sent a hit at me a few weeks ago and I almost lost my life," she admitted to him.

"What? How come you ain't tell me?"

"I know how to handle myself," she said strongly.

"I understand, but you still my wifey," he said, making her feel loved.

"I don't talk stupid on the phone, Kazzy. You know that the feds would be at my door in seconds."

He got off at a Bronx exit. "We gonna see Knight. He just got back from Chicago. But first, I'm tryna knock them walls down."

***

Manhattan, NY

Rilla had been focusing on getting money. He copped a new Bentley truck and a crib. He was able to get a big house outside the hood.

He and Don was doing big things and he knew there would be more to come, especially after the beef with Knight's crew. Knight and his goons had a big lock on the streets in certain hoods, but Rilla planned to squeeze his way into the South Bronx.

Rilla had met a woman last week and she finally called him for a date because she liked his swag. Rilla's date was a sexy woman named Jadaya. He couldn't believe he was sitting across from her making her laugh enjoying dinner.

Chapter 26
Washington Heights, NY

Paco drove through the city with Drop's cousin Von, talking about letting him control Dyckman because everybody he dealt with was scared due to the Cubans.

"I need you to hold shit down, bro. You got the crew," Paco said, stopping at a light.

"Man, you got too much going on, man," Von said.

"Me?"

"Yeah. Everyone know you got beef with some crazy-ass Cubans," Von said not trying risk his life or his crew's lives.

"That's how you feel when shit get real? You slide?"

"No, son, it's just I got shit going on," Von said.

"You on some scared shit?"

"Nah, I'm on some smart shit," Von shot back.

"Okay, good." Paco pulled over on to the curb to let him out.

"I live up the block," Von said, speaking up, seeing Paco was on bullshit with him.

"Get your scared ass out," he said, opening the door.

When Paco opened the car door, he saw Don coming out of a liquor store with two goons. Before Paco could lock eyes with the enemy, Don was on it.

Boc! Boc! Boc! Boc! Boc!

Don hit Von, killing him, as Paco pulled off, swerving a Honda Civic. Paco did 75 mph, trying to avoid getting hit up. He felt like a bitch running, but Don beat him to the punch.

***

Downtown, BK

Knight had been thinking about opening a lounge in Brooklyn also soon. He saw a few spots that would be good areas to open up a club. Knight's plan was to eventually have a chain of clubs and be able to stop selling drugs. Going legit was all he cared about doing with his money. He told Paco to invest in something worthwhile, but he was headed just like Lil K.

Knight saw Kazzy's text, telling him to meet at Millbrook projects ASAP. Before he could reply, he saw Bree and a few of her goons come out of a store in a shopping center area. Bree smiled at Knight and went for her gun and so did her goons.

Bloc! Bloc! Bloc! Bloc! Bloc!

Knight ducked, running into the parking lot, covering his head as Bree and her goons chased him. People heard the shots and started to run all over the place to dodge the gunplay. Knight pulled out his gun when he got a chance and shot at Bree, hitting Bree's arm, and he hit one of her goons in the chest.

The police sirens took him out of his zone and Bree had slid off already.

***

L.A., Cali

Marie sat down with a powerful man named Domingo. He was from Mexico, but he had his hands in the L.A. drug game for over twenty years. Domingo's brother was a cartel leader back home and he controlled L.A.

"Domingo, you have a nice restaurant here," Marie said. with two goons behind her. He had two goons behind him.

"Thanks. I love Mexican food," he said.

"I'm sure you do."

"Now how can I help you?" He gave her a fake smile because he really hated her guts.

"This is the first and last time I'ma tell you to stay out of East L.A.," she told him nicely.

"You hear this?" Domingo said to his cousin, laughing.

"I'm glad you find me funny," she said.

"I think you have let all that power get to your head."

"Are you getting outta L.A. or do I have to get rid of you myself?"

"You and what army, Marie? Do you think you will be able to live in peace in L.A.? I run all the gangs in L.A." He smirked.

"This is why in this game, you have to stay two steps ahead of your opponents," she said. This was the cue for her men to pull out their weapons.

Marie's goons and Domingo's men all pulled out their guns but when Domingo saw what was happening, he felt sick. Domingo's men all had their guns turned on him, even his first cousin, who had been promised a position controlling the drugs in L.A. for Marie's organization.

"You lost." Marie got up and left, hearing twenty- two gunshots killing Domingo. Marie had a flight to catch to PA.

Romell Tukes

Chapter 27
South Bronx, NY

Red sneaked out on her own, scheming on a lick. Last night she watched a gangsta movie and she came to the mindset that she ain't need Lil K to ride on niggas. She waited until Lil K was asleep to sneak out of the house. She drove around looking for victims to rob and kill all on her own.

Red hated the way Lil K always treated her like a big baby. It was hard for her to open up or express herself to him because she knew he would never understand. She knew Lil K had good intentions for her, but sometimes he would do too much.

Driving past Castel Hill projects, she saw two men doing a drug transaction in the back of the projects. She pulled over and watched the man who took the bag hop in the Benz truck. Red followed the Benz through the Bronx streets on a late Friday night.

"I got you, sucker," Red said to herself.

The truck drove into the Soundview area and parked at a two-story house on the corner. When Red saw the man get out of the SUV she made her way across the street with a gun fully loaded.

***

Rilla had just picked up some money from his cousin, who had been running his drug operation in Queens and L.I. He went into his back seat and grabbed the bag full of money he planned to put in his stash house.

"Don't fucking move," a female said, placing a gun to the back of his head.

"Take the paper, but this isn't what you want, trust me," Rilla said before the gun slammed into the back of his head. "Ahh shittt!" Rilla yelled in pain as blood gushed from his head.

"Turn around," Red said and he did as he was told.

When Rilla saw her face, he got lost in her beauty, forgetting about the gun she had to his face. "Who the fuck are you?" he said seeing her evil smirk.

"Red, a.k.a. Red Devil," she said, adding an extra name to herself.

"From Knight's crew? Goddamn," Rilla said, knowing it was over. Out the corner of his eyes, Rilla saw six figures appearing from different shadows dressed in all black.

When Red saw a funny look in Rilla's eyes, she turned around only to be ambushed and tasered by four different Taser guns, putting her down. The six attackers grabbed her body and tossed her in the van that rolled up in the middle of the street. The attackers left Rilla alive as the van drove off.

"What da fuck?" Rilla couldn't believe what just happened. He got in his truck with the money, leaving town for a few days.

He called Don on his way up to Boston and Don laughed, telling him he was good. Don and Uncle Pimp set up that whole move because they knew sooner or later they would be coming for Rilla to get to Don. Uncle Pimp's hoes kidnapped her and brought her to his Brewster, NY mansion. Don knew this would work and it did.

***

Williamsbridge, BX

Lil K woke up in the bed to see nobody there. He thought Red was in the bathroom or in the kitchen cooking.

"Baby!" he yelled, walking through the house. Hearing nothing made him search the whole crib. When he came up with nothing Lil K called her phone, only to hear her phone ring. Red had no friends whatsoever, as far as Lil K knew. He was her only family that he knew of so she couldn't be too far, in his mind.

A while back, Lil K had placed a GPS system in her phone and car just in case something like this happened. Lil K checked the GPS system on the app and saw her car and phone were in Soundview.

"Soundview," he said out loud as if a third party was there next him.

Lil K got dressed and grabbed his Glock 40 with fifty shots in the clip, ready for war.

Lil K drove his Hellcat through the streets. The car roared down the streets, shaking the pavement. He hated coming to the Soundview area of Bronx because them niggas would do anything to catch him slipping.

Lil K located Red's car quickly. He hopped out and opened the door to see gloves and a ski mask in the driver's seat. There was a fully loaded Draco under the seat. Lil K could tell there was some type of foul play. He was sick. Deep down, he knew she was dead.

Chapter 28
Downtown, BK

Mita had to go to city hall in Brooklyn to pick up some important papers. She caught the city clerk minutes before they closed, so she was able to take care of everything in one shot.

Leaving her daily life to hide out under Knight made her upset because she had to pause her life. Mita knew it was for her own safety so she rolled with the punches.

Walking out of city hall, she called Knight to tell him how everything just went. Mita was doing shit for D Fatal Brim's federal appeal motion to help him get out of jail.

***

Don checked the time in his Porsche. He had to meet Fats in ten minutes to talk about the recent events with Red.

When Don and Uncle Pimp came up with the plan, Fats knew he would not be able to achieve it because Knight's crew were all smart, but Fats was overwhelmed with joy when he heard the news of Red's capture. He couldn't wait to kill that bitch.

Don drove past city hall and saw Mita talking on the phone, he couldn't believe it. He pulled over, jumping on the curb.

Mita saw this and reached into her Gucci purse. Mita pulled out a 9mm handgun and started shooting the way Knight taught her.

One of the bullets hit Don in his right upper shoulder. Don screamed in pain, thinking twice about getting out to chase her down.

Mita ran off in her heels as Don made a U-turn. He needed medical attention, so he drove himself to King County Hospital.

***

Long Island, NY

Kazzy was at Knight's crib, going over everything Julie had sent him concerning their new enemies.

"I seen this nigga before, son, word to mother," Knight said. He was looking at the small photo of Batista and his wife.

"Julie said they live somewhere in New York City. We gotta find them, but she said the main source is their son Diaz," Kazzy said.

"Why they both look so familiar?" Knight continued to think hard.

"I don't know, but I'ma look into this Diaz cat some more," Kazzy said, taking a sip of liquor.

"I have to meet with a lady tomorrow about my financial status in the club, then I got you," Knight said.

"We good. By the way, Red is missing."

"What? Wait, our Red?" Knight asked.

"Yeah. Lil K tripping. He can't find her nowhere, boy, facts." Kazzy shook his head.

With Red missing, Knight wondered whether it was the Cubans or Fats.

"We going get to the bottom of it soon," Knight said, seeing Mita come downstairs to see who was there. She knew Kazzy, but didn't like him at all. Mita went back upstairs and slammed the room door.

"Damn, she don't like me, huh?"

"Not at all, brother," Knight said, laughing.

***

The next morning, Knight met up with his financial adviser to go over some documents for the lounge he planned to open up. Knight waited next to his Bentley SUV for the lady, who was a pretty Latin woman.

A BMW coupe pulled up and the woman got out in heels in a skirt. "Hey," she said. Knight's face got stuck.

Knight couldn't believe it. The woman he was staring at was the woman he saw in the picture last night with Batista. "Hi," Knight replied.

"Are you okay? You look like you just saw a ghost." She laughed.

"Sorry."

"It's okay. How about we get started on all of this?" Cynthia said, pulling papers out of her purse.

"Okay."

"You wanna go inside or do the paperwork out here?" she questioned because it was chilly out.

"Inside. Can you help me bring this bag inside?" Knight opened his trunk door.

"Sure," she stated.

When she got to the back Knight slammed the gun to her head, knocking her out. He tossed her in the trunk with her purse.

Knight got in the car and drove off to the Bronx, calling Kazzy, Lil K, and Paco.

Romell Tukes

Chapter 29
Westside, Bronx

Cynthia couldn't believe she was tied up to a car lift ass naked in chains. There were four men standing there watching her.

"Tell me about your husband?" Knight said.

"Fuck that! Where the fuck is Red at?" Lil K yelled as he swung the pipe he had in his hand at her ribs.

She screamed in pain as six of her ribs broke.

"Where's Red?" Lil K yelled with red eyes because he hadn't slept in days.

"I don't know a Red, and my husband is in DR."

"Why is he trying to take over my city?"

"Batista knows a very powerful man who's been telling him to leave you alone, but he hasn't been listening. You're Knight, I assume?"

"Who is this man?" Kazzy thought she was lying.

"I only saw him once, but I believe he's related to you."

"Me?" Knight asked.

"Yes. He tried to stop Batista," she said as her iPhone was going off.

"Look who it is," Paco said, handing Knight her phone.

Knight saw the name Batista and a photo of him pop up on the screen. "Just in time." Knight answered the phone, putting it on speaker.

"Who is dis?" Batista prayed his wife had lost her phone somewhere and someone picked up to return it.

"Knight."

"Where is my wife?" Batista's voice got raspy.

"Baby, they gonna kill me!" she yelled until Kazzy swung the metal pipe across her kneecap like a baseball bat, breaking her knee.

"Now Batista, who are you and what do you want?"

"Do not touch my wife," he said, trying to install fear in Knight.

"Too late. She on her last leg, literally."

119

"It's too late to stop what I have in motion. Sorry. But maybe we can talk about me letting you live if you let Cynthia go."

"This is how I get down, Batista."

Boom! Boom! Boom! Boom! Boom!

"Cynthia? Cynthia? Cynthia!" Batista yelled on speaker, but Cynthia was already dead.

"See you later." Knight hung up the phone.

"It litty, I guess," Paco said.

"Facts," Kazzy agreed.

"You should have hollered at him about Red before killing her. That was dumb as fuck," Lil K said.

"He don't have Red," Knight stated, not liking when people called him dumb, but he knew why Lil K was mad.

"How the fuck you know that, son? You ain't even give him a chance to say if he did or not!" Lil K shot back, getting frustrated.

"He would have saved his wife for the life of Red, don't you think?" Knight said.

"I don't give a fuck! You should have waited," Lil K said.

"Watch who you talking to, bro." Knight was getting upset because he didn't like niggas talking greasy to him.

Kazzy saw the two men about to go at it and stepped in the middle. Before he could say something, his phone went off.

Kazzy saw it was a blocked number and answered anyway. "Who dis, cuz?"

"I got your little friend in here," the male voice said.

"Who is dis?" Kazzy said as everybody looked. Kazzy put his phone on speaker.

"I have your lady, Ms. Red, and you will never see her again," Uncle Pimp said.

Lil K snatched the phone from Kazzy. "Where is she?" Lil K yelled

"This must be Lil K. Cheer up. Y'all killed a lot of my bitches, so I will have fun with this one," Uncle Pimp said.

"Who is dis and where is she?" Lil K said before he heard Red's voice in the background screaming.

"I'm Uncle Pimp, a bitch's worst nightmare."

"What do I have to do to get Red back?" Lil K asked.

"It's been written in pen, player. She mines now," Uncle Pimp said before hanging up.

"Damn, son," Paco said, upset that Red got grabbed up.

Lil K had tears in his eyes. He was hurt for real now. He couldn't think straight.

"I'm sorry," Knight said.

"We gotta find Uncle Pimp," said Kazzy, wondering how he got his number.

Chapter 30
Staten Island, NY

EJ was in the hood with his boys, trapping and preparing to go out bar hopping across town. Since selling for Bree, he had been seeing a lot of money and she was playing fair with him. Even though he felt bad for leaving his uncle on some trading shit, he also understood business wasn't personal at all.

"EJ, your boy just got cut upstate," Depo said, coming out of the building where he lived to see niggas was out.

"Who?"

"Litty Da Kid," Depo stated as his Cuban link swung right to left.

"Man, fuck that nigga. I heard he was fucking punks," EJ said. He had heard the news from Litty Da Kid's sister, who he was fucking.

"I can't put that type of bone on son."

"Bro, I spit facts, that's all," EJ said, seeing a chick in a sundress walk on the block. EJ was on it.

EJ walked towards the female, leaving his goons to hate. It was dark out, but as he got closer up close and personal, he saw she had manly features.

"What the fuck? You a tranny?" he shouted as Don laughed.

Boc! Boc! Boc! Boc! Boc!

A car drove down the block, letting off rounds at EJ's crew, killing EJ and three of his guys. Don hopped in the backseat of the car as it pulled off. In the car were the shooters Gotti sent with Don to send Bree a message about fucking around in their city. Don didn't want to dress up like a female, but nobody else would, so he had to.

***

Atlanta, GA

Bree and Khalid's meetings were starting to annoy her. She flew out to Atlanta to place an order for her next shipment.

The death of EJ fucked up a lot because he was her main source of income. EJ moved so many keys she thought he was giving that shit away.

"Bree, good to see you," Khalid said, entering the back row of a movie theater.

"Perfect place," she said.

"Better safe than sorry. How's life treating you?" he asked, eating popcorn.

"Great. When is the next shipment? I have my people at a hotel with the money right now," Bree stated.

"This week sometime. But what's going on with this Knight situation up there?" he asked, watching the movie.

"You should know more than me, if I'm not mistaken."

"You have a very fresh mouth, Bree. Don't let it be your down-fall to success." Khalid made it clear he was getting tired of her remarks.

"I believe this meeting is over." She got up to leave.

"Take care, bitch," Khalid mumbled as he continued to watch the movie.

Khalid made a call to his daughters, who were now in New York City.

***

Brewster, NY

Red's head was nodding back and forth as she was high off heroin. There were two women there with her in the guest house all day, aiding her in the worst way as Uncle Pimp demanded. Every two hours they had to shoot heroin in her veins. The drugs were uncut and raw.

Red was so high she ain't know if she was coming or going. She started to want the drugs more and more.

This is how Uncle Pimp got his women hooked on drugs, and he knew how to master the mind of a woman. Uncle Pimp had another way to control women. He believed in voodoo. He cast spells on all of his women, and today was Red's first step of being under his curse. Fats wanted Red killed, but Red was so beautiful and Uncle Pimp had faith she could become one of his best trophies if done the correct way.

Red's ankles were chained to a bed, but the chain was long enough to stretch to the bed and floor. She was stripped of all her clothes and giving bra and panties.

The door opened and an older woman with gray hair walked in with a suitcase. When the other two women saw the short lady walk in the room, they already knew what time it was, so they ran out of the room.

Red opened her eyes to see some old bitch in front of her opening a suitcase.   The woman started to pull out all types of weird shit.

"Whooo are youuu?" Red's words dragged with her slur.

The old lady said nothing as she looked at Red with the gray eyes people called soul readers. Red watched the woman place candles all around the room in a circle.

"Fuck you!" Red shouted, still nodding off here and there.

The elder woman started to speak in a language Red never heard before. The woman pulled out some baby powder, throwing it all over Red as she screamed in a language that made Red rock herself back and forth. When Red saw a doll with nails in it, she knew this was some this was some extra brainwash shit, and it was working. Red felt her body get so numb she couldn't move.

"Nooooo," Red said, thinking she saw the devil come out of the wall on her, trying to grab her hair.

"Shhhhhhhhh." The older woman smiled, showing the two yellow teeth she had left.

"Please!" Red cried as the woman continued to shout and dance in circles.

After twenty minutes of this, the older woman had a small bottle of a dark brown drink. She opened the top of the bottom and placed it to Red's lips. Red was trying to refuse the drink, but the older woman had a grip so strong she couldn't resist.

Red tasted liquor as it went down her back throat. After that, the woman stood there talking in her weird language for a few more minutes. When Red saw her blow out all the candles, she felt strange.

Uncle Pimp walked in the room smoking a cigar, wearing a robe and Gucci slippers to match. The old woman smiled at him for the first time as he gave her a head nod.

"You okay?" Uncle Pimp said as he approached Red.

"Mmmmm," she moaned.

"You're so beautiful, but I'm glad to have you. This is your new home and I'm your master now. You will learn to love me, trust me, and do whatever I tell you," he told her, seeing the dope was starting to wear off a little.

"Why?" Red asked.

"Because I chose you, little lady. I've been waiting for you. I plan to give you all you need," he said, getting up to leave her there as two hoes came inside the room to watch over her.

***

Lower Eastside, NY

Behadi and Nasma had a condo so nice they thought they were in a penthouse suite somewhere in luxury.

"What's next? Did he give you the list?" Behadi asked Nasma in the bathroom as her sister took a shower.

"Yeah, I have it!" Nasma shouted as the hot water from the shower head hit the sexy perfect body she worked hard to maintain.

"I'ma go sightseeing," Behadi stated.

"Don't get lost," Nasma shot back, hoping her sister was focused because she knew she had a soft spot for Knight's brother Lil K.

When Behadi helped Lil K recover, she fell for him. She never told a soul, but Nasma could tell her sister had him on her mind.

Chapter 31
Manhattan, NY

Batista and a few goons came out to meet Diaz to tell him about what happened to Cynthia.

"What's the emergency, Pops?" Diaz rushed into a hotel bar where Batista was staying until he figured some shit out.

"Just sit down." Batista's words said with sternness. Diaz sat down. "They killed your mother," Batista said.

"Who? When?"

"The Knight crew." Batista's face tightened.

"What?" Diaz tried to hold his tears back.

"I lost my wife to this shit, so I hope you can make it right." Batista got up from his seat.

"I will," Diaz said, still lost in his thoughts.

Diaz called Yala and went to the Upper Westside for a meeting with a new drug dealer he had been hearing about.

**

Bronx, NY

Kazzy went to check on Lil K in his crib because he knew the news about Red had him sick.   Kazzy always had an extra key to Lil K crib. The house had an odor to it and the place was dark with trash everywhere.

"Lil K, what the fuck, my nigga?" Kazzy said, stepping over beer bottles and pizza boxers.

"What? Go away," Lil K said. He had been wearing the same clothes for two weeks now. Since hear Uncle Pimp's voice and the news of him kidnapping Red, he felt lost.

"Bro, you gotta get up and move around, cuz this shit ain't for you, son," Kazzy told him. Kazzy looked at his brother and felt bad for his little brother.

"Get the fuck out."

"Listen, I know how you feel, cuz I been through this shit twice, but my bitches ended up dead. You still got a chance to save

127

Red, but you can't save nobody if you letting yourself go," Kazzy stated before he turned to leave.

Lil K heard the door close and started to shed a G tear for the pain he was feeling. Red was all he knew. She was his better half, but now he felt like she would never come back.

***

Soundview, BX

Jadaya had been creeping off from Paco to spend time with Rilla in his hood. Rilla was holding on to Jadaya as if she was his trophy. Today was a nice day out so niggas were out.

"You smelling good, shawty," Rilla told Jadaya.

"I smell good and taste better," she flirted as weed smoke filled the air.

***

"Yo, ain't no fucking way, son." Paco was parked in a car up the block with two goons, ready to do a drill.

"What's up, Paco?" one of his soldiers said.

"Nothing at all. Y'all ready?" Paco cocked his Draco.

"Drive-by or walk-up?" his boy Bridge asked.

"Walk-up, and don't miss a beep," Paco said.

"Damn, he got a bad bitch with him," Bridge said, looking at Jadaya next to Rilla.

Paco couldn't believe Jadaya had crossed him for an op, but he was about to show her what type of shit he was on.

Hopping out the car with no masks, they started letting off shots on the block, hitting everything in sight. Rilla left Jadaya and ran into the back of the building as Jadaya ran the other way.

Paco hit Rilla in the ass before he bent the corner, but they cleared the block out.

Chapter 32
Las Vegas, NV

Knight took a trip to Vegas for the All Star weekend. He brought Mita along with him because she was begging to get out of the house. They took a private G-6 jet and they had plans to stay at a fancy hotel.

"Oh my God, it's so beautiful out here." Mita looked over the city as the jet lowered.

"You know how to gamble?" he asked her, closing his personal laptop he took everywhere with him.

"No, but you can teach me," she said.

"I got you."

"Say less, handsome, but remember, what happens in Vegas stays in Vegas." She sat on his lap, kissing his lips, reaching for his dick. "Mmmm," she moaned, getting out his rod and slowly stroking it to life. Once he was rock hard, she moved her thong to the side and lifted up her dress. Mita slowly sat on his dick, lowering herself on his pole, loosening up her tight grip.

"Ohhhh yesssss!" she screamed, feeling him deep in her love box.

Knight had forgotten how good her pussy was because it'd been so long. He grabbed her waist, fucking her hard but slow. The quickie lasted until the jet touched down. It landed hard, almost knocking both on the ground.

"I need some more of that," he said, getting dressed, seeing the long Rolls Royce limo outside.

"Oh, we gonna have some fun, trust and believe." Mita planned a threesome with him and she wanted him to fuck her anally.

***

Knight and Mita sat in the backseat, looking at all the gambling spots and skyrise hotels.

"This city is crazy." Mita was mad at herself for not coming out here sooner.

"How is that appeal looking for my boy?" Knight asked, referring to D Fatal Brim.

"My assistant put in the motion I faxed her, so now we just wait for the court. It means so much more when a DA stamps it," Mita said.

"Thank, you that means a lot to me," he said, kissing her hand.

"Anything for you." Mita meant every word.

"Don't say anything and not mean it, ma," he said.

"I'll show you in my actions then talk is cheap baby" she said as they pulled up to a big hotel.

They pulled up behind a limo to see security getting out as if a rapper was about to climb out.

When Knight saw the man get out, he couldn't believe who he was looking at. Gotti wore a white clean designer suit with Cartier frames to match his drip.

"Wait in here," Knight told Mita, pulling out his burners.

"Wait, what's going on?" Mita said in fear as he jumped out shooting.

Gotti saw Knight shooting two guns at once and took off into the hotel.

Boc! Boc! Boc!

Knight took out all of his goons quickly to see Gotti's fat ass running in the hotel with the baddest Latina woman he ever saw.

"Shit, take us to another hotel. Scratch that. Take us to the jet," Knight told the driver, who pulled off because Mita had a gun to his head so he wouldn't pull off while the shootout took place.

"You almost had him," Mita said, laying in his lap.

"I know," Knight said, a little pissed he let Gotti slip out of his hands.

***

Dade County, FL

Julie had been out shopping all day with three guards for a big party tonight in the Key West area.

Shit had been great. Julie found love in her main client's brother, Kazzy. She hadn't felt this way since she was a kid. She really thought Kazzy could be the one. He was everything she always looked for and wanted in a soulmate.

Julie drove up into her mansion and parked her pink and white Rolls Royce next to her Bentley. She let her guards carry all her bags into the house. That's why she paid them the big bucks.

"Don't drop my shit," she told them, walking inside her home.

Julie didn't see a soul, and she always left a few men behind.

She went to go look out back to see her pool filled with the dead bodies of her goons and her dog with its head cut off. She knew the Cubans had made their move.

Chapter 33
Atlanta, GA

Money was doing big things in Atlanta. Fats was sending him drugs now twice a week, but the only issue was the keys had been cut with so much shit people were complaining. He had to go pick up some shit from Twist, but he made a trip to Nashville, TN. Living on the run was scary, but fun. Money already knew if he had any police contact then he was going out busting.

Pulling up to the trap, he saw two GMC trucks parked outside. He thought he was tripping because they looked like fed cars. Money walked into the house only to be ambushed by four men.

"Don't fucking move, nigga! Walk into the living room," one of the men said and Money did just that.

Money saw Twist and two young niggas on the floor being held at gunpoint.

"You must be Money," Khalid stated with a warm smile and an accent.

"What's going on?" Money asked a dumb question.

"I came to find out who this big time dope boy was from New York out here getting money," Khalid said.

"Now you know. How can I help you?" Money saw the fear of God on Twist's face.

"I want to get money with you. I have pure dope straight from my country, Africa," Khalid said.

"I have a plug, and plus I'm getting my shit for the low."

"You can get it for lower, trust me. I'ma put some bricks and my phone my number in a bag for you. I'ma give you a week to get back to me."

"Or what?" Money asked.

"Let's just say Atlanta will be turned into bloodylantic." Khalid stood to leave him so Money could sleep on it. "Your crew told us you would be here. They gave you up, bro, especially him." Khalid pointed at Twist.

"Thank you, I guess," Money replied.

"Until next time, champ." Khalid and his crew walked out.

When they all left, Money pulled out his gun to see Twist about to say something.

Boc! Boc! Boc! Boc! Boc!

Money killed everybody in the room, took the bag, and left, wondering what the fuck just happened.

***

Bronx, NY

Nippy and a few of his boys were all outside trapping hard, turning up, popping bottles.

"This nigga been owing me 100 dollars for two months," Host said as he saw a fiend he knew coming up the block with another man who looked like a fiend also.

"Who Con with anyway?" Nippy said, looking up the block.

"Nigga, I don't know, fam," Host said as Con got closer with a funny look on his face.

"That's not a——" Nippy saw a Draco get pulled out from under Con's friend's shirt.

Tat! Tat! Tat! Tat! Tat!

Nippy and Host got hit up first as everybody ran away from the gunfire. Don saw his target Nippy hit the floor and his job was done. Don heard Nippy worked for Knight's crew so he was on his line.

The past few weeks, Don had been laying low trying to focus on his ops, but the only move he felt strong about that he did was helping Uncle Pimp set up Red.

Fats was waiting for him in Brooklyn to show him something, but Don wasn't in the mood for any dumb shit.

***

Brooklyn, NY

Fats looked at his daughter Jadaya crying on the floor of his garage in his house.

"I swear, Daddy, I don't fuck with Paco," she said, trying to beg for her life.

"I don't believe you," Fats said, seeing Don's car pull up.

"You don't get it!" she cried.

"Y'all can go inside. I got it from here," Fats stated to his goons, who had snatched Jadaya from the Bronx.

"What's going on, Fats?" Don walked into the garage area to see a pretty chick on the floor crying.

"This is my daughter, who traded on me for Paco," Fats said.

"What the fuck you want me to do?" he asked.

"Nothing."

Fats shot Jadaya in her head, killing her, then went inside his house to have a drink.

Romell Tukes

Chapter 34
Downtown, BK

Don had been laying low in his crib, trying to focus on his next move because Brooklyn was starting to slip out of his hands. The Cubans had been flooding the blocks with drugs way better than the shit he was getting from Fats.

Gotti called him the other night and told him about the shootout in Vegas. Don didn't care because he had his own issues at the moment. He was going to meet up with Fats to talk about all the cut he was putting on the product.

When he opened the door to leave his condo, he couldn't believe who he was looking at. "Ain't this some shit," Don said as he stared at Bree.

"Bad timing?"

"Not at all. How can I help you? But do I kill you now or later?" he stated.

"Can I come in to talk please?" she asked.

"No, we can talk right here," he stated, not moving.

"While you was locked up, I went through it because you had no clue what you was getting into," Bree said.

"What the fuck you talking about? And don't try to use your lame-ass mind games. My pops been told me about you."

"Listen, what I'm about to tell you I been trying to tell you in so many words," she said sincerely.

"Spit that shit out den."

"Fats planted them bodies in the trunk when you got arrested and went to prison."

"What you mean?" Don couldn't believe what she was saying.

"Putting everything together shouldn't be too hard, Don," Bree said before she walked off.

Don stood there dumbfounded, not knowing whether to believe her or not, but he planned to cancel his meeting with Fats until he figured out what he was doing.

***

New York City, NY

Behadi and Nasma were out doing some shopping in the city, amazed at all the designer stores they had been running in and out of.

"I love it out here," Behadi said, carrying bags from Dior.

"Most of this shit is yours." Nasma carried her sister's bags.

"Cheer up."

"What the fuck you mean cheer up, Behadi? We here on a mission and you worried about shopping," Nasma said, walking through the packed streets.

"I'm supposed to walk around ass naked, Nasma?"

"You know what I mean. This shit is fucking up how I get my work done," Nasma shot back.

"You have to live life, sis. You let Daddy brainwash you."

"Don't start that dumb shit." Nasma always defended her dad.

"Whatever."

"It's weird how at night you never home. Where you be going?" Nasma asked. The past couple of nights she had been seeing Behadi leave at different hours of the night.

"Minding my fucking business, and maybe you should do the same thing," Behadi said, getting offended.

"Okay."

"Okay what?" Behadi wasn't feeling the way Nasma was talking.

"Nothing."

Behadi never trusted her own sister because she was just like their dad: a snake.

***

Miami, FL

Paco had to get out the city so he flew out to Miami with Kazzy to mourn the death of Jadaya. He heard about her on the news how they found her body floating on river bank in Manhattan.

Kazzy took Paco out to a Latin bar to have some drinks while Julie was waiting home for him.

"You going be okay, bro? She was fucking da ops anyway," Kazzy told him, patting him on his back.

Even though Jadaya did him wrong, he still cared for her because she was a down bitch until she violated the code. "I'm good, son. I'm on that little Spanish chick on the wall," Paco said, looking at a bad bitch on the wall dancing to a Bad Bunny song with her friend.

"Damn, cuz, she maybe out your weight class," Kazzy joked, seeing how fire shawty was.

"It's too easy, son, watch how I bop in Timbs, son." Paco got up and made his way over to the women.

Within minutes, he had all them laughing and smiling.

***

USP Canaan Prison, PA

D Fatal Brim and Knight chopped it up on the visit floor, talking about everything.

"Good news," Knight said.

"What's that?"

"Mita put in the appeal motion to get your case overturned," Knight told him, smiling,

But D Fatal Brim didn't seem too happy. "I know. I got the government brief last week. Thank you, bro."

"You don't seem too happy?" Knight asked.

"I put in two appeals so when they shot me down, I was hurt. I learned not to put too much into it," D Fatal Brim said.

"I know what you mean, bro, but have hope."

"Hope?" D Fatal Brim shot back with a mad face. "Hope is all we have in here when faith fails."

"How can you have hope with faith?" Knight asked, having seen many men in his boy's situation.

"Life leads us on a road of faith where we put our all into something and when the faith goes left we try to put hope in the right place," D Fatal Brim said before the visit ended.

Chapter 35
Miami, FL

Paco had been in the hotel for days, vibing with his new shawty. She was one of the baddest bitches he had in a long time. He rarely saw women so perfect and she was only in Miami on vacation. Her name was Irma from New York City. She told Paco she worked for an investment company.

"Where do you be at in the city, Paco?" Irma asked, eating the pizza they ordered minutes ago.

"The Heights or Harlem, but I love the Bronx," Paco said, looking at how nice and cute her feet were.

"Oh, my brother be in Harlem and Washington Heights also. He likes it out there," she stated.

"That's what's up."

"Diaz just always into some shit," Irma said as Paco almost choked on pizza crust.

"You're Cuban?" Paco asked, hoping she'd say no.

"Of course. 100%," she bragged.

"Let me guess: your father's name is Batista?" Paco asked, getting out of bed.

"How you know? Oh my God, it's a small world." Irma couldn't believe Paco knew her people. She couldn't wait to tell her dad and brother.

Paco pulled out a gun to see her eyes widen with fear.

Bloc! Bloc! Bloc! Bloc! Bloc!

Paco got dressed and left the hotel room that was in Irma's name.

***

Miami Beach, FL

Julie had been staying at the safe house she had because the Cubans was coming at her all types of ways.

Kazzy and Paco sat in the dining room as Julie cooked break-fast for them.

"Yo, that crazy, cuz." Kazzy couldn't believe they ran into Batista's daughter in Miami.

"Word, son. She started to talk about Diaz and I put two and two together," Paco said, taking a sip of orange juice.

"Y'all know he's going to strike back hard," she said, walking into the dining room with their plates.

This was Paco's first time really around Julie and she was a bad chick. Kazzy really had him a dime piece. Paco was happy for him.

"We ready," Kazzy said.

"It may be a good time to sit back and let him come to you," she said.

"Like people dead?" Paco said.

"No, let him come for revenge, then attack. It's a trap and one of the oldest tricks for an emotional killer," Julie said.

"That's smart if he don't catch on," Paco said.

"He won't," Julie said.

"I'ma go back to the town today," Paco said.

"I'll meet you up there." Kazzy smiled at Julie.

"We got some baby making to do," Julie said, looking at Kazzy.

***

Atlanta, GA

Nasma came down to Atlanta real quick because her dad called her and only her. She walked into her dad crib to see him in the living room reading the Noble Qu'ran.

"As-salamualaikum," Khalid said.

"Wa alaikum salam," she repeated, walking into living room, taking off her heels.

"Nice dress," Khalid stated.

"I came down as fast as I could," Nasma said, hoping he wasn't on no bullshit.

"How is it going in New York?" He looked at her.

"Bad. We still haven't seen any of our targets."

"Is that right, my beautiful daughter?" Khalid had an evil smirk on his face.

"It will be done soon."

"I'm done waiting, so this is what I want you to do. There is a women name Bree. I want you to kill her after you kill Behadi," Khalid said with no remorse.

"Behadi?"

"Yes."

"Why my sister?" Nasma wasn't feeling that at all.

"I see a lot of…how do these Americans say? I lot of betrayal in her eyes. I don't trust her, Nasma, and neither should you," he stated, looking in her eyes.

"Okay."

"Thank you. May Allah reward you," he stated, going back to reading his Qu'ran.

Nasma took an Uber back to the airport as her sister called her phone. She couldn't even answer right now because her mind was twisted.

***

South Bronx, NY

Behadi was parked near MillBrook projects, waiting to catch Lil K so she can warn him. She had been coming here for days, but no sign of him or his brothers, which was crazy because they ran the BX. She called her sister because she didn't see her all day and Nasma was normally always at the crib.

Behadi pulled off, seeing her car needed gas, so she went to the nearest gas station BP. Pulling into the entrance, she hit the brakes, seeing Lil K hop out a BMW with jewelry on.

"Do it now," she told herself, thinking right now was the right time to get out and talk to him.

Behadi's feet and legs got numb. She couldn't move at all as she watched him get back in the car racing off. She tailed him, but she couldn't believe how wet she got off the sight of him.

Chapter 36
Harlem, NY

Yala chilled in the lower basement area on a building, interacting in a dice game with close to a quarter million on the floor.

"I lost 70 bands already, fam. I'm out," Yala said, not trying to lose more money.

"A'ight, son," Venny said, laughing because he already won most of his money in the last five minutes.

Yala had a nice sex date set up for midnight with a new chick he couldn't wait to tear down.

Last week Yala bought his mom a mansion in Long Island and he also got himself a nice two-story house in Westchester County.

Walking outside, he saw two men sitting on the hood of his new luxury coupe.

"What the fuck, bro?" Yala shouted out loud, but the men didn't move.

"You can either get in the truck parked across the street or your mom dies," Kazzy stated.

"What? Who the fuck are you?" Yala looked back and forth between Kazzy and Lil K.

"Listen, dumb bitch, we have your mom. Follow us or she dies, period. Your choice you made has now come back to bite you in your ass," Lil K said, getting out of the car.

"Where is she?"

"The Bronx." Kazzy walked to the SUV with Lil K and Yala was a few feet behind.

Yala was a big-time mama's boy and put his mom before himself.

***

Bronx, NY

Kazzy pulled into the back of a closed down shelter in the south Bronx near Hunts Point. "Here we go, big dawg," Kazzy said, getting out the truck walking into the back exit where Paco had Yala mom tied up at.

"Mom!" Yala said, about to rush to her aid until all their guns pointed at him.

"Hold on, playboy," Lil K said, stepping to him.

"Just let her go. I'll give you anything or tell you anything, man, I swear on my life." Yala cried seeing his mom with duct tape over her mouth, wrists, and ankles.

"Tell us about Batista and Diaz," Knight said, coming from the back room.

"I don't really know Batista," Yala stated only to see Knight pull out a gun.

Knight shot Yala's mom in her leg and blood quickly stained the old women jeans.

"Okay, man, I know he lives in Long Island and I know he likes to go golfing every Friday," Yala stated.

"Good start. Now tell me about Diaz, your plug?" Knight asked as he saw Yala cry.

"Diaz lives in Harlem on St. Nick, but I don't know what building," Yala said before Lil K shot his mom in her arm, seeing her squirm in pain.

"Try again, bitch nigga," Lil K said.

"Friday nights, Diaz goes to this little whorehouse in the Heights on Dyckman and he buys pussy," Yala said

"I know where that's at," Paco stated.

"I guess we're done here," Knight said, killing Yala first and then putting two bullets in Yala's mom's head.

"Easy," Paco said.

"Today is Friday, so Paco and Lil K, y'all niggas go see what's up with Diaz. Me and Kazzy gotta take a road trip," Knight said.

***

Washington Heights, NY

Whenever Diaz came out here, he came alone because he didn't want his goons to see him buying pussy or tricking. Diaz got out of his car, placing his hoodie low covering his eyes as he creeped into the building. On the fourth floor he did the special knock six light times, letting them know he was here.

When the door opened he saw a young woman no older than fifteen, his favorite age. Diaz had a thing for minors. It was his little dirty secret.

"Come," she said as other women and goons surrounded the apartment, but when he saw Paco and Lil K, his heart stopped.

The goons all had their guns out on him. He couldn't believe it.

Paco's boy ran the whorehouses in Washington Heights, so it was easy to set this up.

"Diaz, correct?" Paco asked.

"You know who am I just like I know who you are," Diaz said.

"What good news. Can you tell us about your father?" Lil K asked.

"Let's just get this shit over with, playboy. This is bigger than me, my pops, or y'all." Diaz stated.

"What you mean by that?"

"You will soon see, trust me. This is only the starting line." Diaz laughed.

"A'ight, tough guy."

Bloc! Bloc! Bloc! Bloc! Bloc!

Paco killed Diaz and had his people get rid of Diaz's body.

Chapter 37
Brewster, NY

Red woke up in the middle of the night from a nightmare she had about Lil K. She cried, looking at her chains tied to the bed and the two women sitting on the couch watching her. Since the women had placed a spell on Red she had been feeling empty, and heartless. Red ain't give a fuck if she lived or died. She just wanted a hit so she could go to her own space. The thought of Lil K was the only emotion she had. She did miss him, but the chances of her seeing him again were slim.

Uncle Pimp opened the door and came inside ass naked with a needle and drugs in his hand. "You ready?" he asked her.

"Yes." Red's voice was dry and sweet as she looked at his monstrous cock.

"Today we gonna try something different. I'ma give you this dope then some dick, okay?" he said.

Red was quiet, but the more she looked at the drugs the more Red wanted it. "Okay," she said as Uncle Pimp already had the drugs in the needle and everything set up for her. Once he gave her the shoot of pure dope, she got in her zone as Uncle Pimp slid her panties to the side.

He gave her a whore bath every day so she smelled good, just as he liked. Uncle Pimp slowly entered her super tight coochie, and feeling her warmness hug his dick made him go deeper in her.

"Ohhhh," she moaned.

"You like it?" Uncle Pimp had never felt a pussy like hers. He started to pump faster until he nutted all in her. He ain't never nut so fast and he had sex all day.

Uncle Pimp started eating her cat, making her go crazy. His head game was on a different level. It didn't take long for her to hit an orgasm all over the sheets and on his face.

"I'ma save some for later. You're all mines now. I'ma treat you like a Queen," Uncle Pimp said, kissing her lips, and surprisingly, she kissed him back.

***

Atlanta, GA

Money came out to Club Onyx to meet Khalid to talk business and about money. Last time he saw Khalid it was about to get nasty, but when Khalid offered him a position on his empire, he had to sleep on it. Khalid gave him some keys of dope and it had fiends on the East side of Atlanta going crazy. Money had no choice but to fuck with Khalid because Fats' drugs were fucking up his name.

"Khalid." Money entered the back of the club, where Khalid was alone but Money saw men watching his every move so he knew Khalid had goons in the spot.

"Nice to see you made the right choice," Khalid stated as Money sat down.

"Yeah, I'm ready."

"Good, let's talk business," Khalid stated.

"How much?"

"I'ma give you 300 on me, just to show gratitude," Khalid said in his African voice.

"Okay."

***

Uptown, BX

Today was Rilla's daughter's birthday, so he went to pick her up to go toy shopping. Rilla's daughter was seven years old and smart. She was his world and life besides the streets.

The beef with Knight's crew had been weird because nobody had been dying lately. Rilla knew something was wrong but he couldn't put his finger on it. He knew Knight and his boys were smarter than most crews in the city so he took their quietness as a threat.

"Daddy, can we go there?" his daughter said, pointing to Chuck E. Cheese to their right.

"I thought you wanted to go shopping?" Rilla asked as he pulled into the lot to see a few people is customs waving people down just to grab their attention.

"I want to do both. It's not your birthday, Daddy it's mines," she said, making him laugh.

"Okay, you got it, little mami." Rilla took her into Chuck E. Cheese.

***

"That's you, son. We both can't do it," Kazzy told Lil K letting him know he would have to slide up in there and make an attempt on Rilla's life.

"A'ight, be ready for when I come out. I have a plan," Lil K said following the man in the Chuck E. Cheese suit inside.

Lil K walked inside to see a bunch of kids running around, but when he spotted the Chuck E. Cheese costume, he made his way to the restaurant room following him. Inside the restroom, Lil K saw the man taking a piss.

"I fucking hate kids," the man said to himself, taking a piss, unaware Lil K was creeping behind him.

Lil K hit the man in the back of the gun with his Draco, knocking him clean out. In seconds, Lil K walked out of the restroom dress in a Chuck E. Cheese suit. He spotted Rilla and his daughter playing in the pen full of small balls, having fun. Lil K had a silencer on the Draco as he sneaked up on them where no other kids were around. Rilla saw Lil K and knew he got caught up.

Psst! Psst! Psst!

Lil K killed Rilla and his daughter, leaving them dead in the pool of balls.

When Lil K was leaving out the front door, kids ran up to him, trying to get his attention.

"Have a good day," he told all of them as he heard a loud scream from the play area.

Lil K slid outside and Kazzy saw him rush out.

Kazzy couldn't believe Lil K took it this far. He found it funny.

"Nice suit, killer," Kazzy said as they pulled off.

Chapter 38
Philly, PA

Money drove through Philly with a baddie in the passenger seat blowing weed smoke out her mouth into the air. He was coming to visit his boy TJ in South West to drop off 100 keys he had in the trunk. Driving with that many bricks was dangerous, but he didn't trust a soul so he took it upon himself.

Money had just made it to Philly. He loved the City of Brotherly Love's vibes. He was making a left on 52nd Street when red and blue lights flashed behind him, scaring his friend.

"Bitch, put that shit out," he told her.

"Okay," she said, nervous.

Money pulled over because he knew it was only a small traffic stop. Seconds later, a white cop got out of the patrol car with an evil look on his face.

"Excuse me, sir you ran a——" The cop paused, smelling the aroma of weed in the air coming out the car window. "I'ma need you both to step out," the cop said.

Money's heart dropped, already knowing it was over if they was to pop the trunk. "Okay, take it easy," Money said, about to open the door, but instead he reached in his door panel and pulled out a gun.

Boc! Boc! Boc!

Money hit the cop in his neck and face then raced off to the nearest highway.

"Oh my God, you just killed a cop!"

Money had forgotten all about the chick he was with and pulled over on the highway. Money gave her two dome shots then pushed her out of the car, leaving her on the side of the road.

Not only was he on the run for killing a judge and a DA, but now a Philly cop.

***

Atlanta, GA

Behadi left New York for a few days because she had something on her mind and her period just hit two days ago, so she was on one.

She walked up to the front door of her dad's mansion and rang the doorbell.

Nasma had been acting weird and Behadi wasn't feeling it at all, but she just gave her some space.

Within seconds of standing there, the door opened and Chiai stood on the other side, looking alluring in her Islamic garment.

"Behadi?"

"As salamu alaikum," Behadi said.

"Wa alaikum salam, come inside," Chai said, letting her inside.

"Thanks." Behadi walked inside the large mansion she admired.

"How can I help you?"

"Is my father here?" Behadi asked.

"No, he went to Africa for a few days." Chai saw something was wrong with Behadi.

"Damn."

"I can relay a message for you if it's an emergency," Chai stated.

"No, it's good I got it," Behadi said, pulling out a gun and pointing it at Chai.

"I would act surprised, but that's not me," Chai said.

"I have recorders set up all through your home so I heard all yours and my father's plans," Behadi said.

"Okay, good, I'm proud of you, a step ahead," Chai said.

"Y'all trying get Nasma to kill me, then you was going to kill her."

"True, if Allah willed," Chai said, not showing any type of fear.

"Look how the tables turn," Behadi said seriously.

"It's life, Behadi. You have to play the game to the fullest." Chai sat down on a kitchen stool

"Facts, Chai."

Bloc! Bloc! Bloc! Bloc! Bloc!

Behadi saw Chai's body spin out of the chair as she jerked to the floor and Behadi put two more in her forehead.

154

***
Bronx, NY

Paco pulled over on White Plains Road at a chicken spot he had been to a couple of times. It was eight at night and the darkness always gave the city a dangerous look if you weren't from there. The beef with the Cubans had died down, but Paco knew soon shit would be back to normal.

He walked into the chicken spot and ordered a few drumsticks and wings. Paco saw a beautiful woman walk in behind him ordering the same shit he did. He heard her accent and was turned on off the rip.

"You got a sexy voice."

"Huh?" The woman looked back at Paco, looking him up and down.

"You're sexy and I want your number, ma," Paco said.

"You run this shit on all the ladies?" she asked as Paco grabbed his food.

"I never use the same line, if you want me to be real." Paco made her crack a light smile.

"Respect." The woman paid for her food and grabbed her bag, leaving him standing there.

Paco followed her outside. He wasn't giving up that easy. "Damn, you just gonna curve me like that?"

"Like what?" She stepped into the street, letting cars pass them.

Paco was also parked across the street next to a car dealership. "I know you used to the attention, but I'm——" Paco paused when he really got a good look at the woman, but by then it was too late.

Nasma pulled out a gun. She killed Paco and got in her car, racing off to her next mission, ready to change clothes.

She had been following most of the crew for the past couple of days. Now she was on her way to a nearby town called Mount Vernon, New York connected to the Bronx.

***

Mount Vernon, NY

Lil K had been in the Mosque at all hours of the night to repent and worship Allah. He knew Allah was the only person who could bring Red back, so he made Du'wa (personal worships) asking for him to bring back Red. Tonight, he was the only person in the mosque. Lil K would read and make his prayers as Muslim brothers and sister came in and out all hours of the day.

A woman fully dressed came inside to pray. Her face was covered, so Lil K couldn't really see none of her feathers. Lil K saw her approach him in slow steps. He figured she had an Islamic question.

"Nice to see you again," the woman said, pulling out a gun.

The voice was familiar, but he couldn't place it. "May Allah forgive you. I know this is the shaytan," Lil K said as he looked out the barrel of the pistol.

"Khalid."

"I had a feeling you was from the motherland. You been following me," Lil K told her, wishing he would have brought his gun in the mosque. Lil K felt safe in the mosque so he never brought weapons inside.

"Goodbye. I know my sister will be sad," she said, touching the trigger.

Lil K saw Nasma's head get blown off. When her body dropped he saw Behadi behind her crying.

"We have to go," she said with glossy eyes.

Lil K couldn't believe what took place as he followed her out of the mosque.

Chapter 39
Manhattan, NY

Behadi took Lil K to the low-key condo she bought months ago online while living in Atlanta, GA. She told Lil K everything, and he couldn't believe she killed her own sister for him.

Lil K was overwhelmed by everything she was saying for the last four hours. "Wow, you did all that for me? But why?" Lil K had to know why she would risk her life for a nigga she barely knew. Lil K remember her helping him back to normal after surviving that head shot from Money.

"I'll let you get some rest because now we have to worry about my father," she said, avoiding his question.

"Thank you, Behadi."

"Anytime." She went to the back room.

Lil K couldn't believe Khalid lined them up. He couldn't wait to tell Knight.

*****

Long Island, NY

Mita had been exercising heavily in Knight's living room watching workout videos. Knight was out in the Bronx with his brothers handling some business that he told her when she called.

She heard the doorbell ring and looked into camera monitor Knight had installed to see the UPS man. Mita rushed to the door because she had been doing a lot of online shopping. he bought some shit for her boo. Mita was in love with Knight, but she didn't know how to show it.

Opening the door, she saw the man carrying a box and wearing a uniform but when he lifted his head, Mita's heart dropped.

Don pulled out a gun and pointed it at her face.

Boom! Boom! Boom! Boom! Boom!

Mita collapsed on the floor as blood stained her workout clothes and Don went on his next mission nearby.

***

Knight just got done speaking to Lil K about the Khalid situation and he couldn't believe it. Knight even spoke to Behadi himself and she told him everything from top to bottom. It was crazy how hard the enemy would go to kill you, even if it meant killing their own loved ones.

Knight had to stop by his new club that would open in a few days. After checking on the club, he wanted to go check on Mita. As he drove into the lot, he got a text from Kazzy saying Paco had been killed. He couldn't believe it. Knight thought he was reading the text wrong as he parked the car and got out, reading it again.

"Nah, man." Knight couldn't believe it. His boy was dead.

"Got your bitch ass now, bruh," Don said with a gun pointed at Knight's head.

"A'ight, fam, do you. Get it in blood. We ain't gotta do the wolf tickets," Knight said.

Neither one of them saw a black Benz with tints pull into the lot slowly. The two men were back and forth talking shit until shots were fired.

Boc! Boc! Boc! Boc! Boc!

Bullets tore through Don's back, making his body collapse into Knight's arms in slow motion. Don had blood spilling out of his mouth. He died in Knight's arms before he pushed him on the ground to see the driver get out of the Benz.

"Bree?"

"Hey Knight."

"I should kill you right now," he said as she laughed hard.

"Knight, you're so funny, I swear, and you cute. One day..." she said, climbing in the car.

Knight saw how phat her ass was in her dress and he wanted to fuck the shit outta her, but she came with too much.

Knight could have sworn he saw a baby sitting in the backseat of the car.

Within minutes, he arrived at his house to see Mita slumped in the doorway with a UPS package next to her body.

Knight couldn't believe this. He was hurt. Mita was special to him.

Chapter 40
Queens, NY

Batista and two of his bodyguards were on the way to the airport, where a private land strip with a jet awaited him. There was too much going on in New York so he had made plans to go back home to Cuban. Losing his wife took so much out of him Cynthia was his pride and joy. Then losing Irma took a toll on him if he would have knew she was going to Miami he would have stopped her that day. Now Irma was dead along with her brother Diaz. He tried so hard to keep his family and business separate but it overlapped. Batista never had a clue Knight was this crazy and dangerous so before he lost his life, he planned to get the fuck out of the crazy States.

Pulling into the private jet strip he saw his jet ready. Going back home was big to him because he hadn't been home in a while. His driver parked and he got out, inhaling a deep breath of fresh air. Batista got on his jet and when he walked inside the luxury jet, he saw a man sitting there. He knew who the man was.

"Batista, glad to see you, my friend," Smoke said, drinking wine out of a glass.

"Humo (meaning smoke in Spanish)?" Batista was shocked to see his plug, who was a black man from the Bronx.

"You leaving so fast?" Smoke said as Batista slowly sat down, knowing something was wrong.

"Yeah, I need a vacation," he said.

"A vacation? Are you running away after losing your family like a coward does?" Smoke looked at him.

"I'm no coward."

"That's good to know, Batista, but we have a problem," Smoke said.

"Us?"

"Yeah. There are a few things you don't know about me. When I married your sister, I had a life of my own," Smoke told him.

"I don't understand this?"

"Just listen. You will, kid. I have children and I do love my creation."

"What does this have to do with me?"

"A lot. My sons are Knight, Lil K, and Kazzy."

"Your what?" Batista thought Humo was using the word son as a slang.

"They are my children, Batista, and you crossed the line," Smoke said pulling out a weapon.

Bloc! Bloc! Bloc! Bloc! Bloc!

Smoke killed Batista and tossed his dead body off the jet as Batista's two guards joined Smoke, flying back to Cuba.

***

Smoke had been living in Cuba for a long time now. He married Batista's sister, muscled his way into the family business, which was drugs, and tried to push Batista out in order to gain a stronghold over the drug trade in Cuba.

Batista hated Smoke for the power he had in Cuba.

Nobody knew Smoke had kids. Knight and his brothers didn't even know they had a father. Smoke had a lot of secrets and couldn't wait to tell his son what was going on because Knight didn't have a clue. Right now, wasn't the right time to pop up so Smoke planned to make his way back home to think about his next step.

His wife was going to be very upset about the loss of her brother, but it was a part of the game.

Chapter 41
Downtown, BK
One month later

Fats loved chilling in his condo eating and counting money. This was his everyday life.

Losing Don was only a minor setback. He already had another crew to full his position.

Fats had no remorse for setting up Don years ago and getting him a 75 year sentence. It was all a part of his plan to kill the judge and DA for Don's freedom so he would owe him his loyalty and life at the same time. Having blood on your hands was the best way to lock someone in for life.

The only issue at the current moment was Fats had been getting bad coke and dope from Gotti. This was the first time Gotti shitted on him. Fats had been moving the same trash work for months now.

Money disappeared once more, but what he didn't know was that there was one person who had witnessed him murder the cop that night. Until recently, the witness had been reluctant to come forward.

Knight had also become a ghost, which was his biggest fear because of how dangerous he was. There were a lot of rumors saying Knight was connected to some powerful people and some said he got out of the game.

Boom!

The front door got kicked opened and two masked men ran inside. Fats' gun was under his couch, but he was too fat and slow to get it.

"I don't want your fat ass to move. Where the money and drugs?" one of them asked.

"The drugs are in Redhook, but I have two million on the floor." Fats pointed to his right, knowing this was only a robbery.

Both men took off their black masks and Fats almost cried to see Knight's diamond teeth and Kazzy.

"Bag up da rocks, son," Knight told Kazzy.

"Say less, yo." Kazzy saw how scared Fats was and laughed because he was popping wild shit.

"Where is Red?" Knight asked, sitting down.

"With Uncle Pimp somewhere. I don't know, him and Don came up with that idea. I ain't know shit about that, son," Fats cried.

"A'ight. I finally caught up with your fat ass, boy. You're a lot of work, no lie," Knight stated.

"I'm smart," Fats said.

"Not that smart," Kazzy said as he placed all the money in the bag.

"Knight, there is a lot of talk. Just know that shit don't end here," Fats said.

"It begins," Knight stated.

Bloc! Bloc! Bloc! Bloc! Bloc!

Knight aired Fats out, looking at him take his last breath.

"I'ma take the left staircase, bro, just in case someone heard the gunfire," Kazzy said, walking out of the condo.

"Okay, I'ma take the right, bro, and don't pocket none of that paper, son," Knight joked.

"Nigga, fuck you," Kazzy joked, walking into the stairwell.

When Kazzy made it to the next level, he was tackled and stabbed by two men. The two men were Khalid and Gotti taking turns stabbing Kazzy. Each man stabbed Kazzy over thirty times before leaving out the back exit the same way they came in.

What most people didn't know was that Khalid and Gotti were blood brothers and they learned from a mutual friend that Knight would come to kill Fats tonight, so they were ready. Both men thought they killed Knight, but Kazzy took the fall.

***

After two minutes of waiting outside, Knight went back inside to see what was taking Kazzy so long. Walking up the stairs, Knight saw blood linking down the staircase.

"What the fuck?" Knight walked further up the stairs to see Kazzy's lifeless body in a puddle of blood.

Knight shed a tear into the blood of his brother.

"Love you for life," Knight said, leaving, headed back downstairs.

***

Hours later

Knight called everybody to his club at 3 a.m. to tell them all what was going on.

Lil K and Behadi were the last ones standing.

"Kazzy got killed, so it's only us."

"What?" Lil K couldn't believe it.

"We went to holler at Fats and shit went left. Somebody was on to us and caught him in the stairwell." Knight still had the image of Kazzy's dead body in his head.

"What now?" Behadi asked.

"Batista was killed and now we have to find out who else is on us, like…" Knight had been putting all the pieces to the puzzle together and there was a lot of shit he didn't understand.

"Like what?" Lil K asked.

"I don't know a hundred percent yet, but we will find out sooner or later," Knight stated, drinking hard liquor.

***

Bronx, NY
Two months later

Knight and Lil K came up to see their mom's gravesite for her birthday. Walking up the trail to where their mom was buried, they felt a weird feeling in their gut. As they got closer they saw a man in a gray suit placing fresh pink roses on their mom's grave. The flowers were their mom's favorite flowers so whoever the man was, he either knew their mom well are he took a good guess.

"Who are you?" Lil K ask the man.

"Knight and Lil K, I assume? You both look great," the man said as he turned around

"How do you know our names and our mom's favorite roses?" Knight asked.

"After y'all pay y'all respect to your mother, I have a lot of explaining to do," the man said.

"You still haven't answered our question," Knight said.

"We can build later, but my brothers Khalid, Gotti, and Uncle Pimp want you dead. I'm here to help."

"Your brothers?"

"Why the fuck you want to save us?" Lil K asked.

"I'm Smoke y'all pops. I'll be at the bottom of hill," Smoke said, walking off.

Chapter 42
Princeton, NJ

Knight been living in an upscale rich neighborhood for the past year. He knew he had to get out of New York as far as his living situation. He had a 22,617 square foot mansion with a lush lawn, a cobblestone driveway and a six car garage. Inside was breathtaking, the floors were antique heart pine, firestone fireplace, five bathroom and six bedrooms, two walk in closets, marble kitchen and a massive backyard with a pod and a Jacuzzi. This was home when he wasn't at his condos in the city.

Last year had to be the worst year of his life, as he entered a war he wasn't mentally ready for at all. Going against the Cubans, Gotti, Khalid, Uncle Pimp, and Don took all of his time and energy. Everything led back to Fats, who he had been going back and forth with for years. Now with Fats and Don dead, Knight thought he could breathe, but that wasn't the case. Uncle Pimp still had Red captured somewhere upstate and Lil K was still hurt about that. He wanted his wifey back.

The Cubans were out of the picture. Once Batista and Diaz got murked, the Cubans vanished out of the city.

Bree was still lurking around trying to get in where she fit in, but Knight wasn't worried about too much.

Knight had lost Kazzy and Paco within the same year. Losing a blood brother was hard. He missed Kazzy. He even got his name and face tatted on side.

Lil K was back on his Islamic deen and since it was the month of Ramadan, he was fasting for thirty days.

Meeting his father Smoke, a.k.a. Humo, was at a crazy time in his life. He accepted his dad even though he only saw him a few times and they talked on the phone. In a few weeks, he supposed to meet with his dad so they could go over business because he was itching for a new plug.

Things with Julie were weird since Kazzy's death. She hardly showed her face and whenever he went to Miami he would be seen by one of her goons. Knight knew she was crushed by his death and so was he, but he knew he had to keep shit flowing or shit will roll downhill.

The Bronx was still his, but there were a lot of new hustlers trying to set up shop. Knight had a new weapon on his team. Knight's weapon was M Balla, a Blood kid he saw grow up from his projects, Mill Brook. Last year M Balla came home from beating two homicides. M Balla was a jack boy, so Knight had him and his crew hustling and shutting down any shops that didn't belong to Knight's crew.

Knight still had other drug spots in L.I, S.I, Queens, Manhattan, Yonkers, and Washington Heights.

Knight still had a few clubs in the city and he was spending a lot of time focusing on his investments.

His love life was nothing one could be cheerful about. He ran through women daily, but he wished he could settle down.

Knight had a private call and he knew it was from D Fatal Brim in person, so he pushed five.

***

Havana, Cuba

Smoke and five of his goons arrived at an apartment building surrounded by goons with assault rifles. This was an area Smoke ran in the heart and slums of Cuba. He stashed drugs here and this is where he would have his people cut the coke he got from his wife and her family who ran Cuba.

Living in Cuba so long, Smoke learned Spanish and the culture, which was great.

He got out of the truck and walked up the stairs into the brick building to smell the pure coke in the hallway.

Smoke was happy to meet his son, but losing one took a lot out of him also. Kazzy's death could have been avoided if Smoke would have known what Batista was doing earlier.

Batista was his wife's brother and Batista was getting his drugs from Smoke and his wife. Smoke's wife had ten sisters and three brothers. They had a big family.

Knight made plans to meet him in Cuba in a few weeks because Smoke was ready to supply his son. He was just waiting for the right time.

The Cubans had a lot of beef with other countries like Colombians and their rivals, the Costa Rican sisters.

Chapter 43
Mount Vernon, NY

Lil K stood in prayer, reciting the first chapter of the Quran Al-Faitah.

"In the name of Allah, the most gracious, the most merciful.

All praise and thanks are Allah's the Lord of the Alamin (mankind)

The most gracious, the most merciful.

The only owner (and the only ruling judge) of the day of recompense (the day of resurrection)

You (alone) we worship and you (alone) we ask for help (for each and everything)

Guide us to the straight way.

The way of those on whom you have bestowed your grace, not (the way) of those who earned your anger, nor of those who went astray."

Lil K added another short surah to this in Arabic then bowed his head to the floor before finishing up his early morning prayer.

This was Lil K's new lifestyle. True, he was still in the field, but since Red got kidnapped he lost focus in everything. When he lost himself, he found his spiritual side and he really embraced it wholeheartedly.

This month was Ramadan and he had a few days left of his thirty day fast. Lil K was proud of himself for fasting and staying focused even with a lot of shit was going on in his head.

Every day he thought about Red's well-being because he didn't know what was going on with her. All he thought about was if she alive, dead, happy, or sad.

When Kazzy died, Lil K almost gave up the game because he knew this life was about killing and dying in the streets -or a slave plantation as he called it. Lil K hated the feeling of having one foot in and one foot out of the streets.

Lil K hired a private investigator to find Red and he just got a call from him last night asking him to meet at his office in White

Plains, NY. He hoped the P.I. had some good news because he knew anything could be hopeful.

The only thing Lil K knew was Red was being held at some ranch style house.

Lil K took a shower and got dressed to go see if the P.I. had any useful info.

***

White Plains, NY

Lil K walked into the office of an older black man with a bald head and salt and pepper beard named Mr. Curtis Hopewell.

"Lil K," Mr. Curtis said as he stood, extending his hand.

"What's going on with the case?" Lil K got right to business, staring at the man's hand.

"Well, I came across good news and bad news," Mr. Curtis said, putting his head down.

"What? Where is she?"

"Red was caught on video two days ago robbing a bank with four other females in Manhattan and she and the other four women are now on the FBI's top ten wanted list. They murdered seven people and she was leader."

"This must be a mistake. Red don't rob banks?"

"She does now," Mr. Curtis said.

"How do you know it was her?" Lil K asked.

"Check this out." Mr. Curtis handed him a stack of photos.

When Lil K saw the pics of Red with an AR-15 assault rifle, he knew it was true.

Words couldn't explain how he felt.

There was no denying the fact that the woman in the picture was Red.

"Shit." Lil K was upset.

"I'll continue to do my job and find her before the FBI does, but she's in big trouble, Lil K. I was a cop before I retired, so I can tell you now this is big, young man."

"Thank you." Lil K walked out stressed out.

Chapter 44
Queens, NY

Bree looked over at her baby girl as she fed her dinner. Being a mother full time was crazy for Bree. Even though she had a nanny, she still was considered a full-time mom.

Her Queens home was a regular small house with three bedrooms and a bathroom. Bree also had a few other homes in New York and other cities because she traveled a lot.

The past year Bree had focused on her future and opening more traps in Delaware, Boston, and certain sections of Brooklyn and Queens. Khalid was no longer suppling her and she was glad about that because she didn't trust him at all. A few months before she found a new plug, Khalid was cutting the drugs with all types of shit, making a lot of people overdose on heroin.

Killing Don was the best thing she did in a long time. She only wished she could have killed Fats' bitch ass too.

Bree was on a new level in her life she had a new plug and a new clients, so she felt powerful. She still heard Knight's name heavy in the streets, but more so his worker M Balla. Word was if you had money or drugs, M Balla was coming to get it in the worst way. He was putting fear in the whole South Bronx.

Bree had been going hard in the gym so her body was looking like a snack. She still was a bad bitch.

On Instagram she had over 1.7 million followers, but they had no idea Bree Doll was a queenpin killer.

***

South Bronx, NY

C-Roc and his crew hustled all day and gambled all night in the Castle Hill projects. The PJs was one of the biggest projects in the Bronx run by a nigga named Stress, who was in Miami for the weekend. Twenty goons posted up in the back of the last building doing what they did every night. The crew got big money because there were so many buildings in the hood. One building could make $15,000 a day.

"Yo C-Roc, niggas got 10g'z on Slang dice!" Loyal shouted as he watched the dice hit the wall.

"Next roll bet," C-Roc said as Slang rolled the dice and aced out.

"Damn, son," C-Roc's brother Gold stated because he hated losing money.

While everybody was focused on the crew paying C-Roc, four vans pulled up and gunmen hopped out of all of the vans with weapons. The gunmen had H&K, F&N, and Draco plus some military style shit none of them had seen before.

"Don't reach," a tall dark-skinned handsome brother stated.

"What's all this about, fam? You must not know where you at," C-Roc said, trying to play tough.

The tall man who everybody took as the leader looked around as if C-Roc wasn't speaking to him. In a quick motion, the man rammed the butt of his gun in C-Roc's face, dazing him.

"How many of y'all is out here?" the tall man said, counting to come up with twenty-one. "Ten of you gonna die tonight, so make your pick."

All of C-Roc's soldiers pointed at each other. Even Loyal pointed at C-Roc. He had kids to get home to.

One of the soldiers tried to run.

Bloc! Bloc! Bloc! Bloc!

Each bullet that came out of the tall man's gun landed in the nigga's back, killing him.

"So I'll pick."

Bloc! Bloc! Bloc!

Boom! Boom! Boom!

Tat! Tat! Tat!

C-Roc was still alive as he watched his goons get head tapped. Killing a nigga up close was different than seeing it from a distance.

"I assume you C-Roc, that nigga Stress' slave?" the tall brother asked.

"Yeah." C-Roc's heart pumped fear.

"I want you to tell him it's a new chief in town while in Castle Hill, so he can either get down or stay down."

"Who are you?" C-Roc asked as his brother's blood started to pour on the bottom of his Timbs.

"M Balla, you heard?" The tall man walked off with his goons as friends and family members came out the buildings to see what the commotion was about.

Chapter 45
South Bronx, NY

M Balla pulled into his projects with his young boys as they all bragged about who got the best head off.

M Balla was born in Yonkers, New York, where he had a lot of family at, but he was raised in the Bronx. At twenty-one, he had his head on right his name in the BX was litty like Cardi B. He controlled almost every hood in the Southside with his crew they called mack Ballas. They were about money and turning up.

M Balla was a big homie under his older brother, who was serving two life sentences upstate. They called him J Balla.

Working with Knight was big because he used to look up to him and D Fatal Brim, who was cool with J Balla, his older brother. Everybody from the hood looked up to Knight and his crew, especially him, so when Knight approached him with a plan to lock shit, he was down because his name already had a buzz in the Bronx.

M Balla didn't consider himself a drug dealer because he had a nice set up. He would get the keys of coke and dope and see what hood was doing numbers, then force his way in. When he muscled his way into a hood he would give the drugs to the shot caller of that hood. Most niggas were Bloods anyway trying to make money so it made it real easy for M Balla and his guys to pull up. The main issues would come from Crips and Dominicans not trying to give up their turf.

M Balla sent Stress two messages trying to talk nice so they could all get money but he could tell Stress was hard headed, so he would have to show how a Balla got down.

M Balla knew Castle Hill was a goldmine, but Stress was a Crip and his boys were all sex, money, murda, so he would be up against a lot if Stress didn't flood.

His nickname was the Grim Reaper to most because he would always leave a dead body behind wherever he went.

***

Upper Westside, NY

Behadi just got out of the shower. Water dripped from her long hair, which she had dyed dirty blonde. She had a long cotton towel wrapped around her body as she danced in her room to the old school 702 album.

Behadi was getting ready to go out to a spa to treat herself, something she rarely did nowadays because of how busy she had been. Since last year, she had come a long way from being her father Khalid's personal killer to her own woman. When Behadi came to the States from Africa to kill Knight and his crew, she had no idea shit would go left.

Behadi found out her dad was plotting to kill her. Khalid sent her own sister Nasma to kill her after he told her to kill Bree's and Knight's crews. Behadi had her dad's crib bugged and she got wind her dad was trying to set her up.

Behadi had a crazy crush on Lil K. She first laid eyes on him when he got shot in his head. She helped him back to better health while Khalid had him captured. Behadi killed her own blood sister to save her own life and Lil K's life.

Being a skilled fighter, shooter, and killer, she knew Nasma's thought process and plus she was her sister.

Behadi hadn't seen Lil K since that day, and it'd been crushing her because she thought about him every day.

She been focus on designing clothes. She had also been trying to keep an eye on Lil K. Behadi knew where Lil K was but she didn't know if he wanted to be bothered or not.

Losing his girl Red took a lot out of him and she knew he was damaged, but she couldn't do anything about it except wait for the perfect time to make her move.

Behadi knew her father wanted her dead and he would do whatever to succeed. She wasn't going to let him kill her. She knew Khalid better than he knew himself. He was coming soon but right now, he was trying to find her location.

Behadi changed her name and Social Security number. She also changed her appearance. She had gained some weight in the right areas, making her ass look crazy phat.

Chapter 46
Havana, Cuba

Knight had no idea Cuba was so beautiful. The weather was on point and the trees were some shit a nigga only saw in magazines.

The driver pulled into a huge house.

"Damn, this nigga up," Knight mumbled, seeing Smoke stand in front of his glass French doors with a gang of gunmen who spoke no English whatsoever.

"You come alone?"

"Yeah," Knight said to his dad, getting out of the car.

"I was hoping my little one could have come," Smoke said, referring to Lil K,

"He got some shit going on right now," Knight explained.

"Is he okay?"

"Yeah, personal problems." Knight ain't want to tell Smoke too much of his brother's business. Knight knew if Lil K wanted their father to know about Red he would have told him a long time ago. Lil K told Knight when they first met Smoke he didn't like his vibes and he was out of their lives for over twenty years, so why come back now. Knight saw it in a different picture to get a bigger bag.

"I see." Smoke led Knight into the home and he was very impressed by how classy and expensive it looked. Even the wallpaper looked fancy.

"This shit nice. I can't lie, I need some shit like this," Knight said, looking around as they walked into the office room Smoke used for business.

"Yeah."

"You stay here alone" I thought you had a wife?" Knight asked because he remembered him saying something about being married.

"I do, but she's out of town. She can't wait to meet you, I can assure you," he replied.

"Let's talk money," Knight said, smiling.

"Like father like son." Smoke smiled proudly.

"Facts."

"I know you still fucking with ole girl from Miami, but she not nowhere near my level. I have the best coke and dog food out right now."

"The shit Batista was getting wasn't shit," Knight said.

"He was cutting it, stepping all over the shit." Smoke shook his head.

"If I do fuck with you, how much will you give me the keys for?" Knight asked.

"Low."

"How low?"

"Real low. I got you because regardless, you still my son," Smoke stated.

"A'ight."

"Let me milk the cow while I hold it at the same time. You just watch," Smoke joked.

"Say no more."

"You got a drop off location somewhere?" Smoke asked.

"At the cargo in Manhattan. It's safe."

"You sure?"

"Yeah, I do that when I get shit shipped from Miami," Knight told him.

"Okay, in two days a load with the numbers 72381054 will be there awaiting you," Smoke said.

"Say no more."

"Knight, we blood, but I love money more," Smoke told his own son letting him know if he crossed him, it was on and popping.

"I do too." Knight got up to leave.

Chapter 47
Boston, MA

Uncle Pimp and a few hoes waited outside of an upscale hotel for his main bitch to come out with the state senator of Massachusetts. Doing big hits like this he had to plan closely because a lot was at risk.

Uncle Pimp had been chilling lately. He had a squad of killers on his team, all females.

"That's her, daddy," one of his women said from the backseat of the GMC truck.

"Yeah" Uncle Pimp said as he watch an older white man and a sexy, brown-skinned woman come out of the hotel.

***

Joe and the beautiful lady had been seeing each other for weeks now and he was loving it. Joe was the state senator of Massachusetts. He had a wife and kids, but he couldn't resist a sexy black woman.

It was 3 a.m. and it was time to depart.

"Thanks for the long night," she said in her sexy voice.

"No problem. I aim to please," he shot back, feeling good about the work he just put in.

Once deeper into the parking lot, she saw a GMC truck parked in the spot where it was supposed to be. The woman stopped and acted like she had to fix her heels.

"You okay?" Joe stopped and saw her go in her purse.

"Your time is up," the woman said, pulling out a gun.

Boc! Boc! Boc! Boc!

The GMC pulled up in front of her and opened the back door for her.

"Nice job, but next time finish the job inside like how I told you," Uncle Pimp said before he slapped the shit out of the woman named Sexy Spicee.

"Sorry."

"A'ight, cool," he said as the others laughed under their breath because they were all jealous of her and Red.

As the truck pulled off, Sexy Spicee leaned in Uncle Pimp's lap and pulled out his dick. She started to suck him off slowly and at a nice pace he loved. She got deep enough to feel him in the back of her throat. Every time she gave him head, he would forget what was happening outside of that.

Sexy Spicee was from Miami. She was black and Cuban. They called her Sexy Spicee, but her real name was Nicole. She met Uncle Pimp when she was dancing and stripping in a club months ago in the 305. Uncle Pimp put her through a few months of training and now she was one of his top hitters.

They drove back to their home in Brewster.

***

Brewster, NY

Red was taking a hot shower alone in the private bathroom she shared with Uncle Pimp. Red became one of Uncle Pimp's main hoes and she was gone off the dick. Making love to Uncle Pimp was the best. She was in a different space.

Living with a gang of other women in the same house was crazy, but Red ran the house. Everybody envied Red, especially Sexy Spicee. Red was the one training the women who were fresh in the camp.

She would think about Lil K almost every day, but she felt as if he was just a phase in her life. Losing her memory took a lot out of her, but she remembered most of the events.

Red heard the girls come back and got out of the shower to hear the gossip.

Tonight, she planned to cook Uncle Pimp his favorite meal and have a threesome with one of the other women.

Chapter 48
Hollywood Hills, Cali

Marie loved her new home, which was 27,519 square foot with eight bedrooms and six large bathrooms. The mansion had two pools, indoor and outdoor, pool house, bar, indoor and outside. The white marble floor brought out the stylish house she designed.

Marie was now in the top five of the biggest drug suppliers on the west coast. She had drugs coming in from Mexico to Cali and she had an army under her nose.

Her everyday life was basically the same: sell drugs, kill, travel, and visit her husband in federal prison in PA. Being married to a nigga locked up in jail was hard because she was a person who needed attention. Marie could have cheated on D Fatal Brim many times, but she had self-control. She even went out to go buy a toy, which she would use daily whenever she would get horny.

Marie was in her kitchen cooking breakfast for herself this morning before she went to Texas. Her phone was ringing and she went to pick it up.

"Yes" she answered.

"This is Neko," the man said on the other line.

"Why are you calling me?" she asked. Marie's workers were told to never call her unless it was a real emergency.

"Last night our spots were robbed," Neko said.

"Robbed?"

"Yeah, and six men got killed in the process."

"Fuck." Marie hung up.

Marie stopped what she was doing and got dressed, heading out to Texas to check on her traps.

She knew one thing for sure. Neko better have the money he owed her.

***

White Plains, NY

Lil K got a call from Mr. Curtis saying he had something very important to tell him. When Lil K got the call, he rushed down

White Plains, but the area Mr. Curtis asked him to meet him at was in the hood.

Since the last time he saw Mr. Curtis he couldn't stop thinking about Red. Hearing about her rob a bank sounded crazy. That wasn't even like her at all. He knew someone had to be brainwashing her.

He pulled into the basketball area and called Mr. Curtis. "I'm here." Lil K heard Mr. Curtis' heavy breaths on the other end of the phone.

"Okay, one second. Don't go nowhere please," Mr. Curtis begged.

"I'm not," Lil K said before the phone hung up.

Lil K thought he was acting funny but he paid it no mind as he leaned his head back.

As soon as he leaned back, he saw a few shadows appear in his rearview mirror.

"Hell nah," Lil K said, hitting the push to start button trying to get away from the ambush.

Tat…

Lil K was able to pull off without getting hit, but bullets waved by his face a few times.

Tat! Tat! Tat! Tat! Tat!

Lil K couldn't believe Mr. Curtis just set him up, almost killing him. Mr. Curtis was the only person who knew he was coming here because he wasn't being followed.

The only thing Lil K could think of was why would Mr. Curtis set him up, but he planned to find out soon.

Chapter 49
Bronx, NY

Knight was on his way to see Lil K because he said he needed to speak to him about something very important. With so much beef in his city, Knight had to ride around with a stick on his lap.

The drugs he got from his pops was already moving in the streets. M Balla had the keys moving in the city and whatever was in the dope, the fiends were loving it. He thought about his father Smoke and wondered if he could be trusted even on a business level.

Knight was starving, so he pulled over at a McDonalds to get a breakfast sandwich and a cup of hot coffee. Drinking coffee was new to him, but he had to stay up and handle his business affairs. He got out of his car and made his way across the lot to the fast-food restaurant entrance.

Out of nowhere, a silver car smashed into Knight, knocking him to the ground. The impact was so hard he thought he saw angels and stars surrounding him. When he saw three men over him, his heart started to race at a fast pace.

"Knight, we finally meet again, young'un," Gotti said, smiling.

Knight couldn't believe he got caught slipping in his hometown by Gotti.

"This is my city," Knight said through his teeth.

"It's gonna be mines soon, bet that." Gotti then spit in Knight's face, aiming his gun at Knight's head.

Boc! Boc! Boc! Boc! Boc!

Knight saw Gotti's men body drop from head shots, killing them as Gotti ran off.

Gotti fired a few rounds at the shooter, who hopped out of a black Hellcat.

Bloc! Bloc! Bloc!

Knight could hardly move a muscle as someone helped him up. It was a beautiful woman with sunglasses and a wig on to hide her identity. She placed him in her car and drove off, speeding up the streets, hitting potholes.

"Thank you for saving me, but who are you?" Knight asked.

The woman focused on the road with the gun she just used to kill those two men back there on her lap. "Where is Lil K?" the woman asked.

"I don't know who you talking about"

"You don't remember me, do you?" she asked.

"No. I'm supposed to?" Knight's whole lower body was in pain.

The woman used a GPS to get to a local hospital nearby. When she pulled up near the main entrance, she parked the car and took off her sunglasses and wig.

"Behadi?" Knight remembered her from Africa. He wondered if she was here to kill him or not.

"Yes."

"What are you doing here?" he asked her.

"I'm here to tell you my dad been trying to kill you and Lil K. He been sending people," she told him.

"You saved Lil K in the mosque that day from your sister," he said to her.

"Yes, but I want to find him."

"Give me your number and I will give it to him, but he's very stressed since Red."

"I know, Knight," she said, taking the number and dropping him off at the hospital before pulling off.

Chapter 50
Uptown, Bronx

Knight pulled into lot to see Lil K waiting on him. He was wondering if he should tell him about seeing Behadi.

After the shooting with Gotti, he had chosen to go get a new car in order to move somewhat incognito, knowing that Gotti had seen his other vehicle. He was grateful Behadi saved his life.

"Where the fuck you been at?" Lil K asked seriously.

"I came across a big problem. You have no clue." Knight told his little brother, who looked stressed.

"What happened?"

"Nothing. Why you call me, son?" Knight asked.

"You remember this private investigator dude I told you about?" Lil K looked around.

"Yeah, I think I do. Why, what's up?" Knight remembered a little, but not a hundred percent.

"This nigga just tried to set me up." Lil K was mad.

"The P.I., my nigga?"

"Facts, son."

"How?" Knight couldn't believe it. Shit was getting real.

"He called talking about he had a lead on Red, so I shot out there to White Plains."

"And what happened?"

"It was an ambush, my nigga. They tried to take my head off, boy, word to mommy, son." Lil K wanted blood, but he had no clue who did it.

"You know who did it?"

"Nah, I only saw shadows, but I can't front, they looked like females bro," Lil K stated.

"If that's true, then that could only be one person," Knight said as they both looked at each other.

"Uncle Pimp," they both said at the same time.

"What now?" Lil K asked because his brother always had a plan.

"We start war and hunt them down," Knight said, looking at his little brother.

"What about Red?"

"What you mean?" Knight prayed he would eventually be able to move on because he knew Red was gone and she would never be able to be useful to him.

Knight found this the right time to tell him about Behadi popping up to save his life.

"I saw Behadi."

"Who?"

"Nigga, Behadi, from Africa?"

"Oh, Khalid's daughter?"

"Yeah, she saved my life, bro."

"How she do that?" Lil K remembered the time she saved his life in the mosque from Nasma.

"Gotti had me, bro, and she slid up started to air shit out, word." Knight went back to scene in his head slow motion.

"How is she?"

"She looking good and she asked about you the whole time bro, facts," Knight said, seeing a smile appear on his brother face.

"Oh, damn, she remembered me?"

"She digging you, son. I told her to get up with me soon so I can link y'all up."

"What?" Lil K said as his face frowned.

"You need a new joint, bro. You need some pussy. I'ma call you tomorrow" Knight walked off on him, getting in his car, leaving Lil K to think about Red and Behadi at the same time.

***

USP Canaan, PA

D Fatal Brim walked into his unit, coming back from lunch in the kitchen area where all the prisoners went to eat all three meals.

"Yo, Fatal!" a fat nigga from Chicago called him.

"What, Fat Pat?"

"The correctional officer went in your cell a few minutes ago as shawty did her rounds."

"Damn, you nosy as hell, son," D Fatal Brim said, walking off.

"This a penitentiary, you need to be nosy, it may save your life one day, big homie!" Fat Pat yelled as D Fatal Brim went to his cell on the top tier.

"What's poppin'?" he asked two Bloods posted up outside his cell.

"Us, never dem," one of them said.

D Fatal Brim checked under his mattress to see two ounces of dog food and an iPhone with a charger. He had two C.O.'s working for him, both white women, because there were no black women. There were no black women period in the prison but he was cool with that.

He had been on his case law because Knight's friend Mita, the top DA in New York City, put in a motion for him before she got killed. When he heard about Mita's death he was mad because she was his chance of getting home. The good thing is the appeal was still in the Southern District court.

Things with his wife were good so life was good due to his situation.

Romell Tukes

Chapter 52
Manhattan, NY

Gotti stared at his goons from Virginia he had in the city with him to help hunt down Knight. He still couldn't believe he had Knight in the palm of his hands and he slipped out so easy.

Gotti had been in New York for a while now. He had basically taken over Fats' operations out there in Brooklyn. Losing Fats meant he would lose a lot of money because Fats was his best customer. Not only was Fats his client but he was also his brother. Nobody had a clue Fats, Gotti, Khalid, and Uncle Pimp were all brothers.

Gotti really wanted a chunk of the Bronx, but rumors had it Knight's crew had been pushing the good dope they called China White and it would be hard to go against that. He also knew going at it over turfs with Knight was the wrong move. He had to get him at another angle. Gotti was a mastermind at game playing and tactics, but the only problem with that is Knight wasn't a rookie.

Since getting up with his brothers, things had been great, especially coming together to kill Knight. He and his brothers never had a relationship because they all grew up in different areas growing up. Their father Rich had many children. He was a freak. But when Bree killed him, they all came together.

Gotti couldn't get the person who shot up his men to save Knight out his head. He wondered who the shooter was because. They had to be a professional and following him or Knight.

He knew he would sooner or later he would find out who the shooter was in due time.

***

Soundview, BX

Sniper posted up in his hood selling bundles of dope instead of crack because Soundview had turned into the dope capital of city.

"Yo Sniper, let me get five of them bundles," a dope fiend said to Sniper as he came out of the corner store from buying some loose Newports.

"You still owe me, nigga," Sniper said, ice grilling the dirty fiend, who was his cousin. Sniper was a short cocky little nigga with dreads trying to get a bag.

"We family, Sniper."

"What that got to do with my fucking money, fiend?" Sniper wasn't in the mood to argue.

"I'm good for it, Sniper. I'll do anything

Sniper looked at his cousin as if he was tripping because he also knew his cousin was gay.

"Take this shit and get off my block" Sniper dug into his sweatpants pocket and passed his cousin two bundles.

They both were unaware of the three trucks posted up on the block since Sniper entered the store. A gang of men jumped out on the block with guns on deck. The shit happened so fast neither Sniper nor his cousin saw it coming.

"You Sniper?"

"Yeah."

"I'm M Balla and I know you and your crew run this area, so I'm giving a chance to get some real money," M Balla told him, looking him in his scared eyes.

"I can't because I work for Trap." Sniper's voice stuttered as he looked at the long clips on the guns they all carried.

"Trap?" M Balla laughed because he knew Trap from way back when they got into it over a bitch.

"He serious, bro. I'm out here moving his work, a half key a day."

"Let me worry about Trap, my G," said M Balla, who handed Sniper a bag with two keys inside.

"I want 70% off each key, so do the math. I'll be back in three days, killer," M Balla said, laughing as he left the block.

Sniper was scared to death because he knew who M Balla was, and his name was bad news.

***

Havana, Cuba

Rachela bounced up and down on Smoke's massive dick as he started to increase the pace of his strokes. Her moans filled the room as her breasts bounced up and down with every motion.

"Uhhhhh, yessss!" she screamed as she grinded her hips into his cock, taking in every inch. Rachela clutched her pussy wall muscles around his cock before she hit her climax. Her sex juices poured down his legs.

"You got yours off," he said, still horny.

"I'ma take care of you, papi," she said, crawling between his legs and placing his manhood in her warm mouth.

Rachel slowly licked the shaft of his rod before downing him down her throat. Smoke's rod disappeared in and out her mouth as she used her phat lips to massage the head. She bopped her head up and down, slurping and playing with his balls. "Mmmmmm," she moaned, looking into his eyes as she deep throated him like a champ. "Fuck my face, papi," she said as he grabbed the back of her head and went crazy.

Smoke had no mercy as he banged the back of her throat out. When he came, she swallowed everything before bending her big ass over and getting fucked doggie-style.

Rachela was a bad Cuban bitch with a phat ass she had done, big titties, no waist, green eyes, tannish skin, and long jet black hair. She was sexy.

Smoke had married Rachela years ago and they had been happily married since.

Chapter 51
Atlanta, GA

Khalid sat in his mansion in the Buckhead area with his African guards on standby. He just got back from Africa two days ago. It was always a refreshing feeling to visit home and the motherland. He was unlike his brothers, who let the American culture replace their true African culture.

The death of his wife Chai crushed him, but he knew his daughter was the one who did that because he saw her on camera. Behadi was on his top five list, but killing Knight was number one. He never had so much hate for one person.

He been thinking lately about relocating soon and the place he had in mind was none other than New York City. His brothers were all up that way so he figured it was about time he join the manhunt. Not to mention he had a strong vibe Behadi would still be up there and he had a special treat for her.

***

Long Island, NY

Halt and his crew had a federal agent tied up in a chair next to his wife and grandmother, who were also tied up in the mini mansion they lived in.

"It's no need for me to speak in Spanish since you speak good English," Halt said.

"What do you want, Halt? You come in my home and disrespect my family?" the federal agent said. He had been trying to catch Halt for over ten years now.

Halt was from Washington Heights. He was Smoke's childhood friend. When Halt was wanted for two murders and the R.I.C.O charge, he flew out to Cuba with Smoke. Hiding out for ten years was rough but he enjoyed his time in Cuba with Smoke.

"I want you to make my little charges disappear," Halt told him, fixing his suit.

"I can't."

"You can, and I'ma tell you why." Halt walked over to his family and placed two guns to his beautiful wife's head.

"Hold on, please!" the federal agent yelled, seeing his wife break down in tears.

"Second thoughts?" Holt smiled, looking at his three guerilla guards.

"I'ma try, but I can't make any promises," the fed said as Halt shook his head.

"Which one do you love more: your wife or grandmom?" Halt asked, seeing a scared look on the agent's face now.

"Huh?"

"You heard me. I'm not good at repeating myself."

"My grandmom."

When the federal agent said that, his wife cursed at him in Spanish.

"Okay." Halt placed the gun to his grandmom's head.

Boom!

"Noooooo!" the agent screamed as his grandmom's head popped open like a zit.

"Take care of that shit, or both of you are next," Halt said, walking out of the crib with bloodstains on his slacks.

Since being back in the States, Halt set up shop in his birthplace, Washington Heights. The only name he had been hearing about was Knight and Paco was murdered, but they had a firm grip on the Heights and Bronx.

Halt want to take over. He had the money and drugs, so that's all he needed.

***

Brewster, NY

Red and Uncle Pimp laid in the bed after a long night of rough and raw sex.

"You know how to work that pussy, gurl." Uncle Pimp loved the way she put it down on him. Red would make him cum in two seconds. Her shit was so wet and tight.

"I try." Red blushed.

"To try is to fail."

"Sorry, daddy," Red said.

"Go get the other girls. I want to fly out to Las Vegas tonight," Uncle Pimp told her, getting out of bed.

"What about the enemy?" she asked.

"I know you ready to kill but be patient."

"I am, daddy."

"Just know you very special to me and I wouldn't trade you for the world." He made her smile. That's why she was in love with him.

Red was unaware that Uncle Pimp put a voodoo spell on her so she would fall in love with him. "You mean that?"

"Yeah," he shot back as she got between his legs and started to suck his cock.

Red focused on the tip, then gulped as much as she could swallow.

"Mmmmmm," he moaned as her head bopped up and down in his lap until he nutted down her throat.

***

Abu Dhabi

Bree stayed in one of the most expensive hotels in the most beautiful city she ever saw in her life.

She needed a little vacation out of the States.

She had her week fully planned out already. First she would go shopping at a huge mall located down the street. Bree planned to hit up a few concerts, shows, and big parties to rub shoulders with millionaires.

There were a lot of girls Bree knew who came to Dhabi to sell pussy for a high price and if the price was right, she would too.

Chapter 52
White Plains, NY

Mr. Curtis pulled up to his workplace, tired from his long night of working on a case for a new client in Staten Island. Being a private investigator wasn't an easy task at all. He had to put up with a lot of dumb shit.

When he agreed to set up Lil K for $100,000 he figured it was going to be easy. Since Uncle Pimp missed his target, Mr. Curtis only received a small portion of his money, which was only $10,000. Mr. Curtis was very pissed about that plus to make shit worse, now his hand was exposed.

He walked into his workplace at eight a.m., the same time every day. Walking into his office, he smelled coffee. He hoped he didn't leave the coffeepot on yesterday.

When he turned on the lights, Lil K was sitting at his desk with his feet on the desk top, Mr. Curtis thought about trying to run until he saw the Draco in his hand.

"Have a seat," Lil K said in a calm voice.

"Who, me?"

"No the six niggas behind you, dummy. Yeah, you, champ," Lil K stated, sipping on coffee.

"How can I help you? I'm sorry about the last meeting. My car broke down." Mr. Curtis came up with a quick excuse.

"Shut up. I made us some coffee." Lil K pushed him a cup of hot coffee.

"Thank you," Mr. Curtis took a sip of coffee.

"Uncle Pimp made you do it?"

"Yes."

"How much he pay you, brother? And we being honest here," Lil K told him.

"100,000, but he only paid me 10,000." Mr. Curtis sounded upset about being short-changed.

"I need to find him, and I know you can help me."

"I don't know too much personal shit about him except he lives in the woods, basically, and he recently flew out to Las Vegas," Mr. Curtis said.

"Okay, I'ma take your word for it." Lil K stoop up.

"I get to live?"

"No," Lil K said as he raised the Draco.

Tat! Tat! Tat! Tat! Tat!

Mr. Curtis' body flew out the chair and went into shock on the floor.

***

USP Canaan Prison, PA

D Fatal Brim had just come from a lawyer visit and he didn't know how to take in the news his lawyer told him. The lawyer told him he had a 50/50 chance of getting out now because his motion Mita put in was answered.

The only issue was D Fatal Brim's new judge because the final answer would be up to him if he wanted to give him 25 years instead of life or re-sentence him.

He went back to his cell and said a prayer for his release date because he ain't wanna die in jail.

***

Soundview, BX

Trap came out of a crack house next to the projects on a late night. He had just dropped off ten keys to his little cousin PK, who was on the come up.

Trap was getting big money in the BX. He was taking in for Glock, Big Blazer, and his cousin Rilla, who all lost their lives to the streets.

Walking towards the projects, he picked up his phone, unaware of the six niggas watching him from a distance.

"Freeze!"

Trap heard the cops and placed his hands in the air, hoping the police didn't kill him. Last week NYPD killed a teenager in the hood so he was on point.

"Turn around, dummy," a male voice said.

When Trap turned around, he saw M Balla standing there with a big-ass gun in his hand.

"Who you?" he asked, pretending not to know M Balla.

"M Balla, and I'm taking over your shit, son. Who you work for anyway, nigga?"

"Slim," Trap said.

"Who the fuck is Slim?" M Balla asked

"He from VA, but he live in Yonkers," Trap told him, hoping he would spare him.

"A'ight, fam."

Bloc! Bloc! Bloc!

M Balla and his goons ran in the projects for the takeover.

Romell Tukes

Chapter 53
Yonkers, NY

School Street projects is one of the worst hoods in Yonkers, the hood of the late rapper DMX. The buildings were skyrise buildings with pissy halls and elevators.

Streetz and Zoey ran the hood with an iron fist and they also had a lock on almost every project in the small, violent, and dangerous city. The two were longtime friends and they had been hustling forever, but when they came across a plug while at a local casino, their lives changed for better.

Last year they met a nigga named Uncle Slim who offered them a chance of a lifetime. Uncle Slim gave them 200 keys of dope to divide their first-time doing business and they ain't look back since.

Streetz and Zooy still lived in the hood, pushing luxury cars and flashing jewelry. They also put their whole team on so everybody could eat.

Uncle Slim was on his way from his condo on the waterfront.

***

Uncle Slim, a.k.a. Slim, drove in the backseat of a Rolls Royce limousine. Everybody in VA thought he was dead, but the truth was his death was staged by him and Gotti. Knight had no clue.

Uncle Slim was Knight's uncle and he was Money's father. When he brought Knight to VA, he and Gotti came up with a plan to take over VA and New York. They already had Fats, but he wasn't enough, so they used Knight.

Gotti made up some fake paperwork and showed Knight and it read that Slim was a federal agent working to get a time cut. Gotti handed Knight the gun to kill Slim but unknown to Knight, the gun had fake bullets. The bullets sounded real and gave off the same effect as a real one would. They even used fake blood to make shit look more real and Knight bought it.

After the staged funeral, Slim moved to New York and waited for a perfect time to set up shop in the city. He was able to squeeze his way into Yonkers and the Soundview section of the Bronx.

Now that Trap was dead, all he had left was Yonkers until he meet up with Gotti to brainstorm their next move.

**

Uptown, Bronx

Knight was listening to every word M Balla was saying in the passenger seat of the Range Rover sport SUV.

"Are you sure he said this cat was from VA?" Knight asked again for the second time in the last five minutes.

"I'm positive, bro. The nigga said Uncle Slim from VA," M Balla stated.

"Can't be," Knight said, watching the rain come down on his window and hood.

"You know this nigga or somethin'?"

"If it's the same dude, I killed him a few years back in VA. He's my uncle," said Knight with somewhat of a worried look.

"Damn, son, you peter-rolled your own uncle? Damn, boy, you coldblooded for real," M Balla joked, but Knight wasn't in the mood.

"This isn't making sense at all, son, word to mother, yo." Knight knew he killed him, but now he had to rethink.

"So, what if this Uncle Slim nigga is dude? How you want to go about it? Because Soundview is ours," M Balla said. M Balla's homie already took control of Soundview and the whole projects.

"I'ma think about it and let you know, but until then, just continue to get money," Knight told him before M Balla exited the SUV.

Chapter 54
Queens, NY

Uncle Pimp, Red, and Sexy Spicee were on the private jet making love to their master, taking turns on him, riding and sucking. When the jet landed, the threesome was over and all the other women were upset.

"Let's go, ladies," Uncle Pimp said as he got dressed.

The trip to Vegas was very fun and laid back. They really enjoyed themselves.

There was a limo and a few cars parked around the place but they paid the cars no mind as they exited the jet.

***

Lil K and M Balla watched the beautiful women come out of the jet.

"Damn, them bitches bad, especially them two next to him," M Bella said, speaking of Red and Sexy Spicee.

When Lil K saw Red, his heart almost stopped.

M Balla had two cars full of goons on deck just in case shit got outta hand.

"Them bitches harmless," M Balla said.

"You'll see," Lil K said, jumping out with a gun in his hand, hoping to save Red.

The first person to spot Lil K was Red, and she froze in her tracks. When she stopped walking, everybody focused on Lil K, and that's when shit got ugly.

Sexy Spicee pulled out her Glock and fired first, and that's when M Balla and his crew all rushed out of their cars firing.

Boc! Boc! Boc!

Bloc! Bloc! Bloc!

Tat! Tat! Tat!

Uncle Pimp saw two of his hoes go down. Sexy Spicee hit one of M Balla's goons as Lil K tried to gun for him.

Luckily, the limo was a few feet away so he was able to dive in the limo with Red and a few other women. Sexy Spicee sent a few more rounds at Lil K before getting in the limo and pulling off.

Lil K couldn't believe he fucked up and let her get away. He couldn't get the thought of her out his head.

"Damn, dem hoes shooters. Who the hell was there?" M Balla asked as Lil K pulled off, leaving behind two dead men.

"Someone very special," Lil K said.

"Well, you gotta get someone special attention a better way because that's not it, bro. I just lost two good men," M Balla told him.

"Maybe." Lil K couldn't get her outta his head, but there was something about her stare that didn't look the same.

***

South Beach, Miami

Smoke came out to Miami to get outta Cuba and to visit his girl whom he was cool with and supplied.

He was at a nice bar on the beach waiting for Aliza to arrive with a crew of shooters on standby. Smoke hated coming to Miami because he had enemies with another drug organization. The woman's name was Julie and the two hated each other. Years ago, Smoke tried to take over Miami, but Julie had it in a chokehold. He tried to talk to her about dividing it into sections, but she was against it. Julie still wanted Smoke's head and he was aware of that.

Aliza walked up to him looking sexy, wearing designer heels and low-cut shorts.

The two had a few drinks and talked for an hour about everything from business to family, then parted ways.

Chapter 55
Washington Heights, NY

Halt and two of his goons walked to the back of the corner store to meet up with a Dominican plug. Since moving through the Heights in these past couple of weeks, he'd been exhausted.

"Do we wait out here?" one of Halt's goons asked as Halt knocked on a room door used for storage.

"Yes," Halt said as the door slowly opened with a slow crack.

"Halt, my friend," George said, sitting at a table playing cards with his brother.

George and his brother Frazier were two of the biggest brick layers in the Heights. Both men worked together, but they were out of a connect, so meeting Halt was the best thing that ever happened.

"Gentlemen," Halt said, sitting down, fixing his collar on his expensive button up shirt. Halt looked around the small room to smell a strong odor, and the odor smelled so familiar.

"Sorry for the person in the corner," George said.

Halt looked to see a dead body in the corner in a puddle of blood.

"We not gonna give you no cut cards, Halt, because we are businessmen just like yourself," Frazier said, trying to get to the point.

"I already know our situation. You need a new plug," Halt said with a grin.

"How did you know?" George asked, because he never told Halt about his connect situation.

"I killed your plug because I knew you would come crawling to me, and he was a rapist anyway, so don't feel no type of way," Halt stated.

Both of the brothers looked at each other, not knowing what to think.

"So where does that leave us?" Frazier was the real brains to the brothers' operations. He was very level-headed and business-minded.

"That's why I'm here - because I want to help," Halt said.

"How?" George asked.

"I'ma supply you both with keys at a good, affordable, low price," Halt told them.

"How cheap?" Frazier asked

"Twenty-one"

"Wow! But hold on, how we know this ain't all game?" George stated seriously.

"You will see," Halt said as he stood to leave.

"Thank you," Frazier said before Halt walked out.

Both men had heard of Halt for some time now and they heard he was about his money and was fair.

***

Queens, NY

M Balla and his crew were all in a well-known strip club in the VIP section. There were twelve of his Blood homies in the VIP section chilling, popping bottles of Moet and D'ussé.

"Sniper," M Balla called out to his boy, who was getting a private lap dance next to him.

"What, son?" Sniper's dick was hard as hell and he was zoned into the thick redbone bouncing in his lap.

"You ready for tomorrow?" M Balla asked, referring to the drugs he had to go get from Knight early tomorrow.

"Nigga, yeah."

"Just want to make sure, bro." M Balla trusted Sniper with his life. He was loyal.

"Let me enjoy myself, nigga. You see me getting a lap dance and you talking some dumb shit," Sniper stated.

"My bad, son."

"A'ight."

That night the crew ended up throwing a party at a local hotel with a few dancers.

The police came through and shut the party down so it ain't last long.

Chapter 56
Brewster, NY

Red and Sexy Spicee had just got done training in the backyard of the barn area. Both women were the bottom bitches, and they were over all of Uncle Pimp's recruits. They were the women who taught all the rest of the women how to move. Uncle Pimp was barely there these days so they had to hold down the ranch.

"How did it feel?" Sexy Spicee said as she wiped her forehead then her six pack.

"What you talking about?" Red said, sitting down.

"That day at the airport, Red, you don't remember?" Sexy Spicee stated.

"Nope," Red replied, lying through her teeth.

All the girls knew Red had a short-term memory loss so they knew better than to ask her too much.

Uncle Pimp didn't like his hoes to speak to Red about certain shit. He didn't want her to remember what took place before he kidnapped her and put a voodoo spell on her.

"Forget? I'll see you inside." Sexy Spicee shook her head, feeling sad for the woman.

Red played dumb with everybody. The truth was she couldn't get Lil K out of her mind since the shooting took place at the hospital that day. She missed Lil K, but she was now in love with Uncle Pimp, her master. Red ain't know what Uncle Pimp did to her, but it made her feel loved, so she liked it.

***

Uptown, Bronx

Lil K went to Jumah Friday at the mosque to listen to the Imam give his ceremonial speech, which he did every Friday from 12:30 p.m. to 1:33 p.m. The mosque was full of Muslims from all over the city, women and men. After everybody prayed in rows, people started to leave.

Lil K walked towards the door, heading outside. He saw someone behind him, but he paid them no mind as he continued to walk. Once near his car, he stopped and turned around to see a beautiful woman behind him.

"Can we talk?" she said with her face and body covered.

"For what and who——" Lil K paused as he realized who the woman was.

"It's me." Behadi pulled off her hijab, showing her beautiful face.

"I heard you was out here," Lil K said.

"Yes," she stated.

"Why?" he asked.

"I have a lot of shit to take care of," she said, lying.

"I don't believe you," he told her, seeing her smile.

"Well, you have to,"

"Enough of the bullshit, Behadi, what's really going on?" he asked her.

"I came to warn you and your family," she said.

"From your dad?"

"Yeah."

"You been told me about that, Behadi," he said.

"Well, I have to tell you again," she again stated.

"You wanna get a bite to eat?" he asked her.

"Sure."

Lil K and Behadi went to a seafood spot ten minutes away from the mosque.

"I'm really glad to see you," she told him.

"I feel the same," he said.

"How's everything with you and how long do you plan on being out here?" Lil K asked.

"To be honest, I don't know, but I got a lot to figure out," she said, eating white fish.

"I'm here for you," he told her, not trying to get too emotional.

"Oh really?" She was a little excited about him saying that.

"Facts, but I really want to thank you for helping me back to life when I got hit up," Lil K told her.

"That's all?" she stated.

"Oh, and when you saved me from your crazy-ass sister." He laughed at her.

They enjoyed the whole day in each other's company.

***

Queens, NY

Bree was sitting at home, drinking wine watching TV, in her zone, thinking about more ways to get more money.

She had shit going on in other states, but she had a few states on lock. In an hour she would have to feed her child and put her seed back to sleep.

Bree thought about Knight and how she really needed him on her side to get this money because he had BX on lock.

She almost dozed off until she heard the baby crying, so she went to handle her motherly duties.

Chapter 57
Yonkers, NY

Streets had a trap house on the south side of Yonkers where he sold weed, lean, and molly. He put his little cousin on to a bag and now Lil S was up thanks to him.

"That's all?" Streets asked, looking at all the keys of molly and exotic weed on the living room table.

"Facts." Lil S lit a blunt of the exotic weed.

"I gotta go, but hit my line when you get that bread, bro," Streets told him, getting up to leave.

"Where you going?"

"Me and Zooy about to shoot out to L.A. for a week. He got a video shoot out there with the nigga Kiss," Streets said before turning around to see a gun pointed at his face.

Three gunmen had been hiding in the back the whole time, waiting on Lil S' key words "where you going".

"What's good, son?" Sniper said, ready to blow Streets' head off his shoulders

"This ain't right, bro." Streets saw how calm Lil S was and he knew something was wrong.

"I had to, bro. Sniper my big homie for the set," Lil S said as he threw up Mack Balla.

"Fuck you, nigga, I'ma——" Streets' words were cut short when Sniper slapped him with the butt of his gun.

"Let me talk. Tell me what you know about this Slam or Slim nigga, whatever the fuck his name is," Sniper stated.

"Slim?"

"Yeah, nigga, I just said that, dummy!" Sniper spat.

"Dude real low-key, bro. I only see him when it's time to pick up work."

"Don't make me do this." Sniper said. looking back to his goons. who already knew what time it was with their homie.

"Kill that goofy wing-ass nigga," Lil S cheered.

Streets couldn't believe Lil S was on demon time with him after all he did for him.

"I gave you a shot," Street said, training his gun on Lil S.

Bloc! Bloc! Bloc! Bloc! Bloc!

Every bullet entered his frail chest, killing Lil S in a matter of seconds.

"Now you got one more chance," Sniper stated.

"Okay, I believe he lives near the waterfront by the Metro North train station," Streets said.

"You sure?" Sniper said.

"Word to my mother's grave. son," Streets cried.

"I believe you, playa." Sniper lowered his weapon. Before making his exit, Sniper turned around.

Bloc! Bloc! Bloc! Bloc! Bloc!

"Hoe-ass nigga," Sniper said as he walked out to get in M Balla's Porsche.

"I heard them shots, boy," M Balla said, turning down Hot 97, the radio station.

"Yeah, son, he lives down there near the waterfront," Sniper told his big homie.

"In which building?"

"We don't know," Sniper stated.

M Balla did as Knight asked, but now he had to find Slim.

***

Manhattan, NY

Gotti and one of his goons made their way outside to meet up with two soldiers waiting for their boss. Today Gotti had to make a trip upstate to visit Uncle Pimp, then he had to fly out to VA. He needed to spend some time with his wife, who had recently got back from vacation.

Gotti was a little upset about not being able to kill Knight yet, but he had also been trying to figure out who was his plug. Almost every big time drug lord in the States, Gotti had a close bond with. He did some research, and none of his people were supplying Knight. If so, it would have been so easy to set him up.

Outside, Gotti saw the truck doors open with his goons hanging out dead. Gotti looked around and he saw a woman with an assault rifle and silencer attached to it coming his way.

Psst! Psst! Psst! Psst! Psst!

Gotti snatched the bodies out of the truck and jumped in like a young nigga. His bodyguard got hit in the neck, killing him. Gotti hit the gas and got the fuck away from the shooter.

When Behadi saw her Uncle Gotti's scared ass race off, she got upset that she missed her target.

She'd been watching Gotti for a few weeks now and decided to strike today, but shit went badly, so now she had to start from the bottom.

Chapter 58
South Bronx, NY

M Balla's mom loved to drink when she got off work. Reina was a beautiful black woman who was the mother of three kids. She had used crack when her kids were born, but she'd been clean for over ten years. Her favorite child was M Balla, whose real name was Mack.

She was driving to the nearby liquor store to get her gallon of Henny. Reina pulled onto the curb and left her car on to run while she went inside the store.

After purchasing her drink, she walked outside to see a van parked next to her. The door slid open and three shooters hopped out with assault rifles. Reina screamed before they snatched her up and tossed her in the van.

Twenty minutes later, the van pulled into a project building near a dumpster. The projects were Castle Hill projects, the home of M Balla. Zooy and Slim were in the back taking turns on pistol whipping her.

"Tell us were M Balla at?" Zooy stated.

"Please, I don't know," Reina begged,

"You will pay for his life with yours if you don't tell me," Slim said, staring into her eyes.

"I don't know! You have to believe me!" she cried.

Zooy had been on his way to meet Streets when he saw M Balla and Sniper leaving the building. Zooy used to be in the Bronx in Castle Hill, so he had seen M Balla a few times. When he went inside to see Streets, it wasn't hard to put two and two together about who killed Streets.

"She useless," Zooy stated, pulling out a long blade.

"Kill her," Slim said as Zooy slit her neck and started to stab her nonstop.

When Zooy was done, they tossed her body out near the dumpster.

Slim wanted to find out who this M Balla kid really was and why he was coming for his people. Slim knew it was a direct hit because Streets' killer didn't take no drugs.

***

Uptown, BX

Lil K left his low-key apartment early in the morning at six to meet up with Knight, who was in Long Island. Coming outside something didn't feel right. The block was still full of parked cars. Lil K knew when the vibes were off and this was one of the moments.

He looked around and shit happened so fast. Shooters jumped out of everywhere with sniper style weapons, dressed in all black. The gunmen looked like Africans. Lil K was held at gunpoint. He was outnumbered by ten.

A man got out of a car parked across the street dressed in an Islamic garment.

"As salam alaikum," Khalid said, coming his way.

"Fuck you, nigga," Lil K said. Shots started to go off as if he said the magical words

Tat! Tat! Tat! Tat! Tat!

Khalid ran off, getting back in the car, unaware of where the bullets were flying from.

Lil K saw bullets enter all the men's heads, killing them. He looked around to see nobody and he wasn't trying get hit next, so got in his car, pulling off. Halfway down the block he got a text from Behadi saying he owed her one.

Chapter 59
Downstate Prison, NY

M Balla had recently found his mom's dead body behind his project building in Castle Hill. He had come out of his building that morning to see someone wrapped up in a white sheet and the area was filled with police. It just so happened a sexy Spanish woman he grew up with was in tears because of the loss of his mother. M Balla couldn't believe it was his mom wrapped up like a mummy from the ancient times.

Today he was coming to the Downstate Prison, which was located in Beacon, New York, forty-five minutes upstate from the Bronx. His brother JR Balla was currently locked up doing a 65 year bid in the state prison. M Balla had been holding down his brother since Riker's Island jail. The two had always been close as kids growing up in the BX.

Having their mother pass was heavy on him, so he knew it was crushing his brother, who was locked in a cage.

***

JR Balla been working out all morning for his visit in the prison gym on the universal weights. This was how he remained stress free and full of good energy. With sixty-five years to do for a murder and an attempted murder, prison was his last pit stop.

Being a Blood gang member, he dealt with a lot of politics in the jail, especially being a Mack Balla.

He went back to his unit and got ready for his visit with his brother.

***

JR Balla gave his brother a hug, happy to see him.

"You looking like money," M Balla said.

"Get money, take money. You know the vibes, son," JR Balla said as M Balla's face got serious.

"They ain't tell you?" M Balla asked. He saw a dumb look on JR Balla's face.

"Nah, what you talking about?" JR Balla knew his brother like the back of his hand.

"Mommy got murdered."

"Huh?"

"Mommy dead, bro. Niggas killed her in back of the pj's," M Balla told him.

"No!" JR Balla already had tears rolling down his face.

"I'm sorry," M Balla stated seriously

"You sorry?" JR Balla stated seriously,

"I'ma find out who did this shit," M Balla said.

"I hope so." JR Balla stood up to leave from the visit to go back to his unit to vent before he lashed out.

***

East Orange, NJ

Knight and Lil K drove to a Muslim area in East Orange to pay someone a visit.

"You look a little happy," Knight said, driving through the hoods.

"Me?"

"Yeah, nigga."

"Nah, I just been building with Khalid's daughter. Shawty official," Lil K said.

"I get all good vibes from her." Knight thought Behadi was very nice and a good woman.

"Facts."

"That's what you need though, bro," Knight told him.

"What you mean by that?" Lil K asked.

"I mean you need to get Red off your mind until we figure out what she on," Knight said, challenging Red's loyalty.

"She'll always be with us," Lil K stated strongly.

"We don't know that, my G."

"Whatever. Let's focus on this mission, son," Lil K said, not trying to think about Red crossing sides.

"A'ight."

"How do we know what he look like?"

"We don't," Knight said, referring to Gotti's son.

"So how do we get this nigga?" Lil K asked as Knight pulled over across the street from a mosque.

"He should be out any minute, bro," Knight stated.

"Out the mosque?"

"He's the Imam, or whatever they call the leader of that shit," Knight says.

"Bro, I am Muslim," Lil K said, not trying to kill another Muslim.

"So?"

"Nigga, you sure he's Gotti son?" Lil K asked, trying to make sure.

"Facts."

"I ain't killing him."

"I will," Knight said, seeing a dark-skinned man with a big beard walk out of the building.

Knight got out of the car and made his way to Gotti's son. Before Gotti's son even got a chance to see Knight, he saw fire sparks.

Boc! Boc! Boc!

Knight shot the man in the head, killing him before walking back to the car.

"Easy." Knight got back in the car, pulling off.

Lil K shook his head and drove off with all types of shit on his mind.

*****

SoHo, NY

Khalid knew a few Africans in SoHo who sold clothes and garments at an African store.

He wasn't here to shop. He came to speak to an OG killer he had known for years.

Khalid was putting a tag on Behadi's head and if anybody could find her, he knew the OG would.

He walked into a basement area to smell incense and blood.

Chapter 60
Yonkers, NY

Zooy and his cousin Cry Baby were pulling into a block where they sold pounds of weed at called Riverdale.

"I'ma slide out to the BX later to look for this M Balla nigga with some Mount Vernon niggas," Zooy said to his little cousin.

"Them niggas did Streets dirty, cuz," Cry Baby said in his kiddo voice. He was a twenty-two-year-old killer.

"Word to life."

"The block empty, son," Cry Baby said, looking around.

"Where Black G at?" Zooy said, looking around for the goons who always posted up.

"I don't know, but I'ma go see, cuz," Cry Baby stated.

Cry Baby didn't see Black G's and M Balla's goons watching them.

Tat! Tat! Tat! Tat! Tat!

Cry Baby got hit in his chest and face as six shooters jumped out from all over the place with MP 11's and MP 5's.

Tat! Tat! Tat!

Zooy knew he had no wins as he peeled off, getting away from bullets.

***

White Plains, NY

Uncle Pimp, Red, and Sexy Spicee all were in the stretched limo, on their way to a small lawyer meeting over a lunch at an upscale restaurant.

"Pull over," Uncle Pimp told Sexy Spicee, who was driving.

"Right here?" Sexy Spice said, seeing a cigar shop.

Uncle Pimp loved smoking his cigars on a daily basis.

"Yeah." Uncle Pimp was playing in Red's wet pussy as she sucked his penis in the backseat.

"Cum in my mouth," Red said as she deep throated him and continued to take him down her throat.

Sexy Spicee was a little jealous, but Uncle Pimp ate her pussy that morning so well that she was good for today.

After swallowing his nut, Red fixed her Dolce & Gabbana dress, leaving cum juice on the seats as she got out of the car to see a very familiar face, but it didn't click who she was.

***

Behadi was out buying Lil K some cigars for a gift when she ran into Red. She was so shocked to see Red she didn't know what to do.

Uncle Pimp saw Behadi and went for his gun, and so did Sexy Spicee and Red. Behadi was too fast. She managed to get her gun out first and shot Sexy Spicee in her arm.

Boc! Boc! Boc!

Red weaved away from Behadi's fire and sent a few shots back, trying to block Uncle Pimp.

Boom! Boom!

Behadi dropped the cigars and ran for cover just so she could have room to move around and not get hit.

Boc! Boc! Boc!

A cop car came from out of the blue and ran into the limousine before Sexy Spicee shot at the cop car.

Behadi ran off when she saw the cop get hit in the head five times. She left the scene and so did Sexy Spicee, Red, and Uncle Pimp.

Chapter 61
Upper Westside, NY

Slim took his beautiful Latin wife Aliza on a date in the city on this perfect night.

It seemed to Slim like shit was going bad in Yonkers. He lost Streets and he lost money, something he hated.

"Why the sad face, papi?" Aliza asked, seeing Slim's spirit was off today and for the past week.

"I got a lot going on," he said, not trying to expose too much.

"Can I be any help?"

"No, I just need you to keep looking sexy"

"That's regular."

"I know," he said.

"Really, are you okay? Because before I leave, I want to make sure you're stable," she told him.

"I'm okay."

"I believe you. How's the business?"

"Great."

"In Yonkers?"

"It could be better, but I got it under control"

"Will you be ready for more keys this month?" Aliza asked him.

"Yes."

"I'll call my sister tonight."

"Thank you," Slim said, enjoying the meal and the evening with his girl.

Aliza and her family were the drug suppliers in Cuba and Slim had known her forever.

***

Washington Heights, NY

Halt was dong big things in the Height. He formed a big crew and took over almost every block in the Heights. Thanks to Smoke, he was able to supply the drugs at a low price to his people.

He was at a Spanish restaurant eating his breakfast with five of his guards. Halt was so focused on his breakfast he didn't see the beautiful woman walk inside the restaurant. One of his men tapped him on his shoulder letting him know the woman was there for him. Halt looked at the woman and nodded his head, letting her sit across from him.

"Hey," Bree said.

"Who the fuck are you?" Halt said.

"I come in peace, but on business."

"That doesn't answer my question."

"Bree."

"Okay, how can I help you, and who sent you?" Halt stopped eating and wiped his face with a napkin, looking in her eyes.

"I did my research on you, Halt."

"I see."

"Don't nobody move keys in this city without me hearing about them, so——"

She was cut off. "Hold on, you used to be married to Rick?" he asked.

"Yes,"

"I had a feeling that was you, but your business is no good over here," Halt said, about to stand up to leave.

"Please, I need you," she said, begging.

"Is that so?"

"Yes. I have my own money and clientele all over the east coast, I swear."

"I can't trust you. You killed your own husband." Halt heard Bree killed Rick and robbed him. That was the gossip on the street.

"He deserved it."

"How?"

"He crossed me? What was I supposed to do? This is a jungle. I had my own business to run also," she told him.

"I see. Let me speak to some people and get back at you."

"That's fair. Can I leave my number?" she asked.

"No need for that. I already have your Queens address," Halt said before walking out.

Bree couldn't believe Halt had known who she was the whole time.

Chapter 62
Brooklyn, NY

Lil K and M Balla went out to an NBA at the Barkley center in Brooklyn. It was the Nets vs. the Heat. The game was a blow out, but the energy is what both men really needed.

"This shit was live, bro," M Balla said.

"I hate the Nets."

"Nigga, how you gonna hate the home team?" M Balla said seriously, not understanding niggas who went against the home team.

"There is no rule that says you have to go with the team where you from," Lil K said, walking through the large center.

"Yo, look at all them bitches!" M Balla pointed at a gang of bitches who were surrounding a nigga in a fur coat.

When the man and woman turned around, Lil K's heart stopped, especially when he saw Red again. Lil K ain't see Gotti and his crew behind them.

Everybody came out for the NBA game, but nobody expected this shit.

All hell broke loose. Lil K was the first to set it off and M. Balla's crew followed.

Boc! Boc! Boc! Boc! Boc!

Lil K hit two of Uncle Pimp's girls, dropping them so fast nobody saw the bodies fall in place.

Red and Sexy Spicee guarded Uncle Pimp, shooting at M Balla, hitting three of his goons.

Bloc! Bloc! Bloc!

M Balla ducked between the crowds of people running and yelling to save their lives.

Gotti had a clear shot at Lil K's head and then someone shot him in his hand.

Gotti screamed as he dropped his gun, looking at the shooter, Red. She saw him about to kill Lil K, so she did what was right to save him.

"Red!" Uncle Pimp yelled as cops flooded the place and everybody made their exits.

M Balla and Lil K blended in with the crowd, sliding out the front door.

Seven dead bodies were left behind and the crime scene made the world news.

***

Manhattan, NY

Knight sat in his lounge drinking while watching the news to see seven dead in a big shootout at the Barkley Center in Brooklyn, NY.

In a few minutes he had a date with a woman he met downtown named MeMe. The woman was beautiful. He needed to see what she was really about.

Knight called Valentine and set up a date with his daughter, little Karmala. Not being able to see his little girl often was rough, but he knew his lifestyle would risk his family safety.

His father texted him, setting up a meeting. Knight didn't feel like flying out nowhere this week but he needed to handle some shit.

***

Queens, NY

Behadi went to an African hair shop to get her hair done up for Lil K.

Tonight she was suppose go on another friendly date with him at his crib. She was taking it slow because Behadi knew he was still in love with Red.

Behadi had to find her pops soon before he found her, but she knew Khalid would send someone first to do his dirty work.

She risked it all for Lil K and he didn't understand because she didn't press the issue.

Tonight she was horny and wanted to feel him inside of her, but she didn't want to force herself on him.

Chapter 63
New York City, NY

Behadi couldn't believe Lil K had taken to her to a fancy hotel with a nice sexy setup. The suite was full of roses and candles, all leading to the balcony outside where a dinner date was set up.

They both looked sexy and grown tonight. Behadi wore a Dolce & Gabbana slit dress with heels and a little bit of makeup. Lil K rocked a white suit with a black tie, looking like a real boss.

"I can't believe you went this hard," Behadi said, looking at the city skyline, which was lit up.

"It's only right," he stated, taking a sip of Dom P.

"I really like you, and I know you feel vibes, but it's never been the right time," she said drinking her wine, which made her hornier.

"Until tonight." Lil K had felt something for Behadi when he first laid eyes on her in Africa years ago.

"So what now?" She stood up and walked over to the rail, looking over the beautiful city. They were so high in the air that cars looked like colorful ants.

"I don't know. We can only live for today," he said, getting up, closing in behind her, grabbing her waist.

"I want to live for tonight. I want you inside of me. This will be my first time, so take it slow," she begged him.

"I will, ma." Lil K lifted her dress up to see she had on nothing. He slid a finger into her wet tightness to hear her moan softly as the nice breeze blew under her dress.

Lil K pulled out his erect penis and slowly entered her from behind.

"Ummmm," she moaned, holding on to the rail, arching out her back, trying to take it like a big girl.

Behadi's pussy was so tight he had to work his way in and out as he controlled her hip movements.

"Yesss...fuck!" she screamed.

When he got deeper, her moans grow louder and she was able to take it all.

After her first climax, they went inside the bedroom and he made good ole love to her all night.

Behadi had some bloodstains because he popped her cherry. She had been saving herself for marriage, but she knew Lil K was the one for her.

They enjoyed the night. She even got her pussy and ass eaten for the first time.

***

Soundview Projects, BX

M Balla was in Soundview projects as if he grew up there, shooting dice and chilling with his goons.

He flooded the hood with his guys and they had shit on lock every building. With the crazy history between Knight's crew and Soundview, the whole Bronx was surprised to hear and see Knight take over.

Selling almost 40 to 70 keys a day throughout the city, M Balla had plans to expand to Philly and D.C. M Balla had some cousins in D.C. and Philly so when Knight got back from Cuba, he planned to put his boss on game.

Tonight he was going out clubbing in the city for a few hours with his gang to turn up. He hadn't been going out as much lately since his mother passed.

He had been in Yonkers almost every day looking for Zooy and Uncle Slim, the two niggas the streets were saying had killed his mother. He knew he would find them soon.

***

Havana, Cuba

Today the tropical weather and bright skies looked and felt great in the city of Havana.

Knight jet got off his private jet to see a woman in a short mini dress looking like a snack next to a luxury car. His pops must have

232

sent him a sexy driver to take him around before their meeting. He approached the woman and she was the shit.

"Hey, I'm Knight," he said.

But the woman just looked at his hand and got in the car, ready to leave. Knight thought either she didn't speak English or she was stuck up.

The ride was quiet. He looked at the lovely city all the way until they drove into a poor area. Knight wondered where they were going but when she stopped on a hill in front of a blue building, she got out.

The woman's ass was so phat he couldn't help but stare. She smiled, turning around and catching him staring. She waved him on, telling Knight to follow her inside. He got out of the car to see a few Cuban men on the small streets.

Inside the apartment, the woman jumped in his arms and started to kiss him with her full lips. Knight's hardened cock brushed against her phat coochie as he held her in the air. He kissed her back, placing her on a kitchen counter in the small house. They both undressed quickly and he slid inside her to feel her juices already flowing from her slit. Knight started pounding her pussy out, making her go crazy

"Harder!" she yelled in perfect English.

He went deeper, hitting her spot as she hit a high note. It didn't take long for them to cum.

She sucked his dick, deep throating him and slurping, making all types of noises.

After the oral sex, they went to the back and he fucked her doggy-style. When he thought he was done, she put his pole in her anus slowly, but when she got relaxed, she started to ride his dick.

Knight fucked her in her ass so good she had tears before he got done.

**

The ride back to the nice part of the city was odd. They both had many thoughts on their mind.

"Who are you?"

"Rachela," she said.

"Who are you to my father?" Knight just wanted to know.

"You'll see." She smiled

"I thought you ain't speak English?" he asked.

"I never said that."

"I guess you right," Knight said as they pulled up to a mansion Knight had seen before.

Inside, guards were all over and they all gave Rachela a respectful head nod. Knight thought the woman was Smoke's worker or helper.

"Son, glad you're here." Smoke came out of the kitchen in a suit with a glass of water.

"What's going on?" Knight said as he saw Rachela go to Smoke's side hugging him. He then saw Smoke kiss Rachela on her lips, grabbing her ass.

"I see you met my lovely wife," he said.

Knight tried to keep a straight face, but it was hard for him. "Yeah."

"She wanted to show you around," he said.

"She did. It was nice," Knight said, thinking if he only knew.

"I'm glad you here," Smoke said.

"Me too," Rachela added.

"How's business?" Knight asked him.

"Great," Smoke said.

"I'ma go cook." Rachela walked off with a limp.

"Baby, your leg hurts?' Smoke asked his wife.

"Yeah, I bumped my knee," she lied, blushing at Knight.

"Okay."

Knight couldn't believe what just took place, but he wanted to fuck her again now for the rush.

Chapter 64
Washington Heights, NY

Halt had a surprise visit from a woman named Aliza whom he never heard of or seen. The woman was sexy. She had a Cuban swag and she walked like a diva.

Halt held business meetings in his store or the restaurant he owed.

"Let's talk in English because yo' Spanish is bad," Halt told the woman sitting across from him.

"Excuse me?" Aliza stated with an attitude.

"Who are you and what do you want?" he asked.

"I told you, I am Aliza and I have a business proposition for you."

"You got something for me?" He leaned back, smirking, thinking the sexy woman was trying to give up some pussy.

"I see you have a nasty mind and I'm not here for that," Aliza just wanted to clear the airway before he thought different.

"I'm always open for business," he stated.

"I know you work for Smoke and he works for my sister Rachela, to be honest," she told him, exposing his hand.

Aliza and Rachela were sisters, but her dad was the real plug.

"You want to cut Smoke out the picture?" Halt asked.

"If you put it like that, then yes."

"Who do I look like?" he asked her.

"A businessman."

"True, but there is a big difference between good business, bad business, and double cross," Halt told her.

"It's the game," she said.

"Smoke is like a brother to me so I would never cross him or bite the hand that feeds me," Halt explained.

"Okay but let me tell you this before I go. If you think Smoke is this loyal friend to you, then you're dumber than you look," she said.

"Bye."

"You remember when your brother used to work for Smoke and came up missing? You think he disappeared into the clouds?" Aliza got up to leave the restaurant.

Halt saw her leave and thought back to his brother who came up missing years ago. His brother used to work for Smoke and they were best friends.

***

Dover, Delaware

Gotti and Uncle Pimp planned to meet up at a bike event.

Gotti been exhausted dealing with Knight and his car. Moving to New York, he thought it would be easier to move on Knight.

He needed a clear understanding with Uncle Pimp and they needed a solid plan because he was starting to see Knight stayed a step ahead of game.

Gotti posted up near a crowd of bikes and goons for Uncle Pimp at this public event.

***

Uncle Pimp pulled up to the bike event on a sport bike and Sexy Spicee and Red were behind him on their own bikes.

He came out to meet up with Gotti, most likely to discuss Knight and Lil K. Uncle Pimp had been losing a lot of sleep lately due to his most dangerous ops still being alive.

Teaming up with Gotti was the best bet because he had the manpower. Uncle Pimp had woman power, but every time he lost one, he had to go out and find replacements.

The bike event was packed, but it was a public event so he wasn't tripping, plus he had two of the baddest bitches in the spot with him.

Chapter 65
Yonkers, NY

Zooy and his clique all were on Jackson Street on a dead-end block chilling, selling crack, dope, and pills. Even being hood rich, Zooy couldn't stay out of the hood. He loved the block. People ran in and out of the building all day because his boys sold everything out of it.

The death of Streets still was in the air and Zooy was on M Balla's ass but he couldn't keep up with him.

Yonkers was connected to the Bronx but Yonkers was much smaller. The Bronx was big and it would be hard to track down M Balla. M Balla had so much status in the BX

Slim had his men drop off 100 keys last night and Zooy had to go upstairs to bust all that shit down for his soldiers to be divided amongst themselves.

"Yo, Mess, I'ma go see about this work, son. Call them Elm Street niggas and O-Black niggas down here so I can give them they shit."

Zooy went inside and saw two men coming out of an apartment, but he paid them no mind, thinking they were copping drugs of some type. As he was about to reach for the door handle, he was attacked with long blades.

Sniper and his homie stabbed Zooy all over his body, killing him. When they were done, Zooy lay in a pool of red blood.

***

Sniper and Kenny sneaked out the back and slid off into the alley, where M balla was awaiting them.

"I crushed that nigga, son, word to the set," Kenny said, hyped up.

Sniper and M Balla looked at each other before M Balla pulled out a gun. "You talk too much," M Balla told Kenny.

"I'm sorry. I'll chill out, bro," Kenny said.

"Can't risk it, my G." M Balla then pulled the trigger

Boc! Boc! Boc!

Sniper threw Kenny's body out of the car before M Balla pulled off.

"We gotta find this Slim nigga, brotty," M Balla told Sniper, who was wiping the blood off his hand.

"He not down there by the waterfront, so I don't know, son, and I ain't trying to be riding around strapped up out here in Westchester County," Sniper said.

"A'ight. We out," M Balla said heading back to the Bronx.

***

South, Bronx

Knight had a date with a sexy woman he had been feeling. He was leaving Lil K's apartment. Lil K had so many spots in the BX. He didn't know where Lil K was hiding out at unless he told him.

Walking up the dark street to his car, he didn't see the killers lurking.

Uncle Slim jumped out with a MP4, dressed in all black, from behind a SUV. Four shooters popped out of the cut also with big assault rifles in all black.

"You thought this day wouldn't happen?" his Uncle Slim said.

"Fuck you, nigga, I ain't scared. I lived my life," Knight said.

"I see you doing good for yourself, but now I'ma take over the Bronx, little nigga," Uncle Slim said with a straight face.

"If you man enough," he said.

Uncle Slim got closer but before he got two feet away, it happened so fast nobody saw it coming.

Tat! Tat! Tat! Tat! Tat!

Uncle Slim fell face first to the ground, then his goons got hit also.

Knight pulled out his gun and saw the shooter.

Behadi was in Lil K's crib with him but she looked out the window to see Knight surrounded and helped him.

"You be lacking, Knight," Behadi told him before walking back into Lil K's crib.

"Never. I had it on lock," he lied to himself, happy she was on his team.

Romell Tukes

Chapter 66
Brooklyn, NY

Lil K and Knight had to go out to Brooklyn to meet a cat named Addy.

"What's really good with you and shawty, bro?" Knight asked Lil K, talking about Behadi.

"What you mean?"

"Nigga, what you think?" Knight thought he was playing games. Knight hadn't seen him smile since Red got kidnapped.

"Shit on the up and coming, but I don't know what's going to happen because...you know," Lil K said.

"Red?"

"Yeah."

"Bro, you see what type of shit she on. Dude may got her brainwashed," Knight said.

"Maybe."

"Let go."

"It's not that easy, bro." Lil K still had feelings for Red and he knew she still loved him.

"I know, bro. I was in love with Valentine," Knight said.

"How's my niece anyway?" Lil K asked, changing the subject.

"I gotta slide out to Chiraq soon, plus I gotta go visit the BD's."

"They moving keys, huh?" Lil K asked.

"Hell yeah! I'm sending them fools 300 every other week, bro, word to life," Knight said.

"Damn, that's litty." Lil K pulled up to Brownsville projects.

"Yo, son, I forgot to tell you the crazy shit that happened in Cuba, son." Knight shook his head.

"What?"

"I went to go see pops and his girl came to pick me up, but the whole time I ain't know the bad bitch was his wifey."

"You tried to holler at her like a regular Bronx nigga?" Lil K joked, knowing his brother.

"Naw, son, peep game. She took me to a hood somewhere and we went into this house and shit got crazy," Knight said.

"A shootout?"

"Naw."

"Then what?" Lil K got out of the car, trying to make sense of this shit because it sounded weird.

"Shawty jumped in my arms and we fucked. Her pussy was on a different level, but her breath had a little smell to it." Knight made Lil K laugh.

"You still kissed her?"

"Hell yeah, cuz! We drove back to Smoke's mansion and this goofy nigga kissing on his bitch talking about she wifey."

"Damn, you fucked our stepmom, bro."

"Facts, and I'll do it again, word." Knight walked in the front to Addy's crib, laughing with Lil K, but then he saw Khalid and three men come out of Addy's crib with big guns and assault rifles at their sides.

Lil K saw the movement and went for his gun.

Boc! Boc! Boc!

One of the men caught a headshot and Khalid slid away from the drama out the exit.

The hallway was too small for a shooting, so Knight killed the other two men who weren't able to get a shot off because they were caught off guard.

Addy had connected with Khalid when he heard $500,000 was on Knight's head.

Khalid waited four hours for Knight and Lil K to show so when they didn't, he killed Addy and left the crib.

Knight ran out of the building to see a Bentley SUV pull out of the back lot.

"Fuck, yo!" Knight yelled out loud.

***

Washington Heights, NY

Bree walked into a small bar, dressed sexy as always. It was early in the afternoon, 1 p.m. She had to meet with Halt.

When he called her last night to meet she was happy, hoping to win back her Brooklyn streets with his product.

"Nice to see you," Halt told her as she sat down at a table.

"Likewise."

"I called you to tell you I'm willing to do business with you on one term."

"What?"

"Help me find this Knight kid?" he asked.

"Knight?" She played dumb, acting like she didn't know him.

"Come on, Bree, you and him got history. Facts. I know everything," Halt told her.

"Okay, but it's not an easy task, so I need time."

"Take all the time you need, please."

"We have a deal."

"Great! I'll be in touch soon," Halt said, getting up to leave.

Halt had been thinking about the talk with Aliza and he came up with his own plan. He always had a feeling Smoke had something to do with his brother death but he always gave him to benefit of the doubt.

***

Havana, Cuba

Smoke and Rachela had just got done making love, something they did daily, sometimes with two or four women.

"You did good."

"I always do good. I know you love when I choke on your nut and lick your ass," she said.

"I'm not talking about that, and all that ass licking shit have to stop, ma."

"So what you talking about?" She was lost.

"Doing that to Knight."

"My pleasure," she repeated, meaning every word. "You think he went for it?"

"We will see," Smoke said, hoping his scheme would work.

***

Puerto Rico

Knight had rented a 178 sq. ft. yacht for the weekend to spend with his new female friend MeMe whom he had recently met. The chef was cooking some Mexican food for them as they sat on the upper deck enjoying the view of the ocean.

"Wow, you did it up." She wore a nice purple Gucci skirt and top.

"Somethin' light."

"Huh?"

"That mean anything for you?"

"I have to be honest, Knight. I'm married but I'm not happy."

"I can tell."

"How?"

"It's on your face," he told her, seeing her sad face.

"It's that obvious, huh?"

"No, but I pay attention you."

"Oh, you do? So what's my favorite color?" she asked, smiling.

"Green."

"You right, but lucky guess. Favorite designer?" she asked.

"Versace."

"Damn, you good," she said, laughing since he got it all correct.

That weekend was fun. They didn't have sex, but the vibe was way better than sex.

Chapter 67
Long Island, NY

M Balla and Lil K came out to L.I. on different missions, but they were riding together to pick up Behadi.

When Behadi told Lil K her father Khalid had a close friend from Africa who owned a gun store in L.I., he formed a plan.

M Balla had a SUV full of goons trailing them. Lil K's plan was to rob the shop and get the African man to talk, but he would let Behadi pull up on him first.

"We need more guns anyway, so this is a blessing." M Balla only came for the weapons.

"I know."

"At least that Slim nigga out the way," M Balla said.

"He was our least problem, bro," Lil K replied. "But what's up with that IG bitch you had?"

"Which one?"

"Nigga, the tall redbone bitch with the big ass?" Lil K asked, pulling into the lot.

"I been cut her off."

"She in there talking to somebody, so we just going to mob up in there and if he moves funny, smoke him," Lil K said hopping out of the car.

"Nigga I ain't new to this," M Balla said.

***

Behadi had been in the gun shop for at least forty minutes now talking to Raheem, a good friend of Khalid who grew up with him. While talking, Behadi and Raheem saw two men walking towards the store. They didn't pay them any mind at all, but then they saw two gunmen enter the store with masks. Raheem reached for a gun until Behadi placed her 44 Bulldog to his face.

"Don't you dare," Behadi told him, seeing how hurt he looked back at her.

M Balla's goons came right into the store, filling up bags with guns at a fast speed.

"Where is my father?" Behadi asked as Lil K approached.

"Death before dishonor for my friend," Raheem said.

"Your problem is you were always loyal to the wrong niggas," Behadi said before touching the trigger.

Bloc! Bloc! Bloc! Bloc! Bloc!

"Damn, you could have got more out of him," Lil K said.

"Nah, he's from a tribe where they will die before giving up names or snitch," Behadi explained.

M Balla's crew continued to load up weapons in bags before leaving.

Outside, they ran into a big problem.

Uncle Pimp and Gotti were waiting for them with Khalid and his shooters. When Red saw the beautiful woman next to Lil K, she fired toward them.

Tat! Tat! Tat! Tat! Tat!

She almost hit Behadi twice, but one of M Balla's goons got in the way and she killed him.

Lil K and Gotti went round for round while Red and Behadi battled it out as if they were in hand to hand combat.

Khalid got hit in his right leg by M Balla, who was on his ass and shooting wildly.

A few of Uncle Pimp's shooters got killed, so he knew it was time to go because the shit Lil K was spraying was fucking shit up.

Tat! Tat! Tat! Tat! Tat!

Lil K gave Behadi a look, letting her know it was about time to get the fuck outta there.

Most of M Balla's men were laid out in blood on the ground. Red wasn't giving up. Her gun was still barking towards Behadi.

Tat! Tat! Tat!

Behadi knew Red was Lil K's ex and she wanted to kill that bitch now.

***

South Bronx, NY

Behadi went to her crib with her so-called man, who hadn't said a word since the shooting took place.

"You good?" she asked.

"Why you ask?"

"Your energy is off since you saw your ex."

"Nah, you buggin'."

"Oh, I'm buggin'? Okay. I'll leave you to it. I'm going to sleep," she said, walking to her room, shaking her head.

***

Parkchester, Bronx

Sniper moved his mom out to a nice suburban home with his sister last month with the money he had been saving. Most niggas hustled for petty shit like cars, clothes, or jewelry, but Sniper did it for his family.

Growing up in the ghetto all he vey wanted was a big bag and a better lifestyle. Thanks to M Balla putting all the homies on, he was able to get to a better place in life.

He pulled up to his mom's two-story house to bring her a dozen roses for Mother's Day today.

Walking into the crib, he saw blood all over the walls first and when he looked down, he saw his mom's and sister's dead bodies.

Sniper cried as he looked at the gruesome murders.

Chapter 68
Upper Westside, NY

Aliza had her own penthouse suite in one of the most expensive condo buildings on the Upper Westside. Since Slim's death she was a little overwhelmed with happiness because she was sick of Slim. She hated the fact that she had to carry Slim and basically feed him.

Aliza wanted a piece of New York just like everybody else did but she knew she would have a problem doing it alone. Cutting her sister's throat was just part of the game, but she really hated Smoke. Rachela let Smoke into the riches and empire and that's where shit went wrong. Aliza and Rachela didn't speak to each other in years.

When she found out Smoke had Halt in New York moving weight for him, she needed a piece of the pie. Halt called her and told her tomorrow he would like to talk in the Heights. She knew if she could control Washington Heights, she would be able to slide into the Bronx.

Aliza had a hot bubble bath running so she could relax and get peace of mind. The death of Slim brought a smile to her face, but the downfall was he was bringing in a lot of money.

She remembered the time she met Slim years ago in the Dominican Republic. They talked and the next day they went on a date. Slim was trying to find a plug in DR and she was on vacation. Aliza took Slim back to Cuba and changed his life since that day.

Now he was dead. Halt would have to replace him and hopefully he would be a better replacement.

***

Washington Heights, NY

Halt waited on Aliza to show up so he could talk to her about their new business relationship he came up with his final decision days ago. For some time now he had a strong feeling Smoke killed his brother, but he didn't know for a fact so he put it to the back of his head until now. He knew Aliza wouldn't lie just to supply him drugs, but he didn't feel as if he could trust her as of yet. Halt saw something in her eyes he saw too often: greed.

Three of his guards' attention turned to the door when Aliza walked in rocking a nice colorful spring dress with her hair in a bun.

"Gentlemen, let her in," Halt told his men.

"Halt, glad to see you again," she said, sitting down.

"I came up with a decision," he said

"Okay, that's grea.t"

"I'ma do business with you under one condition," he said

"That is?"

"You let me take you on a date," he told her, seeing her blush.

"Sorry, but you're not my type at all. I like blacks, so you need to come up with another wish," she told him.

"Wow, okay, I guess I gotta take that out."

"Yep."

"We good then, I guess," he said in a low voice.

"I can't hear you?" she said, putting her hand to her ear.

"Let's focus on business," he told her.

"Gladly." She smiled, getting to the point.

Chapter 69
Richmond, VA

Knight and Lil K took a trip to Virginia to get outta New York for a few days. They also had business they came down there on. Last time Knight was out in VA he caught a bid trying to get money in the Norfolk area.

"It's a lot of money out here, bro, trust me. Don't let the country roads fool you" Knight said as he drove the Cadillac down the highway, listening to Lil Baby on the radio.

"I see."

"You sure this nigga's family live out here?" Knight asked Lil K.

"Behadi gave it to me and I know she always on point with shit like this."

"Facts."

"M Balla doing a good job, bro," Lil K said.

"He loyal."

"Word to mother, he carrying us on his back right now," Lil K said peeping his boy's grind and honor.

"You right. Sniper going brazy since he lost his mom and daughter," Knight said

"Damn, bro."

"He thinks it was Uncle Pimp and them bitches."

"Who was it?" Lil K asked.

"To be real, I don't know, but we gonna find out."

"Facts, son. This the house right there." Lil K pointed at a small brick house.

"This nigga got all that money and his people living in this piece of shit?" Knight said.

The house was small and dirty and the yard had two old beat up cars and a swing.

"Niggas ain't shit, son." Lil K got out of the car, walking up the rocky pavement.

"Let me knock." Knight walked onto the porch to see ants and mice chilling everywhere.

Seconds later, a husky woman with a gold grill came to the door, staring at them. "What y'all want?" The woman was country.

"You Gotti's people?" Lil K asked.

"Fuck that piece of shit!" she spit.

A little boy no older than twelve years old walked up to the doorway.

"I guess you his people," Knight stated.

"If you say so. Tell that nigga I need my child support," she said before she saw a gun.

Boc! Boc! Boc! Boc! Boc!

They killed the boy and the woman before getting in the car pulling off.

Killing kids and women was normal to them by now. It still felt bad afterwards, but they didn't lose sleep.

* * *

Cuba

Rachela was on her way to visit her crazy pops. She got out of her car and walked into the large mansion he had since she was a kid.

Rachela's dad, Jose Martinez, had been in the game for years. He ran Cuba. Jose Martinez's daughters were the faces to his empire. They moved most of his drugs for him for years.

Rachela and Aliza never saw eye to eye since they were kids, but their dad always treated them equally with love.

Smoke was in New York, so Rachela had to focus on business. Smoke had been looking for Halt, stressing over the 900 keys he shipped him weeks ago with no payment.

She had her own business to worry about. That's why she was here to see OG.

Chapter 70
Manhattan, NY

Gotti was on his way to his hotel because his condo floor was still getting redone.

He couldn't figure out why Knight and his crew kept getting out of his hands. Every time he thought he had a possible chance at killing them, some shit always went wrong. Gotti had to ride with two car loads full of goons and weapons on deck.

"Yo, bruh, pull into the lower garage area," Gotti told his driver.

"A'ight, you sure?"

"Yes."

The SUV pulled into the back and went under a lower garage area. Gotti's soldiers jumped out with machine guns and he followed their lead.

Walking to the elevator, he texted his girl, who was in the UK, telling her good night. In the elevator, six goons entered first. Then the top of the ceiling opened, a smoke bomb filled the elevator, and gunfire took over.

Tat! Tat! Tat! Tat! Tat!

Gotti couldn't see the shooter because of all the smoke filling the elevator. Gotti fired a few rounds and backpedaled with two goons covering him.

When he got back in the SUV, he raced off as shots hit his SUV, shattering the windows and tail lights.

***

Behadi got in her car and took off before the building security arrived. She had been hiding in the elevator shaft, awaiting Gotti, whom she had been watching for three days.

When she got on the highway, Lil K called.

"Heyyy," she answered.

"What's up, where you at?" Lil K asked.

"On my way to you."

"Cool. How was your day?"

"Nails and shopping, regular shit. What you doing?"

"I'm at the crib," Lil K stated, turning down the TV.

"I'll be there in an hour sexy."

Behadi smiled as he hung up the phone. She was truly in love with Lil K, but she didn't know if he felt the same way about her. The day she got into the shootout with Red, she knew it was some type of jealousy. She wasn't going to let no bitch knock her off her high horse.

***

Queens, NY

Bree was leaving her crib, getting into her G Wagon truck, on her way to see Halt.

Tonight, would be her first shipment. She had to go meet Halt's men at a boat in the Dyckman area. Bree knew Halt couldn't be trusted, but she needed him right now. Halt was her only choice and he was in the city area, so it all worked out for her.

Lately she'd been hearing Knight's name a lot in the streets. She really wanted to know who he was dealing with. She knew he had to have a good plug if he was in control of the Bronx.

***

Washington Heights, NY

Bree pulled up into Dyckman to see a few Spanish men standing there with weapons, ready to deal business. Bree got out and made her way to them.

"Y'all Halt's people?" Bree asked them as they looked at each other with smirks.

"You got the money?" the main nigga asked her.

"You got the drugs?" Bree felt something off about their energy and vibes.

Five men dressed in all black popped out.

Tat! Tat! Tat! Tat! Tat!

Halt's goons didn't see the gunfire coming as they got hit up from behind, killing them.

Bree walked over to the bag of drugs on the floor and picked it up. Bree walked off in her heels as her shooters vanished into thin wind.

She had a few niggas in Queensbridge projects down for her. She called them and asked them to come help her with a lick. Robbing Halt was never her goal at first, but she had to really think before lining him up.

Bree knew that for every action, a reaction would follow and she was ready.

***

Rockland County, NY

Halt got a call from one of his guys at 1 a.m. "Yo," Halt answered

"We have an issue, bossman," his worker said.

"At 1 a.m.?"

"Yes."

"What happened?"

"The chick."

"What chick?" Halt stated, still trying to figure out what he was talking about.

"Bree."

"Did she get the stuff?" Halt knew his people were supposed to meet her hours ago.

"That's the issue. She robbed us," his worker said.

"She what?" Halt shouted.

"She robbed us."

"Where is LV?" Halt asked

"They all dead," his worker said sadly.

"Fuck!" he yelled before hanging up the phone.

If he would have known she would cross him so quickly, he would have never given her chance to begin with.

***

Jersey City, NJ

Smoke was driving in a Maybach, on his way to meet a close friend he grew up with who now was doing big things in New Jersey. His cell phone went off and he saw it was Halt.

"Yo Halt, what's up brother?" Smoke answered.

"I need you to send more meat to me," Halt said in code.

"I did the other night. Did you get it?"

"Yes, but we ran into a problem. A big problem," Halt said, taking a deep breath.

"Okay give me a day or two. I got you," Smoke said.

"Good looks. Where you at anyway?"

"Driving through Jersey City."

"Oh, let me guess, you on your way to see Deem."

"Yeah."

"I hate that nigga," Halt said seriously.

"I know, but he is a big part of our success."

"Fuck him." Halt and Deem had serious beef over a chick they both had been sleeping with years back. Not just any chick, though. It had been Deem's wife.

"I have to go. I'm here," Smoke said, pulling up to Deem's block in the hood.

"A'ight." Halt hung up

Smoke wondered how Halt fumbled on all them keys, but he left it alone and planned to put in a new order.

Chapter 71
Long Island, NY

Khalid purchased a new house in the East Hampton area. The thing he loved about this house was the lower underground tunnel.

He couldn't believe his daughter went this far with trying to protect someone who crossed him. It was now to the point of no return he didn't even consider her as his daughter no more she was his enemy.

Khalid walked into his home towards the kitchen with two of his personal guards. He was looking for the five men who was supposed to guard house. When he stepped foot in the dining room he saw all five men dead with their throats slit and three bullets in their forehead. Khalid saw the lights go out and he went for his gun.

Gunfire started to spark the room from all different angles by his shooter. Khalid couldn't see shit, but he knew his hidden doorway to the lower tunnel was a few feet away in a closet.

Tat! Tat! Tat!

"Ahhhhh!" Khalid yelled, feeling a burn to his upper back before making his way into the closet.

There were locks on the inside of the closet so he locked himself in there and crawled through a small tunnel downwards.

***

"Fuck, where is he?" Knight said, looking around.

"I just saw him," Behadi said with her night vision goggles on.

"Let's go before some weird shit happens." Knight was upset he missed his target again.

Behadi got an alert that Khalid that used his name to purchase a new home in L.I., so she came up with a small plan and Knight was down. Lil K was feeling ill so he chose not to come.

"If I know my dad like I think I do then he's not too far gone. He will want blood" she stated leaving the crib.

"I hope so."

"Oh, no need to hope, trust me, he will."

"We will see." Knight got in his truck.

***

Brewster, NY

Upstate New York in the wooded area, Red was home in her bed asleep. Red was tossing and turning in her sleep in cold sweats, yelling and screaming.

"Oh K, stopppp...pleaseee. Whyyy, whyyy... Noooo!" Red was having a crazy nightmare as she did almost every night.

When she woke up from her sleep she saw Sexy Spicee in a chair sitting next to her in panties and a bra, smiling. This was regular to Sexy Spicee and all the other women in the house.

"Finally up?" Sexy Spice said, drinking a cup of hot coffee.

"What do you want?" Red said in a raspy voice.

"Nothing."

"Then leave,"

"Okay, I will," Sexy Spicee said without moving.

"Bye."

"You need to let him go, Red. He moved on." Sexy Spicee rubbed it in her face, the fact that they saw Lil K with another woman.

"Leave me the fuck alone," Red told her, getting upset.

"I'll see you tomorrow for the mission." Sexy Spicee finally stood to leave

Red tried to go back to sleep, but couldn't.

***

Castle Hill Projects, BX

Every year in Castle Hill there was a big event, and everybody came out to pay respect and show love. Rappers, NBA players, bad bitches and dope boys came out for this big ass gathering and cook out.

"It's packed, bro. Last year wasn't even like this one" Sniper told M Balla and Slaughter Balla.

"No lie, son," Slaughter Balla said, looking at all the variety of women walking around.

"Tonight, I'm thinking about throwing some shit in Club Ace," M Balla said.

"Hell nah, my ex in there and I may real live slap that bitch, bro," Sniper said, making niggas laugh hard.

"You know them Dominican bitches 730, blood," Slaughter Balla said before seeing a handful of women come their way.

"She a wetty, bro," one of the young niggas said, catching everybody's attention.

When M Balla saw Red with a group of other bitches with all big Birkin bags, he shouted before bullets started to fly.

Tat! Tat! Tat! Tat! Tat!

Sniper was the first to get hit in the chest, not paying attention to the scene.

Slaughter shot one of the women before Red took his head off.

Boc! Boc! Boc!

M Balla fired at the woman as the crowd ran everywhere into the crowd, getting low from bullets.

Two teenagers got killed right in front of M Balla as he literally jumped over their bodies.

Boc! Boc! Boc!

Boom! Boom! Boom!

Sexy Spice shotgun roared through the crowd killing a few more people.

M Balla made it into the lot where he saw Uncle Pimp driving off laughing in a Wraith with two tone paint.

The shooting was so big it made the world news due to eight dead and ten people injured.

Chapter 72
Cuba

Today Jose Martinez was awaiting for his guest of honor, a man he was very close to. Khalid was on his way to have a sit down with him. The two had been doing business together for years so they had a close bond with each other and it was always business-like.

Jose Martinez wanted to see both of his daughters for his birthday weekend soon. Both of his beautiful daughters hated his new young wife, but he didn't care. She treated him like a king.

He heard a buzzer and he knew who that was. Seconds later, Khalid and his sexy wife came inside his nice size office.

"Jose."

"Khalid, you look younger every time I see you," Jose joked.

"I don't believe you."

"I kid you not. Have a seat," Jose said once his wife left the room.

"Thanks for inviting me," Khalid said, looking around.

Khalid had a great amount of respect for Jose since their first time meeting each other.

"Sure. How can I be of help to you?" Jose asked.

"Knight."

"Yes, a Bronx kid. He's been a pain in my ass so maybe if I can cut off his supply, I'll be able to get to him easier because I believe he has some strong people backing him," Khalid said as Jose's face didn't move.

"I don't give up my business dealings, Khalid, and you know this firsthand about me." Jose felt a little insulted.

"I know, but you family to me and this kid got my daughter to turn on me and killed everything I loved." Khalid put on a sad face, but Jose wasn't buying it.

"I have dealt with a man named Knight and that's all I will tell you," Jose said with an honest look.

Khalid knew Jose for being honest at all times so he truly believed every word he said. "Thanks."

"This Knight kid must have you going crazy. Let me find out you getting too old for the game," Jose joked.

"I don't think you understand. This kid is a different type of monster," Khalid said with a wicked look on his face.

"I can tell, if he got you scared shitless." Jose could tell he hit a button.

"I'm not scared one bit. I lived my life." Khalid got up, ready to leave before he got disrespectful with Jose

"I'll be here if you need me," Jose stated, going back to his business as if Khalid was never there.

When Khalid walked out, Jose called Rachela. "Hey baby."

"What you doing, daddy?" Rachela asked.

"At home, about to go for a swim," Jose said. He had a close relationship with his daughter.

"Okay, nice. I'm on my way to Dubai."

"Before you leave, I need you to stop by."

"Okay, sure, give me a few hours to get there" Rachela said before hanging up the phone.

Jose wanted to know what Knight had done to put the fear of God in Khalid's heart.

***

Atlanta, GA

Uncle Pimp and a few of his girls took a trip out to Atlanta to have fun and get away from all the drama. They were at a new club that just opened in the Zone 4 area. Sexy Spicee was having a good time tossing money, turning up. She had already tossed 20K on the stage as the beautiful women twerked naked.

"I'ma go use the little girls' room," Sexy Spicee said.

"Go ahead, but be back in two minutes, bitch," Uncle Pimp stated.

"Yes, daddy." Sexy Spicee smiled, walking off because she loved when he called her a bitch.

Uncle Pimp had three young bitches in his ear. He was going to bring them back to New York for training.

He loved Atlanta because the sex trafficking was one of the highest in the States and the country.

***

Sexy Spicee went into the restroom and all the stalls were being used except the middle one so she went inside. She lifted her dress and took a piss, feeling lighter. "Shit," she moaned, feeling the liquor.

"Hola, Sexy Spicee," a voice said above her.

Sexy Spicee looked up to just in time to see Behadi kick open the stall. Before Sexy Spicee could reach for her weapon, it was over.

Psst! Psst! Psst!

Behadi walked out of the restroom and waited outside for Uncle Pimp to come out, but he sneaked out the back when she saw Sexy Spicee's dead body. He was the first to get out of the club.

Chapter 73
Manhattan, NY

Gotti had a ball under his arm for a few days now. Today he woke up knowing he had to get the ball checked because his whole arm was swollen.

He been under a lot of stress lately dealing with Knight crew. Gotti had been losing good men during the process warring with Knight.

Gotti had to go to VA sometime this week to check on his drug operations out there and he needed to rally up on some more goons to bring up to New York.

His driver pulled up to the building where his doctor's office was located. Walking inside, he saw the desk lady playing in her dirty nails looking bored.

"Excuse me, I'm here for Dr. Robin," Gotti said.

The woman looked up at him and sucked her teeth. "Fill this out and have a seat." She passed him a clipboard.

Gotti filled out the form and turned it in before sitting back down and waiting his turn. Finally his doctor came out for him.

"Gotti," she called him by his nickname, as he always requested.

"Hey Dr. Robin"

"What's going on?" Dr. Robin said, sitting down.

"I got a big-ass bump under this arm," he said, taking off his shirt, showing her the big boil.

"Wow, that may be an issue," she said, looking at it.

"It's painful also," Gotti told her, seeing the disgusted look on her pretty face from all the fat hanging from his arm.

"I'll have the nurse draw your blood. And I'll have you scheduled for a test with a phlebotomist," she said, leaving the room.

Two days later, Gotti returned to the doctor's office for the results of his test. When Dr. Robin entered the room, Gotti saw the look on her face. He knew something was wrong.

"Everything good?"

"No," she replied.

"I don't understand," Gotti replied, knowing there was something wrong

"You have tested positive for cancer. That's why you have the blood clot under your arm," Dr. Robin stated.

"Me?"

"Yes. Gotti, I'm sorry, but we will have to start treatment as soon as possible," she said.

"Is it curable?"

"You can beat it now if you take care of yourself," she stated.

"Okay." Gotti couldn't believe the news, but he knew he lived an unhealthy lifestyle.

***

Miami, FL

Rachela and Smoke took her boat on the ocean for a day but they just left the boat deck.

Rachela was in the kitchen putting poison in the food she was cooking while Smoke was asleep. Tonight she planned to put her plans into full motion because Smoke had to go. His time was up.

"What you doing?" Smoke scared her because she thought he was asleep.

Rachela hid the bottle of poison behind a cup.

"How long you been there for, babe? I thought you was asleep," Rachela said, still cooking, but nervously.

"I just got here."

Five of Rachela's goons paced the large fancy boat.

"You hungry?"

"Not really."

"You look hungry, babe. You should really eat something"

"Nah."

"Come on, have dinner with me," she said.

"Okay, let me go wash my hands," Smoke said, going upstairs

Smoke went upstairs and Rachela picked up the phone, calling her goons.

"Five minutes after he starts to eat, come to get him," she stated before hanging up the phone.

Rachela heard a big splash into the water and rushed upstairs to see Smoke swimming away at a fast pace.

"Get him!" she yelled to her goons.

Tat! Tat! Tat! Tat! Tat!

"Fuck…"

Smoke was getting away and she was pissed because now he knew what she was up to.

***

USP Canaan Prison, PA

Marie came out to see her husband today. She had been staying at her PA house for the past few days getting peace of mind. Thing in L.A. were going good, but Marie had been having trouble with one of her rivals trying to squeeze their way into her territory.

The Costa Ricans were her number one enemy for years and now they wore trying to muscle their way into L.A. and a bunch of other states.

She looked really pretty in her yellow and gold Versace dress on the visit room floor. Visiting D Fatal Brim was what she needed because he always knew all the right shit to say. He knew how to make her feel like she was on a different planet or universe. At first she used to think it was all jail talk with him but she started to see things in his actions which made her gain his trust.

Marie hated having to wait two hours after arriving every time just to spend a few hours with her husband.

***

D Fatal Brim was finished with his haircut. He didn't have enough time to get in the shower, so he took a quick bird bath in his sink. He knew Marie was waiting on him. He was the only nigga on the unit who had a bad bitch, so niggas were very jealous of him.

267

"Yo Brim!" Trace Brim yelled from outside his door.

"Yooo."

"A nigga just got stabbed up and the guards about to step back in from outside."

"Damn." D Fatal Brim looked at his cell to see a D.C. nigga trying to make his way to the bubble dripping in blood after his homies stabbed him up because he was too cool with a few New York cats in the unit.

"Get my Mp3 off the charger," D Fatal Brim told his homie.

When the guards came back into the unit and saw the man bleeding to death, they hit the coder.

"Lockdown... Lockdown... Lockdown!" the two guards yelled, trying to save the man's life.

Guards and medical ran into the unit seconds later to save the man's life, but he didn't make it.

D Fatal Brim saw another nigga lose his life and it touched his heart. The dude had two weeks before he went home.

The visits were all canceled after the death, so Marie had to leave. The jail was on lockdown.

***

Brewster, NY

Red had been feel very sick lately for some odd reason, but this sick was a different type of illness she never felt. Two days ago, she took a few pregnancy tests, but they all came back negative. She would let Uncle Pimp have sex with her unprotected always as well as all the other women. Uncle Pimp didn't use condoms on the girls. He told them it was about trust. Whenever a chick got pregnant, he would make them get an abortion so fast they wouldn't even remember they got pregnant. She had been experiencing faintness, dizziness, vomiting, skin discoloration, and serious headaches.

Red went into the kitchen with seven other women, laughing and talking. Most of them hated Red because of the way Uncle Pimp treated her with love and care. Uncle Pimp would treat the rest of them like the whores they were. Since Sexy Spicee's, death Red was number one in the house and she loved the power.

"Y'all bitches go clean the house, then make breakfast, and I'll be watching the camera, so don't spit in the food or you'll end up like Ashely #2," Red said, laughing, walking out back to get some air.

Last week she had caught Ashely #2 spitting in the lunch food and killed her.

***

Atlanta, GA

Smoke was staying at a cheap hotel waiting on his people to Western Union him some money so he could have some bread. He had two hundred dollars on him when he made it back to land yesterday.

Smoke couldn't believe what Rachela tried to do. When he saw her poison his food, he thought he was tripping, but when he saw the way her guards were moving, he knew something was up. Smoke didn't have a gun, but he had always been a good swimmer since he was a kid. The dock wasn't too far back so he had to jump or he would have been a dead man.
He knew firsthand how serious Rachela was and how ruthless she could be.

All he could think about was what went wrong. He tried to call Knight and Halt, but no answer from either one of them.

***

Queens, NY

Halt had just come from trying to hunt down Bree, but she was long gone, like a ghost.

He saw Smoke calling his phone and he ignored it. Halt had taken a lot of weight from Smoke and never paid him. He thought that was his reason for calling, but Halt had nothing to talk about.

Business with Aliza was solid. She was on point and gave him shit at a lower price than his ex-best friend did.

Halt was on his way back to the Heights.

Chapter 74
Africa

Khalid made his way back to his homeland for a while because looking for Knight and Behadi was getting very hard and a lifetime event. He had other business he had to attend to in his country.

Khalid couldn't wait to see his wives and family. It was late so normally all his wives would be asleep in the same room in his castle-like mansion, which he loved.

Walking up to the master bedroom, he wondered where the security guards were at. Normally they would be all around walking around to make sure everything was good. He been gone a few months now so he knew they must have gotten lazy or something.

Opening the double doors to his room he saw three women hogtied up on the carpet made out of lion fur.

"Not so funny now," a voice said, coming up behind him.

Khalid looked behind him to see Behadi dressed in all black with blood all on her hands.

"Little bitch, I'ma fucking kill you, I swear——"

"Khalid, it's over, dumb ass," she told him.

"I thought I raised you right, but I see I didn't." Khalid shook his head

"You raised me to be a killer and now look. It backfired," she told him.

"You have bigger problems than me, Behadi."

"I know, but I can only handle one issue at a time," she said before aiming her gun at his wives.

Boc! Boc! Boc! Boc! Boc! Boc!

Behadi shot Khalid's wives all in their heads as he watched in tears. She then aimed her weapon on him.

"You sucked as a father, by the way."

Boc! Boc! Boc! Boc! Boc!

Bullets tore through his skull, killing him fast. She wanted a slow torturous death for Khalid but she chose to make it quick.

Behadi had to fly back to the States soon so she left the house. All the guards were already dead in the guest house.

***

Uptown, Bronx
Weeks later

M Balla had been focused on money and getting everything in order before he went on vacation to the Caribbean Islands with his new girl.

Tonight, he had a meeting with Lil K and Knight about their ops and the next re-up.

Losing Sniper was still fresh on his mind and he wanted blood. His crew was getting thick. He took over Yonkers and Mount Vernon, thanks to the help of his little cousin.

M Balla came out of the building and got in his Range Rover truck, then nine shooters appeared out of the corner of his eyes.

Tat! Tat! Tat! Tat! Tat! Tat! Tat! Tat! Tat!

M Balla got hit up eight times in his truck, killing him, leaving him slumped on the steering wheel. Gotti approached the window and fired three extra shots into M Balla's head.

***

Cuba

Knight got a text from Smoke phone two nights ago telling him to meet him at Smoke's crib, which was odd because Smoke would call, not text.

Knight pulled up in a cab to the mansion and walked inside to see no security.

"Yo Pops!" Knight yelled into the house to hear an echo.

He heard heels clicking on the marble floors. When he saw Rachela approaching in a lingerie set with a see-through robe, he got horny. Her curves and flat stomach was so sexy he couldn't control his stares.

"Hey Knight," she said with a sexy voice.

"Where is my pops and why are you playing a dangerous game?" he told her, trying to look at her colorful eyes and not her nice boobs.

"Smoke is out the picture for now," she said.

"Huh?"

"Your father is a snake, Knight. You're that blind?"

"We're all snakes."

"He's a poison snake, Knight. He's been trying to set you up this whole time. You're the reason why he tried to cross me, but this is business, so you have a choice."

"Do I?"

"You do. Follow me," Rachela said, walking downstairs into a basement area.

Knight saw Valentine and his daughter Karmala in a small room with a glass window.

"You touch my family and I'll kill you." Knight made her laugh

"That's so outta style that you have to say some shit like that. I'll chop your nipples off and feed them to a tiger. Now that sounds sexy." Rachela smiled

Knight saw Valentine and his daughter were asleep and they looked okay.

"What do you want?"

"I want to supply you and your crew, but I also want to expand to other cities with your help," she told him.

"And they go free?"

"As soon as you say yes, you can take them back with you. It's not as if I give a fuck."

"Okay, fine, send them back home and we do business."

"Deal, friend, and hopefully one day I can get another ride on that magic stick," she said, walking off as her ass cheeks bounced with every strut.

Knight took one look at his baby mother and seed before leaving. He trusted her to return his family.

He thought how he kept finding himself in these type of situations.

Romell Tukes

Chapter 75
Brewster, NY

Red and Uncle Pimp had just ended the lovemaking session. The room was hot and sticky, but it smelled like roses.

"You ready for me to fuck you in your ass, baby?" he asked Red, who laid naked next to him.

"Yes, but can I use the bathroom real quick? I don't wanna give you the doo-doo dick," she said.

"Go ahead."

Red went to use the private bathroom. She flushed the toilet twice, then came right out of the bathroom, shutting off the bathroom light.

"That was fast," Uncle Pimp said, leaning up to see her pointing a big pistol at him.

"You gave me HIV, you hoe-ass nigga!" Red yelled in tears. Two days ago Red went to see a doctor on her own to see what was really going on with her. When the doctor told her she had been feeling ill because the HIV virus was going against her blood cells, she was hurt.

"I should have told you. I'm sorry."

"You gave all of us HIV?" she asked.

"Yes, but I love y'all. Red, you gonna kill me after all I've done for you? I made you!" he shouted.

"Nigga, you ain't make shit! Lil K made me and you took me away from him, you fucking dog!" she said, crying.

"He don't want you now. Red, you're a drug addict, you have HIV, and you mentally off. Just put the gun down, and——"

Boc! Boc! Boc! Boc! Boc!

Red continued to empty the clip until Uncle Pimp had no movement. She dropped to the floor crying as other women rushed the room to see what was going on.

"What happened?" a redbone chick with green eyes asked, seeing her pimp dead.

"He gave us all HIV," Red said.

"I don't got no damn HIV," one of the women said.

"We all do," Red said, getting up to see upset faces, as most of the women were strung out on drugs.

Red took one of his cars and slid off to the Bronx to make her peace with Lil K if she could find him.

***

Washington Heights, NY

Halt had a beautiful daughter who was eighteen years old and on her way to college. He was dropping her off at her mom's house so he could go out to PA.

"When you coming back?"

"Soon," Halt said.

"What's soon?" his daughter asked knowing his soon could be months

"A few weeks."

"You know I'll be in college then," she said as he pulled up in front of the three story house.

"I'll come see you in college."

"What? Oh hell no, Daddy, you'll embarrass me." She laughed.

"You just jealous because them little college chicks gonna be all on your old man," Halt said, getting out of the car to walk her in the house.

"Thanks for the lunch and be safe." His daughter reached for the door and Bree opened the door with a gun.

Halt went for his gun, but Bree put two slugs in his forehead. Bree killed his daughter and then walked over both of them on her way to her car parked up the street.

She had to finish Halt because she couldn't leave loose ends on her behalf. Now she had to put the rest of her plans together.

Chapter 76
Staten Island, NY
Six months later

Lil K and Behadi had a nice crib together in a middle class area and Behadi had a baby boy on the way. Lil K couldn't believe he was about to have a seed. It felt so good about to be a father. Behadi was the perfect woman. The only flaw is she didn't play no games and would kill in a blink of an eye.

"Babe, you cooked?" Behadi woke up, walking into the kitchen to see Lil K and Knight talking.

"Nah, why, you hungry? I'll make something for you," Lil K said.

Okay. What's up, Knight?" Behadi asked.

"You getting big, girl. I can't wait for my nephew to pop out. I'ma spoil that little nigga," Knight stated, taking a sip of tea.

"No you not. I don't want you to spoil him - none of you. I'm tired. I'm going to sleep," she said, walking upstairs.

"What was you saying?" Lil K asked.

"We gotta kill this bitch, but I heard her pops is a very powerful nigga in Cuba," Knight said.

"I think we should wait, play it by ear," Lil K said.

"Why you say that?"

"The product is good and business is booming. We need this because we haven't heard from Smoke."

"Rachela was supplying him," Knight replied.

"We need to focus on Gotti. He been too quiet, son," Lil K said.

"Facts. I saw Uncle Pimp on the news months ago."

"Me too. I wonder who did that and where Red went?" Lil K asked.

Hearing about Uncle Pimp's murder, he knew Red had something to do with it.

"I don't know. I'ma go to Miami for a few months or L.A. maybe. M Balla's brother JR Balla home, and he holding shit down," Knight said.

"All dat money we spent on a lawyer, he better be home," Lil K joked.

"Word. I'm out. I'ma be back when the baby due. Love you."

"Love you too."

***

Miami, FL
One week later

Knight went out for lunch with Stephen, an old friend, and she was looking sexy.

"It's been a while, funny guy," Stephen stated. She was one of the biggest drug suppliers in the city.

"I been busy."

"So I hear," she shot back.

"What you hear?"

"I hear it all, Knight, but that's not why you here."

"I can't come see an old friend?"

"No."

"Too bad. I'm here for no. But how's business?" he asked.

"More money, more problems, same crime wave, I guess," she said as their Mexican food arrived at their table.

"Same here."

"I know who and what you want, so I'ma just give it to you so you can leave because you're kinda fucking up my lunch." Stephen wrote down an address and apartment number and passed it to him.

"This is my condo building," Knight stated.

"Well, you slipping now, boy," she told him.

"It's like that?"

"Yep," Stephen said, watching him get up to leave.

Knight walked out, looking at Gotti's address, which was his building on the third floor, a level above him.

***

Gotti was on bed rest because his cancer had taken over his body. He moved to Miami so he could enjoy his last days. Gotti had a nurse there 24/7 with him helping him because he couldn't move or nothing he barely could talk now. His condition was getting worse by day.

The knock at the door got the nurse's attention and she went to answer it. Gotti heard the gunfire as he looked around the room, praying that wasn't what he thought. Seconds later, Knight stuck his head in the room.

"Gotti, I see you," Knight said, seeing fear in Gotti's face.

"No," Gotti said.

"You lost a lot of weight. You look sick, man." Knight smirked standing over Gotti's skinny body

"Kill me."

"I am, but I just want to see you die slow." Knight shot him in both legs.

"Ahhhh!" he cried.

"I gotta go, Gotti." Knight fired four shots in Gotti's temple.

"Nice job," a female voice said, clapping, coming into the room.

When Knight saw who the woman was, he lowered his weapon. "MeMe?"

"Hey Knight. I've been waiting on this day for years," she said in a strong Spanish accent.

"What's going on?" Knight was lost. He hadn't seen MeMe in a few weeks. The two had been dating on and off for a while but she was always disappearing.

"That's my husband you just killed and my worker, Knight. Me and my sister run the Costa Rican cartel."

"Wait, you're Kailina?" He had heard of them before. Word was the sisters were moving so much weight they could supply every state in America.

"No, I'm Melaie, short for MeMe, but Kailina is my sister," she said.

"This is crazy."

"I know you're in business with Rachela, but I want you, Knight. We could do big things," she said.

"No wonder why you never slept with me or nothing."

"You're not my style, no offense. But let's get out of here. My private jet is waiting. I hate Miami. I have a lot of enemies out here," she said, walking out of the room.

Chapter 77
L.A., Cali

Marie was waiting for Rachela to arrive at her downtown condo. Rachela reached out to her a few days back to set up a meeting with Marie, the woman she heard so much about. Marie also heard about Rachela and her Cuban family. Her father was supposed to be some big-time drug pusher out there in Cuba.

"Boss lady, she's here," one of her guards stated.

"Bring her in."

"Will do," he said, walking off to get the door.

"Marie." Rachela walked into the living in a nice classy white dress.

"Nice to meet you, Rachela."

"Same to you. Have a seat," Marie stated.

"Thank you."

"How can I help you?" Marie asked, crossing her legs.

"Well, I don't know if you know who I am, but my pops Jose Martinez runs Cuba's drug trade and I control all the business affairs," Rachela told her, getting comfortable.

"Okay, that's nice," Marie said, hoping she would get to the point.

"I've been watching you for a while now and I think we will be a bigger and better force together," Rachela stated.

"How can I know I will be able to trust you?" Marie asked.

"Trust is normally earned and I will give you every reason to trust me." Rachela's words were genuine.

"I don't see why I shouldn't give you a chance."

"I feel the same. That's why I'm here" Rachela shot back.

"Just don't back door me and we will get along good," Marie told her.

"I agree."

The women poured glasses of wine and cheered.

***

Staten Island, NY

Two months later

Behadi had a beautiful baby boy. She felt the motherhood vibes and loved it. The only thing she didn't like was breastfeeding. Her breasts produced milk with the slightest move.

Lil K was outta town for the night and she was laying in her bed asleep. Behadi woke up around the same time every night since her son came home from the hospital. One a.m. was the regular time her baby would cry to get fed but tonight, for some reason, the baby wasn't crying. She knew something was wrong so she got out of bed and made her way to the baby's room.

She looked in the baby's crib to see nothing. She panicked, looking around the house for the baby. She ran downstairs and paused when she saw a man in the living room. Her baby was in the man's arms with his neck hanging as if he had been strangled. The newborn was dead. She had tears in her eyes.

"Don't make a move or I will kill you too," Money said, throwing her dead baby on the floor, getting up.

"You bastard!" Behadi cried.

"Tell Lil K that Money is back and I'm looking for him."

Behadi was so hurt that she couldn't say a word back.

"I'ma let you live this time, but next time it's on me, sexy," Money said before walking out the door.

Behadi was in tears as she called Lil K to tell him the news.

***

Philly, PA

Lil K had opened up shop in Philly with his boy Nate. He was seeing big money in Philly.

It was late and he was on his way back to the hotel when Behadi called.

"Holla."

"Money killed our baby!" she screamed through her cries.

"I'm on my way." Lil K went straight for the highway in tears. He couldn't believe it.

Chapter 78
New York City, NY

Smoke had been plotting on ways to repay Rachela for her betrayal and take over her empire but knew that would be a hard task.

He was able to get in touch with Knight through Lil K via text message. Smoke needed to explain to his son what happened and hoped he could help him take over his wife's drug operations.

Halt was a ghost but he swore if he was to ever see him again, he would kill him with his bare hands.

There were two knocks at the door. Smoke went and opened the door to see Knight standing there with red heavy eyes as if he ain't sleep in days.

"Son."

"Save all that son shit, you snake-ass nigga! Why did you find us?" Knight was straight forward.

"What do you mean?" Smoke asked, seeing Knight go for a weapon.

"Don't make me ask you again." Knight's voice got thick.

"I'm not really your father, I'm sorry, but I was close to him. Your dad died years ago in a drug deal gone wrong with Jose Martinez," Smoke told the truth.

"So what was your agenda?" Knight asked.

"Jose sent me,"

"Who is Jose Martinez?"

"Rachela, my wife's, father from Cuba. He is deadly. I met him before I started dealing with Rachela," Smoke said.

"Wow, this shit is fucked up! I had a feeling something wasn't right with you."

"I'm sorry, but your dad was a stand-up nigga," Smoke said.

"Too bad."

"Too bad what?"

"He's not here to save your bitch ass," Knight said before pulling the trigger

Knight killed the man who fronted as if he was his dad. Now he wanted to find out who this Jose nigga was.

First his nephew got killed by Money, who popped up out of the blue, and now this shit.

Knight moved Valentine and his daughter to Texas so they could be safe from Rachela. He needed a plan with MeMe to kill Rachela and move forward, but he didn't really know who he was up against.

There was one person who knew everything about the Cubans, and that was Julie in Miami, but he knew she disliked him. For some reason she thought Knight played a part in his brother Kazzy's death. But she was his only way to help figure out who this Jose Martinez was.

***

South, Bronx

Lil K was in MillBrook projects on a late night sitting in the playground. Earlier today he had to bury his son. That shit crushed him. He couldn't believe it. To hear Money popped back up in the picture, he knew something wasn't right.

Behadi hadn't spoken to him since that night Money killed her son. She was a trained killer and she couldn't do shit.

He was drinking his pain away with a gallon of Henny.

"Lil K," a voice that sounded so familiar whispered.

He thought he was tripping hearing Red's voice and as he looked around, he saw her.

"I should kill you right here," he said, upset.

"I know. I'm sorry," she said, coming closer to him to see a gun on his lap.

"What do you want?"

"To talk."

"Now your pimp dead so you want to crawl back?"

"No, you don't understand, Lil K."

"Please make me," he replied.

"I was under drugs and a spell on some voodoo shit. He brainwashed me!" she cried.

"Now he's dead, so I guess you good," he stated, taking a gulp of Henny.

"I killed him after I found out he gave me HIV," she said, seeing him pause.

"I'm sorry," he said sadly.

"I know it's my fault for all of this, but I still love you," Red told him from her heart.

"Don't blame yourself."

"I have to, now that I fucked up my life," Red said.

"I lost my seed. Money is back," he said

"I'm sorry to hear that, but who is Money?"

Lil K forgot Red had short term memory loss and forgot certain shit and people. "Nobody. I have to go," he said, seeing Behadi text.

"What?"

"I have to go," he said, getting up to leave.

"Bye Lil K."

The way she said bye, he thought it sounded odd, but he paid it no mind.

When he was walking off, he realized forgot his gun on the bench.

Boom!

Lil K turned around, thinking someone was shooting at him. When he saw Red with a bullet in her head, dead with his gun in her hand, he cried to see she had committed suicide.

***

Brooklyn, NY

Bree looked around the while getting out of the car before taking her cute daughter out of the back seat. It was winter time so she had a bubble coat on her daughter and herself. She carried her sleeping daughter into the building and went to the third apartment to her left. She knocked softly on the door and it opened.

"Come in. Nobody followed you and my daughter, right?" he asked.

"No, Money, you think I'm dumb?" Bree told Money.

A few years back Bree and Money had a sexual relationship that didn't last long while they both were living in Atlanta. Bree ended up getting pregnant by him and they kept it on the low.

"Why didn't you kill the girl?" she asked him.

"I know what the fuck I'm doing, Bree."

"I can't tell."

"You do you and let me do me," he told her

"Fine, handsome, but shit changed since you been gone."

"How?"

"Knight is dealing with dangerous people now," she said.

"So what?"

"You're so small-minded," she said, walking to the back room to get away from him.

**

Dade County, Miami

Knight arrived at Julie's last known address in an Uber. He saw a bunch of pink luxury cars lined up so he knew it had to be her. When he rang the doorbell, it flew open. Julie had a choppa aimed at him.

"You got the fucking nerve to come down here," she said, upset.

"You think I would kill my own brother?"

"You're a fucking snake. I don't know what you will do," she stated

"Can I please talk to you, Julie? You know I don't move like that never," he said seeing her in deep thought.

"You only got two minutes." She walked inside, letting him in. They went into the kitchen, where she was making lunch.

"Do you know a Jose Martinez?" Knight asked as the name made her stop doing what she was doing.

"You don't want to bark up that tree," she stated.

"He killed my pops and tried to set me up with Smoke." Knight saw he had her attention now.

"So you killed Smoke?" She laughed lightly.

"Yeah."

286

"He's a dirty one, but his wife Rachela is the one you have to be very wary of. I hate that bitch" Julie said.

"Can you help me?"

"How?"

"Anything," he said.

"Nah, that's not my fight no more. We called a truce a few months back, me and the Cubans."

"Come on, Julie."

"I'm not helping you, Knight. I stuck my neck out too many times for you. Now get the fuck out."

When he was about to get up to leave, he saw a nanny bring a little boy into the kitchen. The little kid looked just like Kazzy. He couldn't believe it.

"Take him upstairs," she told her babysitter.

"That's Kazzy son?"

"None of your business. Now get out please," she said.

"Think about it. We family" Knight said, walking off.

***

Brooklyn, NY

Bree was babysitting, waiting on Money to get back from D.C. He was on the flight to the JFK airport.

The knock at the door made her get up while her baby was sleeping. She opened the door to see Behadi pointing a gun at her face with an insane look.

"Bitch," Behadi said before pulling the trigger.

Behadi walked in the crib to see a baby carriage in the middle of the living room floor. She shot the baby twice in the head, killing him before leaving with a smile on her face now.

Since losing her child, she had been focused on finding Money and when she did, she saw Bree with him, so she waited for the right time.

She would plan to catch Money later on in the near future.

***

Money walked into Bree's low-key apartment to find her dead along with his seed. He already knew Behadi was the person who did this because of what he did to her.

Money didn't even cry. He left and went back to the airport. He needed to get outta New York again because he was still wanted for murders.

***

USP Canaan Prison, PA

Today D Fatal Brim was being released from prison after he gave his time back. He won the appeal Mita put in for him a while back.

Marie awaited for him in a Rolls Royce, looking sexy standing in front of it.

"Oh my fucking God, baby!" she screamed, jumping into is arms, hugging him.

"Hey boo." He kissed her

"I'm so happy! Let's go. Our plane is waiting. We going to L.A.," she said, overly excited.

"A'ight." He couldn't believe he was out.

"I'm so happy, but I need to speak to you," she said

"I'm listening, baby."

"I teamed up with a woman named Rachela. She Cuban," Marie told him getting on the highway. There is only one issue."

"What?"

"She wants Knight dead."

"My Knight?" he asked.

"Yes. There is a big war going on and Knight is down with our enemies," she said.

"Her enemy or yours?"

"Both of us. Them Costa Rican bitches been trying to take everything I worked so hard for," she said.

"Shit."

"I know it's hard, but I need to know who you with?" she asked.

"What you mean?"

"It's me or them." She pulled over, reaching to her side for her gun.

"You, baby. You my wife," he said as she slid her hand on to her lap.

"Good. Love you daddy." She smiled, happy she didn't have to kill him.

***

San Jose, Costa Rica

Knight sat at a round table on a sandy beach behind a mansion on the beach that was very beautiful. Knight sat next to Melaie and her sister sat next to some other nigga who looked mixed, but he looked like he had swag.

"Okay, I'm glad we all here because this is the start of something big. Knight, this is my sister Kailina and her man Wolf. He's from around your way," Melaie, a.k.a. MeMe stated.

"You from New York," Knight said, trying to remember where he heard the name Wolf from.

"Yeah, I'm from Yonkers, NY but I been down here for a few years running the show from behind the scenes, son," Wolf said.

"Okay, I heard of you." Knight now remembered the name. Wolf was a stone-cold killer from Elm Street, a street in Yonkers.

"We about to do big things, bro. You ready?" Wolf asked him.

"Facts."

"Your little brother down with this?" Kailina asked.

"Yes. Whatever I do, he do," Knight said.

"Good. All I ask is please don't cross us," MeMe said.

"I don't cross people unless they cross me," Knight said.

"So we good?" Kailina said.

"Let's get to a big bag," Wolf said before popping a bottle of champagne worth $300,000.

***

Wolf woke up in his large bed surrounded by beautiful Versace drapes. He looked over to his beautiful girlfriend and now baby mother Kailina, whom he called the Costa Rican Princess. Wolf got out of the bed and slid into his Versace slippers walking to the balcony to take a seat and get some fresh air. He couldn't believe how much his life changed in the recent years. He thought back to years ago when he was living in Yonkers on Elm Street in New York.

He grew up a good kid. His mother Rita raised him right along with his brothers CB and Black. When he went to college at NYU his life changed after meeting a Puerto Rican woman named Bella. Wolf's little sister Victoria was killed right in front of him at a high school basketball game by a known killer named Champ.

Nobody knew Wolf was trained to kill. His aunty in the Dominican Republic used to train him growing up and he became a great shooter and fighter. Once he found out who killed his sister, he hunted Champ and his crew down with the help of his newfound friends, Andy and Smurf. Wolf did a murder, but unknown to him, a federal agent named Aguilera watched the whole scene unfold.

One day his female friend from college, Bella, introduced him to her father, and that's when his life changed for good. Bella's father was Agent Aguilera, the cop who saw the murder. He told Wolf if he didn't work for him as his killing machine, he would throw him under the jail for the murder he witnessed. Wolf agreed to the blackmail and started doing hits for Aguilera, but Wolf found it odd that he was killing mostly powerful men and drug lords. As time passed, Wolf found out Aguilera set him up. He sent Champ to kill his sister just so he could blackmail him. After killing Champ, he realized there was a lot more to the situation he didn't know. The Mexican Mafia was trying to kill Wolf, but word was the hit put on his life came from Cali.

He went out to Cali to meet his father, Ryan, who was a hitman for the Mexican Mafia and powerful people. The Mexican Mafia sent Ryan to kill Wolf, his own son but he refused putting his own life at risk.

Wolf was in Cali trying to figure out who wanted him dead, so he ended up killing the Five Families, which was the biggest drug organization on the west coast and Mexico border.

Still with no answer as to who wanted him dead, he uncovered a lot of deep secrets once his father was killed. Wolf got word from the top dawg that the person who wanted him dead was a woman in New York. He couldn't believe the whole time the person who been trying to kill him the whole time was in his backyard. Going back to New York, he couldn't believe the whole time the person trying to kill him was his own mom Rita. His mother was a big drug supplier, but she used her job as a detour. Rita's other son CB came home from prison and they went to war with Wolf. CB had a different father from Wolf. While in prison CB met a Cuba & black man they called OG but the two got close. CB had no clue OG was his dad.

When Rita and CB died, OG broke outta jail with the help of his wife Maryanna, who was Wolf's aunty.

Wolf met Kailina and moved out to Costa Rica with her while still being in-tune with Yonkers, NY.

Kailina had tons of drugs shipped to Wolf's people in Yonkers, NY.

Wolf's and Knight's crew were all on the same team, but he didn't really know him like that. He had heard he was a solid dude. Teaming up with the Bronx jack boy turned dope boy could be good or bad, but he was ready for whatever.

"What you doing?" Kailina came outside in her robe yawning.

"Thinking back," he said as she sat her phat ass on his lap.

Kailina had beautiful tannish skin, green eyes, thick, big booty, big titties, perfect teeth, full lips, curly long brown hair, and a flat stomach.

"You ready to go back?" she asked.

"Maybe."

"What does maybe mean?" she asked.

"We'll see, I guess. I hope your sister knows what she doing"

"She do, Wolf, trust me."

"I do now. Go check on my son," Wolf told her, kissing her lips.

"I want some dick in twenty minutes so be ready."

"I will, ma. Facts." Wolf loved how freaky Kailina was and her pussy was on a different level.

***

Miami, FL
Two months later

Julie and two SUV's full of goons were on their way to meet one of the most powerful men in her city. She'd been focused on holding her city together and expanding which was her plan for years.

Her being a mother now made her see life in a different view and she was starting to see a change and growth. Julie learned to forgive Knight for what he did, but she didn't trust him or want to see him at all.

The Lambo SUV pulled into the racetrack parking lot. She stepped out in heels and a nice black classy dress.

"Let's go, men," she stated, walking into the racetrack station that was used for horse racing. Julie wasn't into gambling but today she chose to place a half a million on a horse.

Her lucky number was three, so she went with horse number three, the underdog.

Walking into the bleachers, she saw the person she came to see and he was surrounded by dread heads.

***

Haitian Black saw the beautiful but dangerous woman Julie coming his way, so he put his Cuban cigar out. He had a lot of respect for Julie because not only was she his plug, but she was a strong Latina woman.

The two met years ago when his Zoe Pound and Top Six goons tried to rob her. The robbery was a set up to see what type of dude Haitian Black was and he turned out to be a good loyal person, so she offered him a spot on her team. Since that day they'd been going strong. Having Haitian Black on her squad was great because he had a strong control over South Miami.

"Hey HB," she called him, short for Haitian Black.

They called him Haitian Black because he was black as hell and had Haiti running through his blood.

"What's up, boss lady?" he shot back as she took a seat next to him.

"I came by to see what the issue is?"

The past month, Haitian Black was taking a lot of losses. He was losing men and his product was being robbed daily from his spots. Haitian Black recently found out who was behind all the mayhem and he couldn't believe it. A woman he use to cop work from now wanted him dead because he had the city on lock with Julie.

"You already know what's going on," he replied.

"Did you find out who is out to fuck up my shit?" she asked with an evil look in her eyes.

"Yeah."

"They dead?" she asked.

"No."

"No? What the fuck you mean no?" she shouted.

"It's Stephen."

Haitian Black's words were like a knife to her heart.

Julie stood up to leave without saying a word, already knowing what had to be done next.

***

Austin, Texas

Stephen had a large mansion on the outskirts of Austin. She had seven acres of land all to herself. She had relocated to Texas a few months back to open up a pipeline to transfer drugs back and forth to Mexico. Home for her would always be D.C. and Miami.

Stephen was moving so much coke she been supplying a Mexican cartel family near the border. Thanks to her plug she was able to move tons of her work all over the south.

The only issue she was having now was in Miami with a woman named Julie. She hated Julie with her soul for two reasons. One reason was because she was stepping on her toes with the drug trade and taking over the city. Another reason was because Julie had a close relationship with Knight, which made her jealous because she was in love with him and still carried feelings for him.

Tomorrow she had to go out to Cuba to meet her plug Jose Martinez. She recently met Rachela out in D.C. a few months ago and they clicked. The two been doing business since and she had the dope on lock but Jose supplied the coke to her uncut and fire.

She went to her room and started packing for tomorrow.

Chapter 79
Artemisia, Cuba

Jose Martinez was horseback riding at his ranch style house. Riding horses was something he been doing since a kid. Riding horses was a stress reliever for him and it was like meditation. Today one of his clients supposed to come and she was a big factor to his operations.

Jose saw his daughter coming from a distance, looking beautiful as always. He was glad she was here because he needed to speak to her. He got down from his horse like he was still a young man with young bones.

"Daddy."

"Baby, how are you doing?" He kissed her on the cheek.

"I heard you was looking for me, papi?" Rachela asked, walking on the grass in her six inch heels, trying not to fall.

"Yes."

"What's going on?"

"I need you to do me a solid." Jose stepped back and looked at his daughter.

"Anything."

"I need you to handle the Angebua Family from Granma." Jose saw Rachela's eyes lit up.

"I thought they were close to you, papi?"

"In business, you have to be aware of those who are close to you the most," he said as he continued to walk.

"What did he do?" She just wanted to know.

"He crossed me and the relationship we once recently shared."

"I don't understand."

"We both agreed to share Villa Clara and he recently killed all my men and took over Villa Clara. That was his plan all along: help me take it from the Lopez Family then cross me." Jose's voice was saddened at the thought of the disloyalty.

"Damn, papi, I will take care of this right now," she said hating to see her father under any type of distress.

"Where is your sister?"

"I don't know. I don't keep up with her," Rachela said.

"Okay, but she's still your sister. I won't be here forever and she will be all you have," he said, knowing his two daughters had a bad relationship since they were kids.

"What happened to the Knight kid?"

"Be patient. He will fall into your hands; trust me," Jose said with a smile.

"Patience is not my best tool," she stated.

"Well, make that something you work on," Jose told his daughter.

"One day."

"Soon. I have to get ready for this meeting," he said, walking toward his house almost a half of mile up the rocky dirt road.

"Who's coming to see you?" Rachela was nosy.

"Stephen."

"How is she?"

"Business is good on both ends. You found a profitable client for our organization."

"I always do," she bragged.

"Not always," he corrected her.

"Most of the time. But after I take care of your problem, I have to tend to the task at hand."

Jose already knew what she was referring to.

Chapter 80
San Jose, Costa Rica

Wolf slow-grinded his hips into Kailina's pelvis, feeling her tight sex muscle grip his penis as he made love to his baby mother.

"Oh yesss, daddy!" She dug her nails into his back, almost making him bleed.

Her juices were all over the silk sheets anytime he had sex with her she would squirt all over the place. Wolf loved her beauty and sex.

"I'm cumminggg!" she screamed, gripping his waist. Her climax came out like a waterfall.

Wolf picked her up in the air and pinned her against the wall, entering her naturally tight love box. "I love you, baby," he whispered in her ear as he started pounding her little out.

"I love you tooooo." She bit his shoulder as he banged her body against the wall with each pound until he nutted inside of her.

Kailina was breathing hard when he put her down, but she wanted more. "Sit down," she said.

Wolf did as he was told and watched her slow gulp his whole manhood. She bopped her head up and down, focusing on sucking dick something she loved to do with him. After the oral sex, Wolf had to rest. If not, Kailina would fuck and suck him all night.

"You're something else," he told her, making her giggle as they both changed the sheets that cost $7,000.

"Look who's talking, freak. You still got my asshole sore from last night," she said

"You wanted it all in you," he said.

"You didn't have to ram it in," she shot back.

"You'll be okay. Anyway, I think your sister made the right choice with Knight and his team," Wolf said as he changed the subject.

"I don't know," she said.

"Why not?"

"Knight got a long history of crossing people."

"Most of the time a person crosses a person because they deserved it," Wolf says.

"What? Are you serious right now?" She got loud.

"Yes. I had to cross people because I saw flaws in their character that could have been deadly to me," Wolf said.

"So you saying if I show you a sign, you will cross me?" she asked.

Wolf didn't answer her because he knew his reply would hurt her.

Kailina was very emotional, unlike MeMe, who was cold-hearted and deadly.

"You know what? I'm sleeping in the other room. Fuck you."

"Shit." Wolf shook his head, not in the mood to argue. He wanted to tell her he was going out to New York in a few days, but she took off.

***

South Bronx, NY

Lil K was on his way to meet his boy J Balla to talk about money and the new product on its way. He had been thinking about taking his relationship with Behadi to the next level. Lil K was madly in love Behadi. He saw things in her he saw in his mom like caring, self-respect, loyalty, and honesty. Her beauty was outta this world and he didn't want to spend his life without her.

She was in Africa handling some business while he was out in the city handling the drugs.

Driving through the Bronx, he realized he loved everything about his city, even the nitty gritty part of it.

He couldn't wait to see Behadi when she got back. Her birthday was soon and he had a big surprise for her.

Chapter 81

Angebua ran his drug empire with two iron fists and a mean crew of killers. He ran a few cities in Cuba, but his new city was Villa Clara a big city and it had a lot of money in it, thanks to Jose, he now was able to control Villa Clara. He wasn't even upset about crossing Jose and backdooring him. Years ago, Jose had Angebua's uncle killed in Havana and Angebua never forgot about that. Teaming up with Jose was all a part of his plan, and Jose fell right into his trap.

Today was church and he was driving two cars deep to the Catholic church he was raised in. As he made a right down a small two-way street, two vans blocked off the middle of the street.

"What's going on?" Angebua said in the backseat, wondering if it was just a traffic stop. Angebua had the police in his pocket so he told his men to stop so they could see who he was.

As soon as Angebua got out of the truck, the doors of the van all flew open and shooters jumped out with assault rifles.

Tat! Tat! Tat! Tat! Tat!

Angebua tried to run, but bullets from Rachela's weapon chopped him down. Her goons continue to open fire on Angebua's men, killing them.

Rachela placed her Chanel heels on the back of Angebua's head and fired four more rounds.

She checked the time on her watch and walked off, knowing she had a flight to catch.

***

South Bronx, NY

J Balla was watching a mean dog fight in the basement of his homie Pit Balla's crib. Dog fighting and selling keys was J Balla's thing. He controlled the Casted Hill section of the Bronx and was working on Soundview right now. Lil K dropped a new shipment in his lap a few days ago and he had been trapping since. J Balla had a rule: no day off in the field unless it was time for a vacation or a funeral.

His dog was losing, but he knew his red nose couldn't fuck with the Roc dog mixed with pit. He only hoped it would put up and good fight and not get killed.

Working with Lil K and Knight was big because they were legends in the town, so fucking with them was big time. M Balla's brother was heavy in the South Bronx because everybody had love for him before he got killed. Now J Balla was taking his late brother's spot.

***

Manhattan, NY

Maryanna was in the back of an Uber on her way to her Harlem brownstone. In a few hours, she had to meet up with worker Rocky in Harlem. She and OG had Harlem in a chokehold with the bricks because they sold weight at a low price. They had been laying low since she broke him outta jail, which he was still on the run for. She was an OG ride or die. She loved him with all the heart she had left.

There was one person she couldn't get out of her mind and thought process because she wanted him dead: her own nephew. Maryanna knew Wolf would be a problem if he was to come back. She wanted a hold on Yonkers, but two hustlers had the small town on lock: H and Chills, she had been hearing through the grapevine.

She had a lot on her beautiful mind and knew without a plan shit would crumble.

Chapter 82
Botswana, South Africa

Behadi loved being home back in the motherland, but she wasn't here to reminisce.

She walked through a small forest outside a small city area to pay her aunty a visit on her dad's side. Killing her vicious evil father always played on her mind, but she knew she had to do what needed to be done.

A small house built outta trees and bamboo sticks held up the small hut her aunty had been living in for years now. Behadi remembered coming here as a child and being tortured by her aunty, who was a spiritual healer. Her aunt did magic and was a fortune teller, plus she worshipped the devil. Behadi was against worshipping anything besides the Most High Allah. She walked into the small hut to see candles and small pieces of wood chips burning.

"Behadi, my little killing machine," her aunty said, staring into the fire not even looking at her niece.

"You dirty bitch!" Behadi had real tears in her eyes thinking about how her aunty used to treat her. She was just like her father.

"You still mad, sweetie? I turned you into a savage, as they will say in America." Her aunty had a strong African voice.

"Today you will pay for everything you done, you old bitch." Behadi pulled out a medium-sized sword.

Her aunty turned around to face Behadi with dark eyes. "I knew you was coming and I know soon you will see happiness in a loved one, but you will also see death. Killing me will only place a black dot on her diseased heart," her aunty said.

"I don't believe in your false tales. Allah is the only one who knows my future." Behadi swung her sword.

The sharp sword sliced her aunty in the neck, making blood squirt all over the place, even on Behadi's face. Without even wiping the bloodstain off her face, she walked off back to the city, which was ten miles up a dirt road, but the shortcut was through a jungle.

Behadi had so many questions. She wanted to ask her aunt before killing her, but she knew Allah would reveal everything to her.

She was staying at a hotel until the morning, when she planned to fly back out to New York.

Leaving Lil K for a few days felt like a lifetime. Their love was to the point where she couldn't breathe without him. She knew he was all she needed.

Tomorrow was her birthday, and she couldn't wait to spend it with her boo.

***

Manhattan, NY

Lil K had a nice set-up on a hotel roof on one of the tallest buildings in Manhattan. The view was so pretty they could see New York and the New Jersey area. There was a candlelit table with flowers and food on the table.

"Oh my God, baby, it's so nice out here!" Behadi said, walking onto the rooftop in a sexy red strapless dress with heels, showing a little skin.

"Happy birthday," he said with his hands out, showing her a billboard that read, "I love you, Behadi."

"No you didn't!" she shouted

"Yeah, but that's not it, baby. You deserve all of me and I want to spend the rest of my life with you, ma, so will you…" Lil K got on one knee and pulled out a box.

Behadi's mind went crazy. She felt like she was about to faint.

"Marry me?"

"Yes, baby!" She kissed him and snatched the box out of his hand, placing the big diamond ring on her own finger.

"I love you, baby."

"I want to make love right here," she said, laying down on the table, moving her skirt to the side, letting him see her pretty pussy.

Lil K wasted no time. They made love on the table and all over the rooftop.

Chapter 83
Columbus, Ohio

Parry was a bigtime plug in Ohio. He moved drugs all through the Midwest area. He had shit locked down.

He was black and Cuban, but raised in Brooklyn, NY. He moved to Ohio for a better come-up in the dope game because New York was a dangerous city. Not to mention he'd had a hand in the kidnapping of very police detective there.

He was driving his Rolls Royce truck to his big mansion in the richest area of the city. Parry's wife was a model from overseas. He couldn't wait to get home to fuck the shit outta her.

Pulling up into his driveway, he parked next to the Bentley truck he copped for his wife. He walked into the house.

"Baby!" he yelled, hearing the living room TV playing loudly, which was rare because his wife hated loud noise.

As he walked into the living room, he saw his wife hanging from the ceiling from a noose. Parry reached for his weapon, feeling that someone was still there.

"Don't do it, brother," a familiar voice stated, giving him chills.

Parry turned around to see his brother OG pointing a big 50 cal pistol at him.

"You're out?" Parry had no clue OG was out of prison because he had put him in jail for life. Parry had ratted on OG and robbed him before he sent him off to prison.

"Nigga, you thought you would get away with this?"

"Brother——"

"Parry, stop. Let's just keep it G. You're dying anyway," OG told him.

"Let me go kiss my son first, at least?" Parry asked.

"No need for that."

"Huh?"

"He's dead in the bathroom tub, Parry."

Tears formed in his eyes. He couldn't believe his own brother killed his son. "You're a monster."

"Like you're not?" OG shot back, raising his eyebrows.

"You took my family."

"And your money and drugs, champ. But I gotta fly back to New York so I gotta go, fam," OG said.

Boc! Boc! Boc! Boc! Boc!

OG emptied his clip into his brother's chest, showing no sympathy. Being in prison with a life sentence, every night he thought about what his brother did to him. He could have had Maryanna kill Parry, but he wanted to do it himself when he got out.

His next plan was to see what was up with him trying to take over Yonkers, NY. Harlem was already his, but Harlem wasn't enough. OG thought about the kid who killed his son CB and hoped he would come out of hiding.

He thought about Wolf daily. He had a hundred ways to kill him when he caught him. Even though Wolf was Maryanna's nephew, she was riding with OG.

Chapter 84
Bronx, NY

Knight had a flight to catch to Costa Rica to meet with MeMe. Since dealing with her, his life changed for better and she was strictly about her business and helping him elevate. Knight looked past her beauty and sex appeal to focus on business.

He left his low-key apartment he had in the Bronx. He thought about taking a suitcase but decided against it.

His phone was ringing and he picked it up, seeing it was his baby mother Valentine's number. Since she got snatched up by Rachela a few months back, Knight had been moving Valentine and his daughter around every first of the month to keep her safe. He knew she hated moving around, but being an ex-cop, she knew it was for her and Karmala's safety.

"Hey Valentine," Knight answered, climbing in his car.

"Knight, you disappointed me, my friend," a male voice replied.

Knight looked into the phone as if they had the wrong number. "Who the fuck is this?" Knight knew whoever the man was had to be Hispanic because he had a strong Spanish accent.

"I'm the man who killed your father, and now I'm looking at the dead bodies of your beautiful daughter and child's mother," the man said calmly.

"Jose Martinez," Knight said.

"I will be sending you a picture text message to remind you of what happens when someone crosses me or betrays an oath. I know I'll be seeing you and the Costa Rican sisters soon," Jose Martinez said before hanging up.

Knight listened to the dial tone, hoping he was lying.

When Rachela kidnaped his family, he was sick about that, but he was grateful she let them go.

He sat there zoned out until he heard his phone chime, letting him know he had a message. Knight was scared to open the text message, which was a picture text.

Upon opening the text, he saw his worst fears. Valentine's and Karmala's heads were both cut off, sitting on a table next to a tiger head.

Tears flowed down his cheeks as he put his head on the steering wheel. He knew one day everything he been doing would catch up with him, and today it did.

Losing his daughter and baby mother hurt more than anything in the world.

***

Lil Haiti, Miami

Haitian Black had just come back from spending time with his family in Haiti, the island he grew up on. He stopped by his little sister's crib to drop her off some money and check on her. Haitian Black was heavy on family values and loyalty. He never let money blind him or choke out his morals as a man. Every Saturday he came to his sister's crib.

As he walked into her crib, he heard water running from the kitchen. When he heard funny sounds, he wondered what his sister was doing. When he saw three men standing over his sister tied up in a chair he reached for his gun, forgetting it was in the car.

"Forgot your piece in the car, huh?" a woman said, walking to the other side of the kitchen.

It was Stephen, looking sexy and thick in her jeans and heels.

"You fucking hoe-ass bitch!" he shouted.

Stephen placed her gun to his sister's head.

Boom!

Haitian Black was so shocked he forgot where he was at for the moment.

Boom! Boom! Boom! Boom!

Stephen opened up Haitian's Black's chest, killing him, seeing his body collapse into the countertop.

Stephen wanted to send a message to Julie that she could pop up anytime. She been laying low in DR and other cities and states, but Miami was still hers.

The beef with Julie wasn't about money. She felt like Julie was trying to steal Knight from her. She planned to spin on Julie until she get dizzy and she was dead. She hated Julie and everything the bitch stood for.

***

Key West, FL

Julie's son and the nanny were on their way to a big waterpark to have fun on this hot summer day.

Julie loved her son she had with Knight's brother Kazzy before he died. With her busy schedule, she had been unable to spend time with her handsome son. Luckily she hired a nanny to help out 24/7.

The nanny pulled into the gas station to get some gas for their trip. She was unaware an all-black was SUV was tailing them. When she opened the driver door to get out, the SUV parked parallel to her and lowered the tints.

Tat! Tat! Tat! Tat! Tat! Tat!

Bullets from MP11 assault rifle killed the nanny and Julie's son at the scene, leaving a bloody mess.

***

Tampa, FL

Julie had been in her Tampa condo for the past few days. The recent news of her son's death fucked her up. She hadn't been able to move out of the bed or talk to anyone - not even her friends and family. With so many enemies, she didn't know who killed her baby, but she was ready to flip Miami upside down for his killer.

Julie heard a knock at her door. Nobody knew about this spot - not even her goons. She went to the door to see a woman prettier than her. She opened the door.

"Julie?"

"Yes, who are you?" Julie caught an attitude

"MeMe from Costa Rica. Can we talk for a second? I'm sorry for what happened to your son, but I believe we can help each other, because I know who killed your son," MeMe said.

To Be Continued…
Jack Boys versus Dope Boys 3
Coming Soon

Lock Down Publications and Ca$h Presents assisted publishing packages.

BASIC PACKAGE $499
Editing
Cover Design
Formatting

UPGRADED PACKAGE $800
Typing
Editing
Cover Design
Formatting

ADVANCE PACKAGE $1,200
Typing
Editing
Cover Design
Formatting
Copyright registration
Proofreading
Upload book to Amazon

LDP SUPREME PACKAGE $1,500
Typing
Editing
Cover Design
Formatting
Copyright registration
Proofreading
Set up Amazon account
Upload book to Amazon
Advertise on LDP Amazon and Facebook page

***Other services available upon request. Additional charges may apply

Lock Down Publications
P.O. Box 944
Stockbridge, GA 30281-9998
Phone # 470 303-9761

Submission Guideline

Submit the first three chapters of your completed manuscript to ldpsubmissions@gmail.com, subject line: Your book's title. The manuscript must be in a .doc file and sent as an attachment. Document should be in Times New Roman, double spaced and in size 12 font. Also, provide your synopsis and full contact information. If sending multiple submissions, they must each be in a separate email.

Have a story but no way to send it electronically? You can still submit to LDP/Ca$h Presents. Send in the first three chapters, written or typed, of your completed manuscript to:

LDP: Submissions Dept
Po Box 944
Stockbridge, Ga 30281

DO NOT send original manuscript. Must be a duplicate.

Provide your synopsis and a cover letter containing your full contact information.

Thanks for considering LDP and Ca$h Presents.

<u>NEW RELEASES</u>

A GANGSTA'S PARADISE by TRAI'QUAN

THE MURDER QUEENS 2 by MICHAEL GALLON

FOREVER GANGSTA 2 by ADRIAN DULAN

GORILLAZ IN THE TRENCHES by SAYNOMORE

JACK BOYS VS DOPE BOYS by ROMELL TUKES

BLOOD OF A BOSS **VI**
SHADOWS OF THE GAME II
TRAP BASTARD II
By **Askari**
LOYAL TO THE GAME **IV**
By **T.J. & Jelissa**
TRUE SAVAGE **VIII**
MIDNIGHT CARTEL IV
DOPE BOY MAGIC IV
CITY OF KINGZ III
NIGHTMARE ON SILENT AVE II
THE PLUG OF LIL MEXICO II
CLASSIC CITY II
By **Chris Green**
BLAST FOR ME **III**
A SAVAGE DOPEBOY III
CUTTHROAT MAFIA III
DUFFLE BAG CARTEL VII
HEARTLESS GOON VI
By **Ghost**
A HUSTLER'S DECEIT III
KILL ZONE II
BAE BELONGS TO ME III
TIL DEATH II
By **Aryanna**
KING OF THE TRAP III
By **T.J. Edwards**
GORILLAZ IN THE BAY V
3X KRAZY III

STRAIGHT BEAST MODE III

De'Kari

KINGPIN KILLAZ IV

STREET KINGS III

PAID IN BLOOD III

CARTEL KILLAZ IV

DOPE GODS III

Hood Rich

SINS OF A HUSTLA II

ASAD

RICH $AVAGE III

By Martell Troublesome Bolden

YAYO V

Bred In The Game 2

S. Allen

THE STREETS WILL TALK II

By Yolanda Moore

SON OF A DOPE FIEND III

HEAVEN GOT A GHETTO II

SKI MASK MONEY II

By Renta

LOYALTY AIN'T PROMISED III

By Keith Williams

I'M NOTHING WITHOUT HIS LOVE II

SINS OF A THUG II

TO THE THUG I LOVED BEFORE II

IN A HUSTLER I TRUST II

By Monet Dragun

QUIET MONEY IV

EXTENDED CLIP III

THUG LIFE IV

By **Trai'Quan**

THE STREETS MADE ME IV

By **Larry D. Wright**

IF YOU CROSS ME ONCE II

ANGEL IV

By **Anthony Fields**

THE STREETS WILL NEVER CLOSE IV

By K'ajji

HARD AND RUTHLESS III

KILLA KOUNTY III

By Khufu

MONEY GAME III

By Smoove Dolla

JACK BOYS VS DOPE BOYS III

A GANGSTA'S QUR'AN V

COKE GIRLZ II

COKE BOYS II

By Romell Tukes

MURDA WAS THE CASE II

Elijah R. Freeman

THE STREETS NEVER LET GO III

By Robert Baptiste

AN UNFORESEEN LOVE IV

By **Meesha**

KING OF THE TRENCHES III
by **GHOST & TRANAY ADAMS**

MONEY MAFIA II

By **Jibril Williams**

QUEEN OF THE ZOO III

By **Black Migo**

VICIOUS LOYALTY III

By **Kingpen**

A GANGSTA'S PAIN III

By **J-Blunt**

CONFESSIONS OF A JACKBOY III

By **Nicholas Lock**

GRIMEY WAYS III

By **Ray Vinci**

KING KILLA II

By **Vincent "Vitto" Holloway**

BETRAYAL OF A THUG II

By **Fre$h**

THE MURDER QUEENS III

By **Michael Gallon**

THE BIRTH OF A GANGSTER III

By **Delmont Player**

TREAL LOVE II

By **Le'Monica Jackson**

FOR THE LOVE OF BLOOD II

By **Jamel Mitchell**

RAN OFF ON DA PLUG II

By **Paper Boi Rari**

HOOD CONSIGLIERE II

By **Keese**

PRETTY GIRLS DO NASTY THINGS II

By **Nicole Goosby**

PROTÉGÉ OF A LEGEND II

By **Corey Robinson**

IT'S JUST ME AND YOU II

By Ah'Million

BORN IN THE GRAVE II

By Self Made Tay

FOREVER GANGSTA III

By Adrian Dulan

GORILLAZ IN THE TRENCHES II

By SayNoMore

Available Now

RESTRAINING ORDER **I & II**

By **CA$H & Coffee**

LOVE KNOWS NO BOUNDARIES **I II & III**

By **Coffee**

RAISED AS A GOON I, II, III & IV

BRED BY THE SLUMS I, II, III

BLAST FOR ME I & II

ROTTEN TO THE CORE I II III

A BRONX TALE I, II, III

DUFFLE BAG CARTEL I II III IV V VI

HEARTLESS GOON I II III IV V

A SAVAGE DOPEBOY I II

DRUG LORDS I II III

CUTTHROAT MAFIA I II

Romell Tukes

KING OF THE TRENCHES
By **Ghost**
LAY IT DOWN **I & II**
LAST OF A DYING BREED I II
BLOOD STAINS OF A SHOTTA I & II III
By **Jamaica**
LOYAL TO THE GAME I II III
LIFE OF SIN I, II III
By **TJ & Jelissa**
BLOODY COMMAS I & II
SKI MASK CARTEL I II & III
KING OF NEW YORK I II,III IV V
RISE TO POWER I II III
COKE KINGS I II III IV V
BORN HEARTLESS I II III IV
KING OF THE TRAP I II
By **T.J. Edwards**
IF LOVING HIM IS WRONG…I & II
LOVE ME EVEN WHEN IT HURTS I II III
By **Jelissa**
WHEN THE STREETS CLAP BACK I & II III
THE HEART OF A SAVAGE I II III IV
MONEY MAFIA
LOYAL TO THE SOIL I II III
By **Jibril Williams**
A DISTINGUISHED THUG STOLE MY HEART I II & III
LOVE SHOULDN'T HURT I II III IV
RENEGADE BOYS I II III IV
PAID IN KARMA I II III
SAVAGE STORMS I II III

318

AN UNFORESEEN LOVE I II III

By **Meesha**

A GANGSTER'S CODE I &, II III

A GANGSTER'S SYN I II III

THE SAVAGE LIFE I II III

CHAINED TO THE STREETS I II III

BLOOD ON THE MONEY I II III

A GANGSTA'S PAIN I II

By J-Blunt

PUSH IT TO THE LIMIT

By **Bre' Hayes**

BLOOD OF A BOSS **I, II, III, IV, V**

SHADOWS OF THE GAME

TRAP BASTARD

By **Askari**

THE STREETS BLEED MURDER **I, II & III**

THE HEART OF A GANGSTA I II& III

By **Jerry Jackson**

CUM FOR ME I II III IV V VI VII VIII

An **LDP Erotica Collaboration**

BRIDE OF A HUSTLA **I II & II**

THE FETTI GIRLS **I, II& III**

CORRUPTED BY A GANGSTA I, II III, IV

BLINDED BY HIS LOVE

THE PRICE YOU PAY FOR LOVE I, II ,III

DOPE GIRL MAGIC I II III

By **Destiny Skai**

WHEN A GOOD GIRL GOES BAD

By **Adrienne**

THE COST OF LOYALTY I II III

By Kweli

A GANGSTER'S REVENGE **I II III & IV**

THE BOSS MAN'S DAUGHTERS I II III IV V

A SAVAGE LOVE **I & II**

BAE BELONGS TO ME I II

A HUSTLER'S DECEIT I, II, III

WHAT BAD BITCHES DO I, II, III

SOUL OF A MONSTER I II III

KILL ZONE

A DOPE BOY'S QUEEN I II III

TIL DEATH

By **Aryanna**

A KINGPIN'S AMBITON

A KINGPIN'S AMBITION **II**

I MURDER FOR THE DOUGH

By **Ambitious**

TRUE SAVAGE I II III IV V VI VII

DOPE BOY MAGIC I, II, III

MIDNIGHT CARTEL I II III

CITY OF KINGZ I II

NIGHTMARE ON SILENT AVE

THE PLUG OF LIL MEXICO II

CLASSIC CITY

By **Chris Green**

A DOPEBOY'S PRAYER

By **Eddie "Wolf" Lee**

THE KING CARTEL **I, II & III**

By **Frank Gresham**

THESE NIGGAS AIN'T LOYAL **I, II & III**

By **Nikki Tee**

GANGSTA SHYT **I II &III**

By **CATO**

THE ULTIMATE BETRAYAL

By **Phoenix**

BOSS'N UP **I , II & III**

By **Royal Nicole**

I LOVE YOU TO DEATH

By **Destiny J**

I RIDE FOR MY HITTA

I STILL RIDE FOR MY HITTA

By **Misty Holt**

LOVE & CHASIN' PAPER

By **Qay Crockett**

TO DIE IN VAIN

SINS OF A HUSTLA

By **ASAD**

BROOKLYN HUSTLAZ

By **Boogsy Morina**

BROOKLYN ON LOCK I & II

By **Sonovia**

GANGSTA CITY

By **Teddy Duke**

A DRUG KING AND HIS DIAMOND I & II III

A DOPEMAN'S RICHES

HER MAN, MINE'S TOO I, II

CASH MONEY HO'S

THE WIFEY I USED TO BE I II

PRETTY GIRLS DO NASTY THINGS

By Nicole Goosby

TRAPHOUSE KING **I II & III**

KINGPIN KILLAZ I II III
STREET KINGS I II
PAID IN BLOOD **I II**
CARTEL KILLAZ I II III
DOPE GODS I II
By **Hood Rich**
LIPSTICK KILLAH **I, II, III**
CRIME OF PASSION I II & III
FRIEND OR FOE I II III
By **Mimi**
STEADY MOBBN' **I, II, III**
THE STREETS STAINED MY SOUL I II III
By **Marcellus Allen**
WHO SHOT YA **I, II, III**
SON OF A DOPE FIEND I II
HEAVEN GOT A GHETTO
SKI MASK MONEY
Renta
GORILLAZ IN THE BAY **I II III IV**
TEARS OF A GANGSTA I II
3X KRAZY I II
STRAIGHT BEAST MODE I II
DE'KARI
TRIGGADALE I II III
MURDAROBER WAS THE CASE
Elijah R. Freeman
GOD BLESS THE TRAPPERS I, II, III
THESE SCANDALOUS STREETS I, II, III
FEAR MY GANGSTA I, II, III IV, V
THESE STREETS DON'T LOVE NOBODY I, II

BURY ME A G I, II, III, IV, V

A GANGSTA'S EMPIRE I, II, III, IV

THE DOPEMAN'S BODYGAURD I II

THE REALEST KILLAZ I II III

THE LAST OF THE OGS I II III

Tranay Adams

THE STREETS ARE CALLING

Duquie Wilson

MARRIED TO A BOSS I II III

By Destiny Skai & Chris Green

KINGZ OF THE GAME I II III IV V VI

Playa Ray

SLAUGHTER GANG I II III

RUTHLESS HEART I II III

By Willie Slaughter

FUK SHYT

By Blakk Diamond

DON'T F#CK WITH MY HEART I II

By Linnea

ADDICTED TO THE DRAMA I II III

IN THE ARM OF HIS BOSS II

By Jamila

YAYO I II III IV

A SHOOTER'S AMBITION I II

BRED IN THE GAME

By S. Allen

TRAP GOD I II III

RICH $AVAGE I II

MONEY IN THE GRAVE I II III

By Martell Troublesome Bolden

FOREVER GANGSTA I II

GLOCKS ON SATIN SHEETS I II

By Adrian Dulan

TOE TAGZ I II III IV

LEVELS TO THIS SHYT I II

IT'S JUST ME AND YOU

By Ah'Million

KINGPIN DREAMS I II III

RAN OFF ON DA PLUG

By Paper Boi Rari

CONFESSIONS OF A GANGSTA I II III IV

CONFESSIONS OF A JACKBOY I II

By Nicholas Lock

I'M NOTHING WITHOUT HIS LOVE

SINS OF A THUG

TO THE THUG I LOVED BEFORE

A GANGSTA SAVED XMAS

IN A HUSTLER I TRUST

By Monet Dragun

CAUGHT UP IN THE LIFE I II III

THE STREETS NEVER LET GO I II

By Robert Baptiste

NEW TO THE GAME I II III

MONEY, MURDER & MEMORIES I II III

By **Malik D. Rice**

LIFE OF A SAVAGE I II III

A GANGSTA'S QUR'AN I II III IV

MURDA SEASON I II III

GANGLAND CARTEL I II III

CHI'RAQ GANGSTAS I II III

KILLERS ON ELM STREET I II III

JACK BOYZ N DA BRONX I II III

A DOPEBOY'S DREAM I II III

JACK BOYS VS DOPE BOYS I II

COKE GIRLZ

COKE BOYS

By Romell Tukes

LOYALTY AIN'T PROMISED I II

By Keith Williams

QUIET MONEY I II III

THUG LIFE I II III

EXTENDED CLIP I II

A GANGSTA'S PARADISE

By **Trai'Quan**

THE STREETS MADE ME I II III

By **Larry D. Wright**

THE ULTIMATE SACRIFICE I, II, III, IV, V, VI

KHADIFI

IF YOU CROSS ME ONCE

ANGEL I II III

IN THE BLINK OF AN EYE

By **Anthony Fields**

THE LIFE OF A HOOD STAR

By Ca$h & Rashia Wilson

THE STREETS WILL NEVER CLOSE I II III

By K'ajji

CREAM I II III

THE STREETS WILL TALK

By Yolanda Moore

NIGHTMARES OF A HUSTLA I II III

By King Dream

CONCRETE KILLA I II III

VICIOUS LOYALTY I II

By Kingpen

HARD AND RUTHLESS I II

MOB TOWN 251

THE BILLIONAIRE BENTLEYS I II III

By Von Diesel

GHOST MOB

Stilloan Robinson

MOB TIES I II III IV V VI

SOUL OF A HUSTLER, HEART OF A KILLER

GORILLAZ IN THE TRENCHES

By SayNoMore

BODYMORE MURDERLAND I II III

THE BIRTH OF A GANGSTER I II

By Delmont Player

FOR THE LOVE OF A BOSS

By C. D. Blue

MOBBED UP I II III IV

THE BRICK MAN I II III IV

THE COCAINE PRINCESS I II III IV V

By King Rio

KILLA KOUNTY I II III

By Khufu

MONEY GAME I II

By Smoove Dolla

A GANGSTA'S KARMA I II

By FLAME

KING OF THE TRENCHES I II

by **GHOST & TRANAY ADAMS**

QUEEN OF THE ZOO I II

By **Black Migo**

GRIMEY WAYS I II

By Ray Vinci

XMAS WITH AN ATL SHOOTER

By Ca$h & Destiny Skai

KING KILLA

By Vincent "Vitto" Holloway

BETRAYAL OF A THUG

By Fre$h

THE MURDER QUEENS I II

By Michael Gallon

TREAL LOVE

By Le'Monica Jackson

FOR THE LOVE OF BLOOD

By Jamel Mitchell

HOOD CONSIGLIERE

By Keese

PROTÉGÉ OF A LEGEND

By Corey Robinson

BORN IN THE GRAVE

By Self Made Tay

MOAN IN MY MOUTH

By XTASY

<u>BOOKS BY LDP'S CEO, CA$H</u>

TRUST IN NO MAN

TRUST IN NO MAN 2

TRUST IN NO MAN 3

BONDED BY BLOOD

SHORTY GOT A THUG

THUGS CRY

THUGS CRY 2

THUGS CRY 3

TRUST NO BITCH

TRUST NO BITCH 2

TRUST NO BITCH 3

TIL MY CASKET DROPS

RESTRAINING ORDER

RESTRAINING ORDER 2

IN LOVE WITH A CONVICT

LIFE OF A HOOD STAR

XMAS WITH AN ATL SHOOTER

Jack Boys Vs Dope Boys 2